WHAT MIGHT WE KNOW

NOVEL 2 IN THE SERIES
SCRAPBOOKS OF THE SOUL

MARILYN HAMMOND, PHD

ISBN: 978-1957176109

Email: scrapbooksofthesoul@gmail.com

Cover art by Marilyn Hammond, PhD
Exterior and interior design by Jennifer Leigh Selig, PhD

EMPRESS
PUBLICATIONS
WWW.EMPRESSPUBLICATIONS.COM

SCRAPBOOKS OF THE SOUL

Explore the mesmerizing universe of **Scrapbooks of the Soul**, a compelling series of novels where fiction merges with profound inquiry. Each book is a rich mosaic, filled with diverse fictional characters who delve into the mysteries of the soul, sleeptime dreams, brain hemispheres, and the intersections of spirituality and science. Their dialogues, embellished with insightful footnotes, navigate through themes of whole-brain Christianity, and the intricacies of psychological, generational, and cultural healing.

These stories are more than narratives; they are a reflection on human experience, encompassing long-standing friendships, resilient relationships, and our struggle with life's opposites. The series offers a unique perspective, suggesting our reality is shaped by our perceptions and interpretations. Engage with **Scrapbooks of the Soul** to discover a world where each page mirrors the complexity of life and the varied interpretations that define our existence.

Novel #1 *Deep Hints and Clues*
Novel #2 *What Might We Know*
Novel #3 *An Empty Ache*
Novel #4 *Sit With It*
Novel #5 *Backyard Talk*
Novel #6 *Approach Boldly* (Plus Series Index)

DEDICATION

In loving gratitude to Heather who resourcefully found help for computer and other technical needs

TABLE OF CONTENTS

CHAPTER ONE

Sobbing Stefan

Widow Ann Dramm lived in a high-rise in Stamford CT. In addition to her two daughters and their families, Ann was connected to local friends and her artistic/psychological involvement with a maternity center. She stayed in touch with Beth in Austin TX, only survivor of the Texas Trio which had included Matti and Gabby, now deceased. In addition, Ann had ongoing contact with Julia Montel in Clarksdale KS, the newborn that Ann's graduate school roommate Matti placed for adoption many years ago. Ann's friendship continued with Julia's mentor Lenore, the retired psychiatrist with whom Ann journeyed to the homestead site of Lenore's grandparents in Kansas.

These out-of-town friends telephoned, texted, e-mailed back and forth with Ann. Julia recently told Ann a story involving Stefan, Julia's brother-in-law suffering with COPD, living in Golden Acres a skilled-nursing center in Clarksdale, whom Ann met when she visited Julia and family. Julia found her husband's brother, Stefan, insufferable. Until one day.

Julia's husband, Marc, took an obituary in the local newspaper to his brother in Golden Acres. Stefan looked at the obituary, choked-out the words, "That sorry bastard," and began to sob; body shaking in his wheelchair. Marc was stunned, while Stefan searched for a handkerchief in his robe pocket, his pajama pocket, Marc walked to a bedside table and brought a box of tissues to Stefan who took a while to recover before he could speak the memory the obituary triggered.

When Stefan was four or five years old, at the Montel Furniture store, in a back freight area where the man in the obituary, big Joey Hall worked, this somewhat mentally challenged adult, grabbed young Stefan, sexually molested him, while sitting on a chair, with Stefan on lap, one arm slung over the boy's shoulder and body, hand fondling the young boy while masturbating himself with Stefan's hand. Joey threatened he'd tell Stefan's parents what a bad boy he was if Stefan ever said anything to anybody.

Stefan remembered running to the show room to find his parents. He saw only his mother, who was with a customer. He'd been trained to never disturb his parents when they were with a customer. His father must not have been at the store. Stefan didn't remember what happened next.

"After that I hated the store. That crazy S.O.B.," Stefan wept. "I resisted going to the store and stayed with Aunt Sophia, instead." He asked Marc, "Do you think he ever messed with you?" Marc said not that he remembered. Stefan concluded, "This is one helluva secret I kept from even myself. I still smell his stinking body, his foul breath, oh god . . ."

Marc was overwhelmed with compassion for his brother. Julia was devastated with regret of her annoyance of Stefan. Now, when a prayer was said for uncle Stefan at mealtime, there was such importance, such tender regard for him in the understanding of Julia and Marc. They were grateful deceased mother Rose never knew his traumatic story.

As Stefan's health declined, he asked Marc to get in touch with both his children. They visited their father in the few months before he died, and as requested, he was buried in the cemetery alongside his parents, after a private family Mass celebrated by the local priest.

The uncovering of Stefan's trauma as a young boy shed a completely different light on his life and personality. Julia prayed for Stefan as hard as she could remember praying for anyone. When Julia prayed that Stefan rest in peace, she meant it from the bottom of her heart.

Julia's sandpile experience kept unfolding her own story. Insights flooded-in about prickly parts of her personality: Her insistence that the family in which she grew up had healthier family dynamics in every way compared to the Montels. Yet, how did Marc turn out to be so patient and selfless, and why did her family need to be so perfect in her eyes? What was her need to compete about this? She came to realize how pompous she'd been about sex; dismissing the possibility that Marc might have ideas about sex, or sexuality in marriage, as if her psychiatric training made her an expert on the subject. Clear also, was her cheeky arrogance about Stefan being a vapid specimen of humanity, which endured to some degree until the day, not long before he died, when he gently declared, "Julia, this life is imperfect, unpredictable, and unfinished."

Memories returned to Julia: in elementary school after telling a classmate she was adopted, the young classmate said, "You mean your mom gave you away!" When she was older, a chance comment in a biology class that a woman knows a baby is hers, but a man doesn't have this certainty except now with DNA, awakened the possibility her biological father didn't even know she existed, which of course, she now knew was so. Cal Hanover hadn't known.

Stefan was correct when he said, "Life is imperfect, unpredictable, unfinished." He was perhaps an underdeveloped sage, Julia wondered to herself. Stefan later told her, "The good priest who visits me first uttered the words about life being imperfect, unpredictable, unfinished." Somehow, these words seemed to soothe Stefan.

Julia was acutely aware her acid test was whether she was becoming reconciled within herself to her birth mother Matti. She knew she needed to retrieve Matti's computer from Lenore, with no idea that Lenore planned to bring the purple leather notebook which contained documents from Matti's computer, to Julia.

CHAPTER TWO

Logan Lives

Ann Dramm had become a bolder woman through therapy. Then, dealing with the loss of Mel, absorbing Aunt Gloria's details of estrangement within the family, due to religion. Followed by Gloria's death, the burials in Steelton, exacerbated by Ann moving from her home of many years to a high-rise loft. This now bolder woman was reeling with change.

Ann found comfort talking regularly with Lenore by telephone and learned, most amazingly, that Logan from Lenore's long ago medical residency in San Francisco had not died in a rock-climbing accident in Oregon as reported by a female friend in the Bay area. It was a bizarre mix-up of nearly identical names and occupations. Alive and well, the Logan she'd known and "been in love with" as a medical resident, telephoned, which sent her head, heart, and her future into a spin.

Lenore's unusual Logan-death-mistake began with an error. However, the error was not in the obituary which stated that surgeon Logen S. Bradshaw died in a rock-climbing accident in Oregon. The error began when a friend from Lenore's medical training days in San Francisco e-mailed Lenore the obituary along with words of shock, surprise, regret, that the life of Lenore's long-ago love ended so tragically. Later, Lenore blamed herself for dismissing the spelling "Logen," as a newspaper typo, for the emotion-laden words of sorrow of her medical school friend inclined Lenore to ignore the spelling.

Lenore explained the error to Ann, "The fact is that a surgeon, Logen Samuel Bradshaw of the San Francisco Bay area did die in a rock-climbing accident. However, my long-ago romance was with Logan Savidge Bradshaw, a surgeon who lived in Seattle. Their middle initial was the same. "The day Logan telephoned me was surreal."

Her friend from medical school days had contacted the Logan Lenore had dated. His situation was that after two divorces, two adult sons, and grandchildren, Logan was retired and living in his boyhood home in Seattle. Events moved swiftly after Logan telephoned Lenore. The two first met in Denver, then San Francisco, eventually Clarksdale, and finally Seattle. By then, Lenore was dealing with hypotheticals regarding the prospect of marriage.

Did she want a man daily in her life? She was well-adjusted to living alone. Logan had said after being with her in Clarksdale, and finding that cable TV sports would make his beloved Seattle Mariners and Seahawks available, he could handle living in Clarksdale. Was this realistic? Having always lived in a city; could he survive in the town of Clarksdale? What did two divorces say about his marriage compatibility quotient?

Lenore met his two sons and their families in the Seattle area and found them lovely people. He met Lenore's children and grandchildren when he was in Clarksdale and there seemed to be mutual amiability.

Lenore had shared on the telephone with Ann the initial reuniting with Logan, "At the airport, we hugged and a familiar compatibility seemed present. I remember having this amusing thought that no one would suspect a senior citizen rendezvous was taking place. Strangely, by the time we were on the shuttle to the hotel I felt like a younger me, as if the years in-between had not happened. It was a throwback to that earlier time in San Francisco.

"By the time we met at the Denver airport, because of e-mail and telephone, we already knew basic facts about spouses, children, grandchildren, how life had treated us, and we'd exchanged photos. Therefore, sitting across from each other in a beautiful restaurant the first extraordinary evening together, we talked about people we knew in common from the past.

"After a night of wonderful sleep in separate rooms, day two was more direct, pointed, and real. Logan told me how he'd always liked my naturalness, freshness, and lack of contrived social conventionality, which he'd had way too much of growing up. He explained both of his wives were over-socialized, just as his parents had been.

"He spoke of his two wives. The first, mother of his two sons, to whom he was married over twenty years, and the second wife of two years, which he knew was a mistake even before the wedding ceremony. He turned the conversation back to me and said he needed more psychological sophistication and thought he used to tease about my deep interest in psychiatry because he admired that part of me. He said he liked my mind, the simplicity of being with me, my independence of thought, and the searching, ponderous topics I liked to talk about.

"He remembered best our walks in nature, Muir Woods, sitting and talking while at the ocean or in the mountains. His words burned into my very being. I asked why we stopped seeing each other. He said he wanted to ask me the same question. He felt the weekend with his parents went OK, but when I didn't return a telephone call or two, he assumed he was wrong about the weekend. He added that knowing my tendency for probing thought, he surmised his mother may not have worn well with me.

"His honesty was almost too much for me. I wanted to go away from it, yet found myself defending this obvious trait of mine by saying what drew me into psychiatry was a probing love of the inner world. For me, there is no greater mystery than the human personality. I felt no need to apologize for being morbidly intense, but did so anyway.

"He slyly said there is more to me than morbid intensity, and we laughed that he cleverly reinforced the description of morbidity while yet moderating it. We had always laughed easily together.

"I returned to the question of why we stopped dating and what he said about my not returning telephone calls. I reminded him of a slipshod system of taking telephone calls in the place I lived in those days before cell phones, where notes about answered calls were tacked to a cork board by a door to the outside with people rushing in and out the door and possibly some of the notes becoming detached and lost. Or people were too busy to write a note alerting someone to a telephone call, or handwritten notes were impossible to read.

"This was also a time when a research project I was working on had ended, data was being reviewed, preliminary writing begun for an article to be published. I was on overload. And perhaps unconscious forces were at work. He said maybe it was fate."

CHAPTER THREE

Rendezvous

Lenore continued, "Logan wanted to know why fate had been kinder to me than him because my marriage endured and his hadn't. I told him I did not know fate's secrets. He raised an eyebrow and smiled at my answer, an old, familiar gesture of his. Earlier he'd kissed me on the cheek when my old habit of head tilt/widened eyes, showed itself. He said he found the gesture endearing years ago, as if I was giving him my rapt attention. I didn't mention his raised eyebrow.

"He wanted to further clarify why we stopped seeing each other and said, 'You weren't avoiding me?' I told him I wasn't, and that I suffered terribly assuming he was avoiding me.

"He did not dwell on the subject and simply commented that it was good we both now knew neither of us had rejected the other.

"And then he asked me if I still went to church every week like I did years ago. He'd asked me on the telephone whether Dennis was Catholic. Why was he bringing up the religion thing again? This time he said, 'Catholics seem to stay married.' He was talking out loud, it seemed. Was he concluding this is why my marriage lasted?

"I remarked I wasn't sure Catholics stay married more than other groups these days now that women have career opportunities and thus the option of getting out of an unsatisfactory situation, plus the fading of divorce stigma, along with more effective birth control, thus liberating women and bringing choices previously not available.

"Logan was raised Presbyterian. Logan's youngest son Frederick is an ordained Presbyterian minister. His eldest, Franklin, a neurologist."

Lenore continued, "On a park bench in Denver after a leisurely walk we talked about books we'd read in recent times. Thrilled that we'd read some of the same books, I turned towards him, impulsively touching my hand to his cheek, he returned my gesture putting his arm around me. We were on the same page as years ago.

"When I returned from Denver, my children had the audacity to ask whether we had sex. I think they were teasing me, but I gave a serious answer and said, 'No, no, no. There was too much involved to clutter the situation with sex. I know I was overwhelmed about being together and happily retreated to the silent safety of my own hotel room. I think this was true for Logan, too.

"Weeks after Denver, we met at the San Francisco airport. I hadn't been to San Francisco since medical residency, and thus I expected the city to hold more excitement for me than for him, for he'd practiced medicine there for a few years before starting a practice in Seattle, moving with his wife and sons, for she also was from Seattle. The family frequently returned to San Francisco over the years.

"Strangely and surprisingly, I first found myself second-guessing the way I'd spent my life in Clarksdale compared to San Francisco and its charms. Any bits of comparison vanished when Logan started talking about death. He spoke about having recently made explicit, detailed, legal documents to curb end of life treatments for himself, except palliative care, and given copies of the documents to his sons. He said embracing death as a part of life is liberating, and he hoped there would be increased civil discourse about the inevitability of death, which will then eventually moderate the exorbitant money spent on unnecessary end-of-life procedures. Only a senior citizen rendezvous includes talk about death."

CHAPTER FOUR

Marriage

Logan said after his first marriage, and then the impulsive second marriage dissolved, he reverted to his Presbyterian upbringing when he no longer had confidence in himself, for "what good is a surgeon who has lost confidence?"

Part of his recovery from two divorces returned him to wood carving, "As a child on vacation with my parents I watched a man carve a tiny bear out of wood and never forgot the magic of that experience. Wood carving helped me heal from the broken relationships." Logan would eventually build a mostly glass hut in a small clump of trees behind the octagonal home in Clarksdale, where he could whittle in the hut in solitude under the endless expanse of Kansas sky.

When Logan first came to Clarksdale, Lenore learned of his interest in saving the earth. He explained, "I've been influenced in the view that the earth is sacred from the writings of Thomas Berry (1914-2009), a Catholic priest, cultural historian, pioneer in ecology, who was shaped by the ideas of Teilhard de Chardin. Berry posed the idea that patriarchal institutional Christianity concentrated so much on the redemption of humanity, that it left out mother earth, the natural world, as a means of divine revelation."

Logan's first Clarksdale visit was busy. He met Lenore's children, grandchildren, Julia Montel and family, was treated to a tour of Montel furniture store, saw the location where Dennis's pharmacy had been, the golf course, the regional behavioral center outside town where Lenore spent her psychiatric career.

Lenore told Ann, "Much about the Kansas earth resonated with him. He spoke about one day hoping to see native prairie tall grasses. He mentioned the earth spirituality of the Plains Indians, the ecological disaster of the dustbowl which you know my ancestors experienced, the High Plains Ogallala Aquifer, fracking, and other concerns. He spoke of the ancient inland sea that once covered the High Plains, and fossils found from that time. He was intrigued that Dennis planned the house to coincide with sunrises and sunsets. When he was in Clarksdale, we walked to the highest elevation of the six-acre property and watched the sunset. Everything fell into place for us here in Clarksdale."

After Logan's stay in Clarksdale, Lenore went to Seattle, where she was again in the house that had tormented her years earlier. She met Logan's Presbyterian minister son Frederick, his wife, and two sons, ages 9 and 11, and saw the special bond between eleven-year-old Aidan with autism, and his grandfather Logan. Electronic devices kept grandson and grandfather in touch when apart. Frederick and family recently purchased Logan's boyhood home from Logan and would soon be moving there. Lenore met and felt comfortable with neurologist son Franklin, his wife, their adolescent son and daughter.

Lenore and Logan married in Seattle. His minister son, and Jesuit Geoff, Roman Catholic priest who'd spent a short while at Lenore's parish in Clarksdale, now teaching at the Jesuit University in San Francisco, took part in the ceremony. Lenore's children and grandchildren were there, alongside Logan's family.

Newlyweds Lenore and Logan lived several months in the unusual octagon house in Clarksdale and several months in a condo in Seattle. Back and forth, they were on planes, spending time with their families, enjoying being together, savoring their unlikely life together.

Lenore had confided in Ann before the marriage, "I have questions about marrying Logan who is twice-divorced. Yet, the circumstance between us is unusual. Whatever attracted us to each other when we were young interns is still there. I might be inviting difficulty down the road. We've signed legal papers about finances, liabilities, end of life issues. Life is a gamble, an opportunity, one decision after another. We'll see how this plays out in the long run."

CHAPTER FIVE

Realtor Tess

Lenore, now married to Logan, living alternately in Clarksdale KS and Seattle WA, kept in touch with widowed Ann Dramm in Stamford CT. Years earlier, the chorus of birds in a tree in a pasture in central Kansas on Lenore's grandparents' farm site had cemented the women's friendship. They would remain friends for life.

Ann Dramm was never without friends, and not long after her husband Mel died, Ann formed a friendship with Tess Schultz, the realtor who helped Ann buy a loft and sell the large home she'd shared with Mel. Tess, whose actual name was Teresa, was a strong personality, the oldest of eight children in her family, who knew even in adolescence, two things she wanted when she grew up: money, and no babies. Her parents had to work and struggle too hard to raise their brood. She worked her way through college and became a realtor who worked every day of the week, marrying and divorcing three men who were no match for her will, work ethic, competitive drive.

When the real estate deals Tess orchestrated for Ann were finalized, the two women became friends, and not long after that, Tess retired, except for an occasional real estate listing and checking in with the property manager in charge of Tess's properties around town. Though financially well-off, retirement left Tess adrift in new waters.

Tess was fascinated with Ann's inquiry into Catholicism, as Tess was a "lapsed" Catholic; the word "lapsed" made Tess laugh her throaty laugh. Tall Tess with brown short-medium hair, chic clothes worn with a flair, neither thin nor thick in stature, a charming tiny lisp accenting perfect pearly white teeth, was an altogether attractive personality who knew how to make one feel safe in her care while she tended to an individual's housing needs, whether buying or selling.

Tess was an extreme extravert with a razor-sharp mind. Strangely, this lapsed Catholic and Ann began attending inquiry classes together at a nearby Catholic Church. Ann did this after learning from aunt Gloria that religion split her father and his father forever, and she wanted to know more how that might have been so. Tess attended classes to catch-up with what she'd missed out on all these years away from church.

They learned Vatican II (1962-1965) was the brainchild of Pope John XXIII (Angelo Roncalli) shortly after he became pope at the age of 77. He died at the age of 82 when the council was only about a fourth of the way completed, and the new pope who oversaw the rest of the council was Pope Paul VI (Giovanni Montini).

They also learned some today believe Vatican II was a godsend, a vision that continues to unfold. Others regard it a catastrophe, the church losing its traditional way, falling into permissive relativism.

Tess told Ann, "I started avoiding Mass in high school and gave-up the whole church thing in college. I look back now and realize I've always had a good "B.S. detector" in me. I can sniff-out manipulation, coercion, using fear and guilt to control people. I cannot abide repressive people or ideas. The church was repressive in ways, and I think I knew this at a fairly early age. I could intuitively detect self-righteous clichés, pious platitudes, and burdens of obligations, duties, rules handed-down from on high. I began to smolder as I got older. You can quote me on that," and she laughed her generous laugh.

"I see that now. Sin, sin, sin. Never-ending sin. You can tell me I'm stupid, corrupt, limited, underdeveloped, undeveloped, a poor excuse for a human being. Tell me I cheat or lie, and I can agree or challenge your statement. But don't keep haranguing about sin even as a prelude to talking about redemption and salvation. Later, I learned the word sin, translated literally from ancient Greek, means to miss the mark, as in the game of archery; to make bad choices, thus living one's life poorly, without proper aim, to miss the point of one's life, which makes sense to me.

"However, I didn't know that, and I had an overdose of sin-talk. I thought Jesus came to help us sinners. I wondered: don't we change with grace? I wanted insights, enlightenment, hopefulness, growth possibilities, wisdom. Maybe the church needed some of what psychology knows today, to get new words to use, for their phrases were downtrodden, oppressive, life-sucking, draining, to me. "Good news" is what Jesus supposedly brought, but what came across to me was the downside of being alive. I gave up on church. Decided I could do better on my own.

"Today I hope the bishops and such are down on their knees for mishandling priest pedophile cases, and maybe they are. Contrition is good for everybody, especially those teaching others about contrition. Hierarchy should be thanked for what they contribute, but hierarchy is not God Almighty. They're more like executives in a corporation.

"I should never have married; not even once, let alone three times. I didn't understand myself. I caved-into the cultural norm of marriage; didn't want to be an old-maid or spinster; such unflattering terms."

Tess wondered about her three marriages and questioned whether some of her anger at oppressive church hierarchy might be connected to her own oppressive expectations she had with her short-term husbands, which may have been connected to feminine rage, not about pregnancy, labor, delivery, care of children, but male lack of appreciation for what these entail.

Tess ruminated that women stretch their bodies and very beings to accommodate new life, while men traditionally kept their same workload, though it is true these days fathers are more involved with caring for babies and children.

CHAPTER SIX

Anti-Anxiety Pills

Tess reflected to Ann, "I think a deep sense of injustice accompanied me into three marriages along with an agenda for changing each husband, wanting him to work harder, work better. Anyway, I quickly became impatient and dissatisfied with the guys I married. They seemed unmotivated, lethargic, slothful, next to my overdeveloped work ethic, which probably isn't a balanced way to live, but seemed the best way to me. Maybe I married lazy guys so I could be a big sister to them and take care of them like I did my siblings."

Ann, from her days of therapy, paid attention to her dreams. Tess didn't. Ann told Tess she says to maternity center residents, "Dreams are to you, from you, about you," hoping to interest Tess in her dreams.

Ann and Tess didn't always talk about religious stuff. Yet when they discussed other matters, their conversation seemed to drift back to religion. Like the day they were talking about recent events at the maternity center when Tess skipped to the topic of soul, "I now know what soul is. I found it on the internet. You know the infinity symbol ∞; the 8 on its side? Well, soul is exactly where the two circles meet. One circle is Spirit, the other is Matter. Soul is the internal combustion engine where spirit and matter mix. It's where the basic ingredients of life come together and drive us crazy. It's where the potential for agony and ecstasy dwells." Ann remembered mandorla, when two circles overlap; the mandorla door at Lenore's octagon house.

That day Tess also had a list of non-gender labels for God: Presence, Process, Source, Infinite, Ultimate, The Holy, Energy, Life, Love, Being, Spirit, Transcendence. "The words must be capitalized, of course," she explained. Ann used many of these words herself and realized Tess may have heard some of them from her. Or who knows what one learned from the other.

Tess needed a sounding board for her ideas, and Ann was a seasoned listener. Tess related, "The priest last Sunday talked about the bible story Mary and Martha. Well, I'm all Martha. He talked about integration in the personality. Neither only Mary or only Martha. Relating the bible to ordinary experience makes it meaningful. I wish the Sunday bible readings could be always this relevant. I'm trying to discover and recover the Mary in me. I think a recent dream was about a Mary-trait part of me.

"In the dream, a pile of dead cows was lying in the street in front of the house where we lived until I was nine years old. I noticed that the cows were not dead, but just barely alive, barely breathing. It seemed I needed to step into the center of the pile but didn't want to do that because I might become "infected," whatever that meant. The dream felt very important.

"Using what you and my therapist told me about relating with dreams, I thought about a cow. A cow, spending much of her life walking about chewing her cud, yet she is exceptionally productive: birthing calves, providing milk for calves and humans, dung for fertilizer. After death, meat for nourishment, leather for purses, shoes, sofas. In a masculine-dominated culture, calling a woman a cow or a heifer is degrading, humiliating, an insult.

"Also influenced by you, I think my dream was about a feminine 'cow-Mary' aspect of me, which had almost died in me. I was afraid to step into the center of this issue, afraid to get infected, be affected by it, changed, made different by it.

"The dream scene was before I was nine years old, which I believe means that at an early age I abandoned what you call the "inner world," of deep prayer and inspiration, and adopted instead the outer world agenda of prosperity, success, progress; doing over being. It is hard for me to "be," just "be." Clearly, I adopted the idea that hard work will get you everything you can ever want or need. Babies were a hindrance to that kind of straightforward goal-oriented drive. This isn't yet crystal clear to me, but it's something along those lines.

"I've been taking anti-anxiety pills for years. I'm riddled with fear. You know I retired because I was afraid of becoming demented or dying with my personal properties not turned to cash. Both of my parents had some dementia before they died. So, when I forget the slightest anything, I see that as a sign of dementia.

"I used to smoke, so if I cough or see someone in public using an oxygen pack, I see my future with chronic obstructive pulmonary disease (COPD). At the time I was helping you buy your loft and sell your home, I was barely keeping my act together. I sensed you were a person with something I needed, and so I sought you out when our business transactions ended.

"Back to Mass, I'm coming to understand Mass as a gathering of energy built around a ritual, and between the potential energy in the ritual and the energy that each person brings, the Mass is an event of holy energy, grace. Each person is a vessel of grace."

Tess did her husky laugh, and said, "In my next life I am going to be a theologian. Women may not yet be allowed to be priests, but can become theologians. I read this someplace. I believe this is the best way to enlighten and influence male hierarchy and bring more balance to outdated patriarchy."

CHAPTER SEVEN

Patriarchy

Tess's fears of old age, illness, and death had her thinking about inviting her niece Dempsey to move to Stamford. Dempsey was the eldest of Tess's nieces and nephews. Tess had several times before suggested Dempsey, now in her forties, leave Terryton CT, where Tess had also grown up, and where Dempsey seemed to be languishing. Tess had always loved Dempsey even after Dempsey became stuck in a moribund mindset. Dempsey was family, and Tess needed family at this time in her life.

All of Tess's siblings were alive. As the eldest, she'd likely be the first to die. She had the financial means and long-term insurance to take care of herself when infirm, unless another economic recession came along and damaged what she put together. She would like to relax and enjoy day by day being alive with fewer worries about the future. She had been looking for inner peace when she met Ann.

In therapy Tess remembered holiday family celebrations with German-Irish heritage grandparents, aunts, uncles, cousins, where the women fixed all the food, while simultaneously looking after the children, including diaper changing which men never seemed to be aware of. The men and children were fed before the women ate and then washed dishes, all the while men relaxed and conversed in another part of the house. This seemed an unfair division of labor even before she knew what division of labor was. Something hadn't seemed fair to young Tess.

She was in college alongside the social change of the 1960s-70s, which challenged many cultural conventions and fit well with her innate sense of what was fair and unfair. But no, she was not inclined to protest in the streets. She had no time for that, with her own job, working her way through college while living at home, still helping her mother when possible.

So while hippies, beatniks, flower children were doing drugs, dropping-out, and living in communes, Tess was solidifying the belief that hard work, money, and no babies, would be the key to the life she wanted.

And now, the presence of Dempsey could ease Tess's worries and Tess could help Dempsey fulfill her potential. However, Dempsey did not immediately accept Tess's invitation.

Tess easily looked at herself, "I stopped accumulating marriage certificates and started accumulating real estate. I bought more and more properties while working as an agent seven days a week just like my mother worked with babies, children, and household seven days a week, except I wasn't awakened by business during the night, as she was with the needs of children. Child-rearing is underestimated by those who haven't been close enough to it.

"I am a so-called "fallen-away" Catholic, away from the church for many years, only recently returning to Mass, I've overdone most things in my life including marriage. I seem allergic to patriarchy. No, my father was not an awful person. Actually, he was a fine person, husband, father, with the gender role mentality of the day, which my mother had also.

"My fixation gathered steam when I realized that after all of the female efforts in birthing, babies were given their father's family name, just as we all had our father's family name. Our mother's family name went away. The arrangement didn't really offend me, it mostly mystified me and I wasn't sure it was fair.

"I once heard a remark that Holy Mother the Church, the Catholic church, had not always been a good mother. I thought, *how could the Church be a good mother when priests, bishops, archbishops, cardinals, the Pope, are all men! Even God is male.*"

Reading about the roots of patriarchy, Tess learned a good bit about what simmered inside her below conscious awareness.

Long ago, a breastfeeding woman could not take her baby on a hunt, for the baby might cry and ruin the quiet needed to kill prey. Thus, women and children stayed close to protected living areas, while men ventured to more distant hunting grounds. This division of labor safeguarded survival, and with it brought different experiences and brain development for males and females through many eons including later centuries of literacy when men were educated but women were not.

Women always know a baby is theirs. A man (before DNA) testing could not be sure, unless he closely controlled the woman. Once males understood their role in pregnancy, female virginity became important to males; far more than literacy for women. Thus, different experiences were allowed or restricted and brain pathway development for males and females was different.

Female sexual anatomy is interior, dark womb, (receptivity) where new life comes into being, similar to right-brain-hemisphere intuition. Male sexual anatomy mirrors left-brain-hemisphere probing, penetrating (analysis), able to impregnate experience with rational clarity. Today, it is sometimes said a certain female is very left-brain, or a specific male is more right-brain, though, indeed, each of us has only one brain, so it is the brain-hemisphere activity that is being cited.

Tess remembered in college finding it strange that Freud believed women had "penis envy," which meant females feel incomplete without a penis. "Oh my, I knew there was something wrong with this. I knew even as a student that the envy was about male domination, privilege and choice, simultaneous with female subordination. It wasn't about anatomy. Freud was wrong."

Tess was clear, "In weddings today, the veil over the face of the bride is a throwback to arranged marriages, the groom not seeing the bride until it's too late. Hello! Surprise! to the groom. And the father "giving" the bride to the groom is archaic."

Lingering questions kept popping up for Tess: Was humanity moving toward figuring out this masculine-feminine, Yin- Yang, brain-hemisphere mystery? What was masculine energy, feminine energy, or is there such a difference? How do these questions apply in our own lives? For

Tess, the subject of feminine/masculine energy was a monster she couldn't let go of, for it was a nagging part of her own story.

CHAPTER EIGHT

Homecoming

To help Tess get her mind off of her own dreads, she had begun reading *Interior Castle*, written over 400 years ago, by St. Teresa of Avila, Teresa, her patron saint. Tess was impressed with Teresa writing about self-knowledge:

> Self-knowledge is so important that, even if you were raised right up to the heavens, I should like you never to relax your cultivation of it . . . none of our friends and relatives are as near to us as our faculties, with which we have always to live, whether we like it or not . . . let us look at our own shortcomings and leave other people's alone.

This was good advice. Tess found herself thinking about the injustices of patriarchy again. "I remember my dad on his days "off" read the newspaper at length while my mother went from one task to another interrupted by the needs of children and others, whereas study, intellectual development, require uninterrupted time. Did women support patriarchy? Yes, of course. Generation after generation most women internalized the idea of their own subordination, learned to mistrust their own experience and devalue it, to please male authority, avoid disapproval, to be protected and financially supported.

"For centuries and centuries, men organized and ran the world. Catholic hierarchy today with pope, bishops, clergy, laity, is like the old feudal system: king, prince, dukes, all the way down to serfs. Corporations today start with a CEO, and progress down to worker-bee staff. It's one-way humans organize themselves. Can there be other ways? How can the hierarchical system be modified to work better for families today juggling both parents working outside the home along with child-rearing and household chores? Women used to be "housewives," as if married to the house. Strange term.

"Yet, somebody has to keep home fires going or the light and warmth grows dim and can die. It was comforting to find my mother home at the end of the school day. Especially in winter the smell of food cooking for the evening meal created a cozy feeling.

"I liked Jesus' mother Mary in elementary Catholic school; made a May altar in her honor and remembered October as a special month of the rosary. Two months (May and October) of the year dedicated to remembering Mary. One-sixth of the year, I realized when I learned my fractions. Not bad. I always liked her far better than grumpy God the Father. Mary is one reason I kept a fondness for the church.

"Strange as it may seem, I love the spiritual tradition(s) of the Catholic church, despite certain doctrines, dogmas, and sometimes downright sinfulness in this human institution. I walk into Mass and feel as if I have come "home." Each Mass is a kind of homecoming for me after having been gone so long. Of course, what I'm coming home to is what Jesus made available to humanity; that's the mystery celebrated in Mass; the creative energy of the universe flowing through him to us earthlings, and all creation. This makes sense to me.

"I'm glad the church didn't implode in the years I was away, though the pedophile scandals are their own kind of implosion and explosion: unmarried, childless, male hierarchy protecting itself, its colleagues, the organization first and foremost. To be fair, expertise on pedophilia was sometimes sought by church officials, but the disorder does not seem treatable. Still, there is deep sin on the part of the hierarchy covering-up the pedophile scandals. I believe people in the pews would be more forgiving if there was more contrition from the hierarchy on this.

"I remember we could see only the face and hands of the nuns in elementary school. They were covered-up. Why? A long history, I'm sure, but part of that history is that women have been required to cover their bodies, such as burkas some Muslim women wear today. Females have been defined as seducing sexpots against defenseless, righteous males, "respectable" women at times have covered themselves to show they were sexually serving only one man and were under his protection. Non-respectable "public women" who dishonestly veiled or covered themselves were punished severely for misrepresenting themselves. Women have, indeed, been treated as "sex objects."

"Perhaps men feel they have been unappreciated as breadwinners, but have their bodies been exploited like women's bodies? Of course, we really need to respect each other as partners, participants, in the game of life and death. Death is always hanging around."

For Tess, the prospect of death was always hanging around.

CHAPTER NINE

Metaphor

Tess realized, "I've developed the habit of searching for personal meaning in the scripture readings at Sunday Mass, which I wish someone had encouraged me to do when I was younger. But then, I may have discovered this sooner on my own had I continued going to Mass. However, I was so entrenched in the standard meanings provided, I doubt I would have been independent-minded enough to search for my own understanding.

"Last Sunday Luke 12:32-48 talked about possessions, purses, treasure. I can relate to all that easily, and then it says "Where your treasure is, there will be your heart be also." My heart was in my work; I treasured success and progress. I do not regret this; just wish I'd been more balanced between work and relationships, including relating to myself. And then it talks about the master coming when not expected, the servant doing what the master wants, and that much will be expected from someone who has been entrusted with much. Now that I am learning about myself in therapy, I realize I would have served myself and others better had I remained connected to a long-term, ongoing relationship with wisdom greater than my small self-sufficient self which ran on will-power.

"Success and progress could take me so far, but are not sufficient to deal with old age and death. Success and progress are optimistically shortsighted; not adequately long-term realistic. I am convinced humans are designed to be intimately, personally, experientially, connected to something bigger than our little brains know most of the time. This is about 'knowing' rather than merely 'believing' in God."

Tess lived in a brownstone. She recently told Ann she'd been using metaphors to talk about the renovations of the brownstone related to the transformations taking place in her personality in therapy. Updating the kitchen was like becoming aware of Tess's thoughts, which she took in, ingested, chewed on, digested; what nourished her ideas and expectations, whether she was aware of what she fed on in her thoughts and emotions, what she savored, what was junk food and should not be swallowed. How she satisfied her personality hungers and thirsts. What were half-baked reactions, well-seasoned impressions; "things" that should be kept on ice for the time being, or put on the back burner. When something was "eating" at her. Tess enjoyed playing with metaphor, which she knew Ann could appreciate.

The bathroom, too, has many personality parallels, for it is where one gets rid of bodily waste. What in our life is a waste of our time, energy, or talent? Do we know how to get rid of crap in the personality or outer life? Excrement is also fertilizer; we can learn a lot from the crap that goes on inside and outside us. Urine is not solid, but fluid, ideas, emotions, inklings flowing through us, needing elimination. There is also psychological letting go, like urinating, defecating. And spiritual letting go, as in the phrase, "let go and let God." The bathroom is where we cleanse the body, refresh the breath (of life) by brushing teeth (the most enduring part of the body, bodies can be identified from dental records); identity. Showering and bathing, washing off what we've picked-up from others, the outside world, personal residue (worries, troubles, fears), being washed away. Washing hair is like cleansing one's thoughts, just as hair growing out of the head needs to be cleansed, renewed. Whether showering or bathing, one is naked in the bathroom, vulnerable, like in deep prayer.

The bedroom is a place of rest and renewal. Sleeping is certainly a change from waking consciousness and dreaming is a special state of being. Tess knew not being able to sleep; insomnia. Pure agony. "I've taken pills for insomnia, too. Ah, *rest in God.* I like the phrase very much."

The *living* room; a unique name for a room. This is the room in which we are most likely to invite others; the room they see before the other rooms. It is sometimes called the *front* room. It's like the part of our personality we share with others. Unlike kitchen, bathroom, bedroom, our intimate needs are not (usually) dealt with in the living room.

Tess was a person who had lived as an adult almost exclusively in the living room area of her personality with far too little time in the more intimate areas of her personality. It pained her to admit being shallow and superficial about herself. In the house renovation she realized again how much effort and money is spent outfitting kitchens and bathrooms and regarded this as symbolic of what it costs to intimately care for the deep, below the surface, personality. It's what she was learning about herself at this stage in her life.

A nagging question remained despite the many things Tess was learning about herself. Why wasn't her niece Dempsey responding to Tess's invitation to new life in the city?

CHAPTER TEN

Enabler

Dempsey was the first child of Tess's next-in-line sibling brother Harold and his wife Paula who were young when she was born. Dempsey had a brother two years younger who had been able to navigate his way through life, but Dempsey, despite a college degree, struggled with low paying jobs, broken-down cars, wobbly friendships, weight problems, and what she herself proclaimed as "not having a life."

Dempsey and her dog Mister were finally coming to live with Tess for six months. The dog and six-month parameter emerged as Tess began trying to sell Dempsey on the idea after initially not hearing back from Dempsey. Her dog and a trial time period were assurances Dempsey needed before saying "yes."

Because of her own therapy, Tess understood some of what happened to Dempsey psychologically—what damaged Dempsey. First, there was Dempsey's name. Tess's brother, Dempsey's father, always a boxing fan, immaturely suggested that his firstborn, whether boy or girl, be named Dempsey, after Jack Dempsey, boxing champion. His equally immature wife thought his idea was "cute." That's how Dempsey got her name.

And then, looking puffy as a normal newborn, the baby's father gleefully mentioned too often how the newborn looked like she'd been in a fight. And he talked like that for months. By the time her brother Max was born (named after Maximillian Schmelling, German champion boxer) her father told the story of their namings many times. Had newborn Max been a girl, she would have been named Maxine, but called Max, after Schmelling.

Poor Dempsey bore the brunt of her father's immaturities, and later she would find, his insecurities. And if there was one thing she was not, it was a "fighter." Life knocked her down (metaphorically) way more than she could fight back.

Tess's sister-in-law Paula went along with Harold's childish humor, which Tess felt was particularly detrimental to Dempsey, who was the apple of Tess's eye when she was little. Though always having a soft spot for Dempsey, Tess was now clueless on how to approach living together with Dempsey and Mister, her dog.

Tess was planning: Dempsey could do therapy. But she won't have insurance! Gulp. Swallow. Acid-reflux. Maybe it would be therapeutic if Tess started calling her "D" instead of Dempsey. How could this happen artfully and not offensively? Tess changed her name from Teresa to Tess, but that was her decision not someone else's. Had Tess created a mess inviting Dempsey?

Tess couldn't stop wondering and worrying. Would Tess and Dempsey eat the same food? Would they eat together? How soon would Dempsey get a job? Would she get a job? Would Tess prepare meals? Would they watch television together? Tess had put a small TV in the second bedroom, Dempsey's room. Would the dog sleep with Dempsey?

The dog's name was "Mister," not because he was male, but because as a puppy he sneezed a lot, probably allergies. He was often "misting" the air around him. He was a "mister." Tess's image of dog sputum flying through the air brought another attack of acid-reflux.

Enabler, enabler, enabler. The words echoed in Tess's ears. Her therapist expressed caution about her becoming an enabler for Dempsey, repeating her marriage pattern. Tess was hoping Ann Dramm could be of help, as Ann herself, long ago, had issues with her own self-confidence and surely would have advice about Dempsey. Tess also knew Ann didn't give advice unless asked; and even then, Ann approached the conversation carefully—relating something out of her personal experience with depression, as well as being a seeker, wife, mother, grandmother.

When renovating the brownstone, Tess had a two-car garage built, accessible from the alley. Dempsey wouldn't have to leave her car on the street. Tess wished Mister would live on the back porch sun room with screened European-style roll-out windows bringing year-round comfort. That's what the window advertisement touted. Tess was pleased with how the sun room turned-out. It was no longer a porch, but a sun room with a ceiling fan for Mister's warm weather comfort.

Tess thought a lot about Mister. He was problematic to her. She wished he wasn't coming. Yet, Dempsey was critically bonded to him. Tess could tell that Mister was a large part of the equation.

Tess began praying for practical guidance so that other nieces and nephews weren't getting annoyed or feeling aunt Tess was running a boarding house for them, too, though no one else seemed as needy as Dempsey. However, Tess scarcely knew some of the younger ones.

Tess was taking the chance she could handle whatever came down the pike. She prayed for a big dose of commonsense, knowing that commonsense is not all that common.

CHAPTER ELEVEN

Dempsey

The day arrived. Dempsey was in Stamford, not far from Tess's brownstone. Dempsey was lost, she told Tess on the telephone. Actually, she was but blocks from the brownstone. Tess noticed the parking space in front of the house was open, hoped it stayed that way, and told Dempsey.

The April day was coolish, pleasant, late afternoon, with no recent moisture, and Tess was grateful for that as she watched out the living room bay window, imagining taking suitcases from the car through the front door and up the stairs to Dempsey's room, which was closer than parking in the garage in back, going through yard, sun room, kitchen, living room, and then up the steps to her room while Mister stayed safely in the yard.

Tess had planned ahead. Yes, indeed, planned ahead: bought extra over-the-counter anti-reflux medication yesterday. Dempsey may need some tablets, too, Tess humorously suggested to herself, as a dark older car moved slowly, slowly, stopped in front to check the house number, parallel parked expertly, driver's door then opened, and it was Dempsey standing outside the car wearing round wire glasses, which Tess found most unattractive on her niece.

Tess was immediately out the front door, down steps and to the sidewalk, curb, at the back of Dempsey's car where she was with her small dog in her arms. They hugged as best they could with Mister between them.

Tess offered to take whatever indoors, but first Dempsey wanted to know if Mister could potty out back, whereupon they traipsed through the house, to the sunroom back door, where Mister was put out on the top step, and he barked furiously. Dempsey went outside with him until he had performed his duties. She then suggested bringing in things from the car with Tess staying in the house, opening the front door as she brought everything in, and kept Mister from charging out the door.

Dempsey had had a plan. Tess was somewhat relieved, for in her planning she had imagined she was the only one with a brain. However, in Dempsey's plan, Tess was forced to hold fidgety barking Mister wanting to escape to Dempsey while the door was left open for bringing in her belongings. Tess felt acid-reflux agitation while Dempsey brought in guitar, laptop computer, printer, several boxes of books, dog carrier, dog bed, and then sacks, sacks, sacks, one or two large plastic yard bags full of stuff. There were no suitcases. Dempsey finally said, "That's the end of it."

Tess thought she saw potato chips and other snacks sticking out of some bags. At the end of the sack onslaught, Tess gave directions for driving to the alley, down the alley, and into the garage which would be open for her. The house number was on the garage.

Meanwhile, with barking Mister and acid-reflux, Tess watched out of the sun room glass door as Dempsey opened the small door of the garage into the back yard. Dempsey was at the right place, as Tess lowered the garage door with the opener and opened the sunroom door so Mister could bolt outside. He was yipping and jumping up as Dempsey picked him up, cradled him in her arms and then put him down while seating herself on an iron chair at the black round iron table in the back yard and lighting a cigarette. She had told Tess she occasionally smoked.

Tess joined Dempsey outside at the table. An old smoker herself, she found the smell and the habit offensive. *Mister mucous was now sitting on his smokestack mother's lap!* It pained Tess to recognize her own dark, unkind humor was showing itself. If Dee had been a stranger Tess would have accepted the wicked humor which often erupted in her, but this time it brought pain because it made fun of her niece, whom she loved dearly.

Tess noticed today the furtive, darting glances, even when Dempsey smiled, as if watching the reactions of others. Always watching. Dempsey had become hyper-vigilant in an unsettling way.

Tess made small talk at the iron table about Dempsey's trip. Dempsey said little. Finally, cigarette smoked, they went inside where Tess suggested they tour the basement, which was one reason she bought the brownstone. Washer, dryer, clothes line, large sink with table next to it, a few boxes of storage were all that was down there, along with a new furnace and a wine refrigerator –Tess's wine cellar.

Tess offered to help take sacks upstairs to Dempsey's room, but Dempsey said she'd do it, as she put Mister in her room and closed the door whereupon he barked and Tess heard him scratch the door!! Tess winced though Dempsey immediately put Mister in her arm and took one sack at a time upstairs until she got to bigger items, when she put him in the back yard where he barked and whined and may have scratched at the glass weather door. Tess tried not to hear and didn't go to see what Mister was doing.

Then, Tess went to the kitchen beginning to prepare the evening meal. Dempsey asked if Mister could stay in the kitchen with Tess, for she had a doggie gate to place in the doorway between the kitchen and living room. Mister and Tess were now in the kitchen together with him incessantly banging against the doggie gate to get to Dempsey as she hauled her final stuff upstairs.

At last, Dempsey was downstairs holding Mister while seated at the petite table in the kitchen. Tess's life had changed enormously within the hour. She and her house had undergone alterations not anticipated. Tess noticed Dempsey's jacket on an ornamental brass garment fixture in the entryway. Well, yes, Tess did sometimes hang her own jacket there momentarily. But no garment was to stay there for long. All garments were to go upstairs. Hopefully, Dempsey would realize this on her own. Tess already mentioned the hooks on the wall to the basement for seedier coats, jackets, etc., when showing her the basement, where Tess hoped Mister would spend a good bit of time. Tess's hope would be not come to be.

Dempsey watched while Tess put the meal together: broiled salmon, small golden baked potatoes, green beans, tossed salad, wheat roll and butter; fruit salad for dessert. Tess had always had a need to eat well or she felt sluggish. Sluggish was like lazy to her, and she did abhor lazy.

They would eat at the petite table in the kitchen with the doggie gate keeping Mister trapped with them. Tess asked Dempsey if she would like coffee, tea, milk, water, beer, wine, as she waited while Tess finished preparing the meal. Dempsey wanted only water and offered to get it for herself, which she did. Learning where things were was important for her to become acclimated to living here.

Dempsey sat at the table while Mister sniffed the floor, cabinets, the gate, begged Dempsey to hold him, but she didn't. There was strained talk about Dempsey's parents, her brother Max, and other relatives. Tess asked questions. Dempsey gave short answers. The conversation depended on Tess.

Finally, food was ready buffet style. Dempsey took tiny bits of everything. Tess should have asked whether Dempsey liked salmon, etc., before assuming. Tess was in the midst of berating herself when Dempsey said she had stopped for fast-food shortly before arriving at the house, as she didn't want to be a bother.

Tess should have communicated better, she scolded herself. Must she anticipate everything? Must she always lead? Must she follow Dempsey's lead? Tess knew she had a lot to learn. Tess asked what Dempsey preferred for breakfast. Dempsey said it depends. Often she skips breakfast, or stops for fast-food if she's going to work. She doesn't buy many groceries. She'd rather buy something simple and easy and be done with it. Can she feed Mister in the sunroom? He hasn't eaten since this morning. No wonder he was jumping at Dempsey's chair. Tess thought he was wanting to be held.

Mister was quite small and strange looking: a Pekingese face, long brown hair head and shoulders and his hind quarters the body of a Chihuahua. Looking at Mister reconfirmed Tess's belief that all dogs need to be spayed or neutered unless under 24-hour surveillance by responsible owners. Mister was an ill-proportioned mutt.

The meal ended, Mister was eating in the sunroom, then out for potty/sniffing in the yard while Dempsey watched him from the sunroom, smoking a cigarette with a window rolled-open. He didn't stay outside long. It was dark outside. Dempsey said she wanted to go upstairs and start putting things away. "Thank you for everything," she said, and vanished upstairs with Mister.

Tess tidied the kitchen; watched the evening news recorded earlier, didn't know what to do with herself in her own home. Responded to texting. Drank a glass or two of wine while reading a little more in the newspaper, a tad more TV watching, then shower, etc., was propped up in bed in pajamas deciding to read her current book, but felt restless. Out of bed, back downstairs checking to see if doors were locked. And then headed upstairs wanting to take Dempsey's jacket from the brass hook, but didn't. *When would Dempsey mention a job?*

Tess felt frazzled.

CHAPTER TWELVE

Arrival

It was very early the next morning when Tess awakened with slight nausea. *Stress,* she told herself. Or maybe her gall bladder was acting up. She remembered the adage that one who is her own doctor has a fool for a doctor. Yet, she persisted self-diagnosing. Was nausea a new stress symptom in her body?

Grateful to have slept through the night. Tess was always grateful for a good night's sleep, knowing well a poor night of sleep. The reasonably predictable retirement life she'd created over these past months was now disrupted with Dempsey and Mister. She felt ashamed this was so. She felt shame for feeling relieved that Dempsey's older car was in the garage and not on the street for all the residents of this upscale street to see. Another part of Tess felt like a mother lioness willing to do anything to help Dempsey, to protect her. Tess was suffering the tension of opposites within herself. "Tension of the opposites." Her therapist used the phrase.

Recently, Tess's first action in the morning was writing down how she felt physically. Sometimes she remembered a dream and jotted that down, too, but didn't remember any dreams this morning. In the kitchen Tess swallowed an anti-acid pill and water, along with hot oatmeal, tea, and then went back upstairs to the comfort of her bed, with door open to her bedroom so when Dempsey emerged from her room, *I can tell her I am ill. Don't want her to think I am a late sleeper, which indicates lack of discipline. I am so full of myself I am almost amused, even in my depleted state with low-grade nausea.*

Propped in bed, warm, and as comfortable as one can be with queasiness, with closed eyes, the words in Tess's mind were *Let go and let God.* A church around the corner has this saying in its large, neon sign. She told herself to relax. She said the "Hail Mary" again and again. She dozed a bit.

And then, it came to pass, Tess was grateful Dempsey started a temporary job not many days after arriving. Mister and Tess continued to learn about each other while Dempsey was at work. Tess wished Dempsey wouldn't be so secretive, for she never mentioned she already had a temporary job lined-up when she came to town through the temp-agency she'd been working with in Terryton. Tess's stress level would have been lower had she known this.

Dempsey preferred temporary work, for she did not like competition or office politics, and felt she avoided these as a "temp." Also, she could give herself a vacation between jobs if she chose. In her own words, "I'm an underachiever in many people's eyes." She paid more for medical insurance, but "I put that into my budget," she told Tess, who was worried about this.

Tess double-thought everything related to Dempsey. Cautiously, very cautiously, so as not to offend, Tess highly recommended her hair stylist, a guy who was outrageously expensive, so Tess would pay if Dempsey wanted to try him out, for he was an artist matching hair style and face.

A week later Dempsey said "yes," to Tess's offer and got her hair styled, changing her appearance drastically. When she came home with her medium brown hair sculpted into a chic cut, she seemed to walk taller, as if her five-foot-six height knew itself. Her demeanor was more energized and livelier. The next day she wore contact lenses to work; her blue eyes alive. Not long after that she purchased eyewear that enhanced her naturally attractive features.

Tess hadn't seen Dempsey smoke since that first day she came and guessed she was extra stressed that day, too. And Dempsey was eating better. She fixed a nutritious lunch to take with her to work; was up early and off to work in a timely fashion; was very caring with Mister, taking him on walks, bathing him with special shampoos in the utility sink in the basement.

Tess was more accepting of the little mutt, even finding him amusing. Tess just wished Dempsey would talk more. Most evenings Dempsey and Mister went to her room where she apparently read or sometimes Tess faintly heard TV from Dempsey's room.

Dempsey insisted upon cleaning the kitchen, since Tess did the cooking. Frankly, Tess would have enjoyed talking more with her, for even at meals she answered what she was asked or reacted slightly to what Tess initiated. How can a personality be so shut-down, Tess wondered.

Dempsey thanked Tess after every meal, and every night before going to bed said "Thanks for everything. Sleep well." What had happened to Dempsey? Tess's days included contact with people from real estate, for she still booked listings. People who knew people who knew people contacted her when they were ready to sell their property. This was a source of income, and a joy to remain connected to people, for Tess needed people in her life.

On weekends, Dempsey took Mister to a dog park, or went shopping but seemed to buy little. She even went to a movie by herself. Tess made it clear she would certainly enjoy a movie with Dempsey. Otherwise on the weekend Dempsey washed her clothes and got them ready for the next week, changed and washed her bedding, vacuumed her room, not wanting the woman who cleaned house to do anything extra because of her.

And then Tess found Dempsey went to Mass one Sunday evening saying she was going to the grocery store getting supplies for her weekday lunches. When Tess told Dempsey of her worry about Dempsey being gone so long, she confessed she'd gone to Mass and then the grocery store. Tess could no longer endure Dempsey's secretive ways.

"Dempsey, I feel as if you're trying to make yourself invisible around me; as if I'm some sort of ogre you have to tiptoe around. What have I done to make this happen? Too directly Tess asked "Do you have some kind of social phobia?" "Probably," Dempsey replied with her familiar nervous laugh. Tess's heart did a piercingly sad flip-flop seeing adult Dempsey display behavior of a frightened child. Tess wanted to hug

Dempsey and say, "I'm sorry, I'm sorry, I'm sorry. Me and my big mouth. Oh, no. I never want to hurt you or make you feel uncomfortable. But what has happened to make you reclusive, withdrawn, so afraid?"

Tess saw Dempsey's fear and knew, she Tess, must learn to walk a fine line between drawing Dempsey out without seeming confrontational. Tess talked with her therapist about this. Dempsey was comfortable around Ann Dramm, who was old enough to be Dempsey's mother. Ann's occasional presence was a ray of hope during this tense time.

CHAPTER THIRTEEN

Thanksgiving

Tess knew she must practice unconditional love, and for someone like Tess who was impatient with "weakness" or "insecurities" in others, this was going to be most difficult. Dempsey was gentle, thoughtful, not invasive

Tess began to settle-down with Dempsey, thanking her whenever possible, telling Dempsey how glad she was in the house during a recent sick-spell—nausea, again. Tess's words of thanks sometimes seemed to embarrass her niece. Tess wondered whether Dempsey was this sensitive at her job, and whether she preferred temporary work so she could move-on and not relate to others.

Dempsey had said temporary work allowed her to work on projects, complete them, and then go on to other projects. She liked learning new things. Dempsey had her own rationale. And then, an inspiration came to Tess.

Tess remembered how the two of them used to play card games when Dempsey was ten or so. That evening they began playing cards with Mister whining to sit on Dempsey's lap. Tess appeased the demanding little creature by fetching a bar stool with a back from the basement, topped it with a pillow and from his high perch Mister could watch what they were doing, or sleep at his leisure.

They played cards every night after the evening meal for several weeks, and after the newness wore off, one or the other would again remember the cards, fetch the bar stool for Mister, and the three of them contentedly passed evenings connecting through card-playing. They could relate in a way that wasn't too close for Dempsey. Talk, talk, talk didn't work for her. Maybe she was on the autism spectrum, Tess thought to herself, but then decided not to become a diagnostician.

They began to refer to Mister on his high throne as Master. He responded to his new name as well as old name. Dempsey and Tess shared this bond of levity about Mister/Master.

Dempsey went to work every day. Tess kept up with real estate listings and the properties she'd decided not to sell, which provided nice monthly cash flow. Also, Tess was in touch with many from her active real estate days. She continued reading *Interior Castle* and learned St Teresa suffered greatly by being misjudged by male spiritual advisors of her day who did not understand her many psychological-spiritual experiences.

This remarkable woman more than four hundred years ago, in a culture far different from ours, was able to hold onto her courageous search for her own truth, her own self-knowledge, and thus help her Carmelite sister-nuns find their own soul-truth. She wrote of the need to be cautious about giving advice.

> Let us look at our own shortcomings and leave other people's alone . . . there is no reason why we should expect everyone else to travel by our own road, and we should not attempt to point them to the spiritual path when perhaps we do not know what it is . . . Go to a man who has both spirituality and great learning if such a one can be found . . . Should your confessor not be a very spiritual man, someone with learning is better; or, if you know such a person, it is best to consult one both spiritual and learned . . . I have had the experience of timid, half-learned men whose shortcomings have cost me very dear.

Meanwhile, Tess, Dempsey, and Mister became less of a dysfunctional family. Thanksgiving came. The three spent the snowy day with six house guests in the cozy renovated brownstone, fireplace ablaze, food aromas increasing as each guest brought potluck to go with the turkey, dressing, and main dishes Tess and Dempsey prepared, working in tandem in the kitchen, reminding them of Schultz family gatherings. They both had the name Schultz and declared Mister's last name was also Schultz. Yes, they were becoming a family—perhaps.

Thanksgiving afternoon the group watched football on TV mounted above the fireplace with toasty fire aglow below. Tess and Dempsey were overall moderately interested sports fans aware of Super Bowl, World Series, NBA Finals, some college teams, and followed their own favorite teams.

Dempsey was helpful organizing the buffet dishes brought in by these friends of Tess who sometimes brought new folks to this tradition which started years earlier. This year Tess asked to host Thanksgiving in her renovated free-standing brownstone.

Dempsey seemed to fit in with this loud group that laughed a lot. Tess expected Dempsey to disappear upstairs with Mister after the meal, but the two stayed downstairs with everyone until the last guests left. Tess's friends assumed Tess's niece would be as gregarious as Tess and engaged Dempsey with this expectation, which had an effect on her.

After guests departed, a remarkable thing happened. Dempsey began to talk about herself. It was as if the departed Thanksgiving group left her energized, whereupon she talked about her usual distance from people.

She spoke about her name Dempsey, perhaps not aware that Tess knew the story of her father naming her after Jack Dempsey, the boxer, wanting his child to be a fighter. She said she both liked and disliked her name: people tended to easily remember the name, but it was also an albatross around her neck representing her father's self-centered expectations, and her reticent mother's lack of standing up to her father's bravado.

She felt her young mother had the insight but not the courage to push against the immaturities of her young husband, and she felt her father loved her but wanted his firstborn to be a boy rather than a girl.

"My mother lives the life my father has arranged for her. My father loves me but didn't and doesn't know how to encourage me with me in mind. My mother loves me and understands my father's emotional limitations, but somehow caves into him. Max continues doing the right thing, exceeding my father's expectations.

"Overall, I feel as if I was born not a failure, but markedly mediocre, extremely, boringly average. When I said I wanted to major in medieval literature in college my dad said he couldn't imagine a more impractical degree. And I suppose he was right; I've had to learn computers to earn a sparse living. I do not blame my parents for my awkwardness. I believe I am naturally drawn to the inner world and easily overwhelmed by the outer world of superficial chatter, meaningless activity.

"I enjoyed today with your friends because the football game gave a common focus and the group didn't have to manufacture conversation to fill the room, the time. Or at least chatter often feels awkward and mindless to me; blather, prattle. I chose to study medieval literature feeling I would acquire a wider, richer vocabulary than American English. And why did I want such a vocabulary? Only with time and reflection did I realize I wanted an enriched vocabulary so I would know better how to chat with others as well as express longings within myself to myself.

"My father shed tears when I told him I was moving to Stamford. I didn't know he cared so much. But yes, I do know he is deeply concerned about my welfare, and what seems to him my tepid approaches to life. He knows you are as independent and capable as he is. He says you are the trailblazer; the first of all the family cousins to go to college. That whole side of the family; the Schultz side, is confident and determined.

"Today, Thanksgiving, it's appropriate I tell you how grateful I am to be here with you, knowing you are the provider of stability, a kind of fortress I seem to need, which I don't like to admit. It's painful for me to say this out loud. I can survive on my own, but not thrive. Perhaps I should have married, but the opportunity never arose. I never feel lonely here with you, and I know how loneliness feels. Mister fills my life, too. Thank you for letting us live with you, aunt Teresa," as if she was a little girl again and Tess was her young aunt. Their eyes filled with tears.

CHAPTER FOURTEEN

Diagnosis

Tess's queasiness continued. Medical exams showed liver abnormalities—liver cancer was suspected—biopsies followed—liver cancer was confirmed—second opinions agreed—a port was installed in Tess's right upper chest—chemotherapy began–there was nausea, weakness, fatigue, a foggy brain. Tess collapsed into catastrophe, calamity. This was her fate. The worst she'd feared had arrived.

Tess asked Dempsey to please quit her temporary job and stay home to help with medical appointments and other practical matters. She was weak and nauseous after just one chemo treatment. But, of course, the words "liver cancer" knocked her down before chemotherapy was put into her body. It knocked Dempsey down, too. The diagnosis changed everything. Mister seemed to sense the change, for he was unusually glued to Dempsey.

There were decisions, other than medical, to make. Should they e-mail or telephone family and friends about the medical diagnosis, or maybe not yet. Once people knew, there might be too much contact, too many offers of help. Maybe they would tell only Ann Dramm. But the more people they told, the more might be praying. They had a praying family. They had to tell the entire Schultz family.

Dempsey's brain was clogged with fear, and she couldn't imagine what Tess was going through. Tess alternated between spurts of frenetic talk and quiet: "I should have gone to the doctor earlier. Would that have made a difference? I remember when a friend, suffering from bladder cancer, said he felt the day would come when we would look back on medicine's primitive methods to treat cancer: cutting (surgery), burning (radiation), poisoning (chemotherapy). He died from his cancer. I wonder if I'll die from mine. My physician has not mentioned what stage cancer. I haven't asked. I pretend what I don't know won't hurt me. Is that why I ignored bouts of nausea I had in recent months along with the abdominal distress?

"Dempsey, please send a donation to the Carmelite nuns to whom I have often sent money, this time requesting prayers for me. I could do this myself, but my mind is paralyzed by the words "cancer of the liver." I wonder if the antidepressants and sleeping drugs I've used for years overtaxed my liver. Too late now. This thought fills me with regret. Yet, it may be time for me to end my time on earth. The over-abundance of elderly people is becoming a financial burden on advanced societies around the world. Practical finances concern me.

"Yet, money couldn't have put together a plan as grand as you coming to live with me when you did. Finances aren't everything. Yet, I liked making money. I feel a sense of accomplishment and satisfaction that I have been able to help family and others with money while alive and after I'm gone. I'm grateful for the wisdom of keeping rental properties to continue cash flow. Yet, why did I suffer so much anxiety making money that I needed pills to quiet myself. Or, was my anxiety not about making money, but about old age, sickness, the inevitability of death? I'm getting confused about which is what. Yet a point of clarity never leaves me, and that's the comfort of having you and Mister with me, Dempsey."

With chemo treatments, Tess was rocked with nausea. despite taking pills to lessen it. "Good cells are being killed along with the bad ones," she remarked. She slept a lot. Dempsey researched what foods were best for Tess to eat. Tess listened carefully to Dempsey's findings and concluded quickly, "I've had healthy eating habits. I'm not going to eat bizarre concoctions now, especially with nausea robbing me of my appetite."

Dempsey understood what Tess was saying. Since living with Tess and eating well, she'd reduced her clothing size and felt remarkably better physically and psychologically. Dempsey researched alternative cancer treatments and learned that early detection isn't the whole story, for some cancers are aggressive while others aren't.

Dempsey shared her findings with Tess, whose physician suggested sunlight can be helpful treating liver cancer. In her decisive way, Tess said "Let's go to Florida for sunshine." And between bouts of nausea, she was propped on the couch or in her bed making lists of what must be done for their departure. At times she sat in a rocker in the bay window area downstairs to get the little light available on the north side of the house this time of the year in Connecticut, and tried sitting in a chair at south side windows in Dempsey's bedroom. The so-called sun-porch below Dempsey's bedroom was not heated, therefore too cold for winter lounging, and not very sunny anyway.

Even in her depleted state, Tess remained a woman of decision. After conversation with her oncologist, locating a suitable cancer treatment center in south Florida on the Gulf coast, she implemented her plan. In a few days' time she leased an upper-level residence not on the beach, but with a Gulf view. Dempsey requested medical records be sent to a physician there, re-directed mail; stopped newspapers; contacted people who needed to be contacted; cleaned-out the refrigerator; began packing bags.

It came time for Dempsey to pack Tess's luxury SUV with computer and printer as well as other belongings, and two women and a dog were driving south for an extended stay in Sandshell, Florida. Tess knew it would take grit for her to withstand the travel, but her very comfortable SUV helped, as they headed for Christmas in Sandshell a town of about 40,000 population, half way down the west (Gulf of Mexico) side of Florida.

The night before they started south to abundant sunlight, Dempsey went into Tess's bedroom to tell her good night as she had come to do since the diagnosis. The fearful self-consciousness which hounded her so much of her life, was gone, as she said, "Is it OK if I say a prayer with you?" Tess easily answered, "Of course." Dempsey knelt by the side of the bed, held Tess's hand, and said a prayer for Tess's body, mind, spirit and emotions. Dempsey was surprised at her own words.

At that moment, Dempsey remembered her mother or father kneeling at the side of her bed, holding her hand, and praying for her when either one put her to bed. They did this with Max, too; a long-ago tenderness she'd nearly forgotten.

Tess added, "Bless Dempsey and Mister." This became their nightly ritual with minor variations.

Traveling to Florida, they didn't talk for long stretches. Reclined at a comfortable angle, Tess slept a good deal in the passenger seat rather than the back seat, to avoid nausea from car sickness. Mister had the backseat to himself except for some overflow items from the back area. Tess assessed the situation, "We are a cozy threesome, though one is nauseous and weak, heading down the interstate in search of sunlight to help heal a cancerous liver."

Caring for aunt Tess and implementing the nuts and bolts of the trip to Florida catapulted Dempsey into new areas of maturity and responsibility. She was becoming a more confident person, and wanted to believe she was becoming a more confident "woman," but that felt too much for her. She felt rather sexless in her identity. Tess had long been her idol, role model, mentor, and now by default Tess was the reason Dempsey was growing into her capacity for change; engaging new facets of her being, and at a fast pace, too.

They spent the night in a hotel. It was late afternoon with sun still bright when the two women and dog Mister arrived at their destination in Sandshell, entered the security gate number, parked close to the attractive overhang jutting out from the entrance to their apartment building. Mister went potty in the grass at the edge of the parking area. Then, up the elevator to their fourth-floor residence, which was the top floor. Unlocking the door, the first glance inside pleased them with many windows on the south and west. They would be able to watch sunsets.

There were two bedrooms and two baths as well as the kitchen, eating, living area all in one, yet creatively distinct. The furnishings were attractive; lovely, actually. After bathroom visits, "Dear god, it's good to be here," Tess exclaimed, as Dempsey helped her get situated in the expensive-looking recliner. The long road trip had depleted Tess.

Dempsey began unloading the SUV. On one of her trips to the back of the SUV, a male appeared and in a distinctive deep voice offered to help. If he said his name, she didn't remember it. Not comfortable with his offer, she thanked him, closed the back of the vehicle with only one sack retrieved from it, and scurried inside to the elevator. Once the elevator door closed, she felt safe and noticed her heart thumping and accelerated breathing as the elevator took her to the fourth floor.

From a window inside their new home, she saw a pickup truck driving out the gate, which she assumed was the fellow with the deep voice. She did not return to unpacking the vehicle, but instead started putting things away in the apartment until later when she felt calmer about continuing the work of unloading while keeping a wary eye in every direction. This is a gated community, she reminded herself. "I should feel safe, but I don't."

CHAPTER FIFTEEN

Florida

Before dark Dempsey took Mister on a walk. *My ferocious guard dog will protect us,* she smiled to herself. He did bark relentlessly when necessary. She also had pepper spray with her. Their walk twice around the building inside the gated community was uneventful and they were back upstairs in the apartment in time to share their first Florida sunset with Tess who was obviously pleased with the sublime scene and said, "Despite cancer cells, life is good; beautiful."

In the mornings when she had more energy, Tess would reflect: "Another fine December day in Florida, sun gracing the glistening Gulf waters. I never tire of the sea; this elevated view almost makes me forget the queasiness.

"I'm not real old and would like to live longer, but if my life is to end soon, I'm not leaving children or grandchildren or a long-time spouse. Mostly, there are friends who will do fine without me, and you who will do OK without me, though I cannot survive now at all without you. Thank you for being in my life, and I hope I am not too burdensome. I am grateful beyond words for you, and Mister," she smiled. "I'm glad we're related."

Tess spoke of her deceased parents, (Dempsey's grandparents). "I expect to encounter them again in some form, and that pleases me. The religious holidays of All Saints and All Souls put me in touch with the original sacredness of Halloween before it became something else." Even in my days away from the church I always prayed for those who had died. I never stopped praying in general. Someday soon I'd like to make a visit to church to experience the quiet; a kind of "sanctified silence." I like those words. I know I can't make it through Mass unless I get to feeling better than I do now. My immune system is compromised. I shouldn't be in a crowd. Perhaps they have someone who will bring Communion to us. Will you please check?"

Dempsey realized her old dread of telephoning and making requests of any sort vanished when she was doing it for Tess. Dempsey was busy. She plopped into bed every night physically and mentally exhausted, yet fulfilled with grocery getting, meal making, laundry, e-mail, texting and telephone.

Online, Tess purchased an attractive head scarf and turban because of thinning hair. Tess's choices about beautiful things helped Dempsey grow her underdeveloped sense of beauty. They brought colorful table napkins with them so that meals would "please the eye as well as the stomach," Tess observed. Despite the appealing napkins, Tess's appetite remained weak; even pitiful.

Meanwhile, on walks so Mister could potty and sniff, he made friends with siblings Cynthia 7, and Charles 10, who lived in the same apartment complex. After school, the children were often kicking a soccer ball, shooting at a basketball goal, riding bicycles in the space behind the building, while an older woman, Mrs. Arndt, seated on a comfortable wooden bench, was with them. The children stopped what they were doing to pet Mister, talk to him, and Cynthia remarked his tail wagged so fast it might fall off.

Amazingly after a few days, Dempsey shot baskets with the children upon them coaxing her, and she rode Charles's bicycle which amused them immensely. She astonished herself that activities of her youth remained with her, though rusty, and that here she felt free enough to "play" for a bit before returning upstairs to Tess and the illness ravaging her.

Then, with Christmas a week away, Cynthia suggested maybe Mister could come to Christmas in their apartment so she could give him a

Christmas gift. Charles said nothing, but looked interested. Cynthia said she would get Mister a treat, a chew bone, or something he would like for a gift, and added she could also draw Mister a picture, at which Charles had big-brother disapproval mixed with embarrassment written all over his face at Cynthia's silly suggestion that a dog could appreciate one of her drawings. Undaunted, Cynthia said she would put Mister's presents under the Christmas tree with the family gifts. Cynthia remained unaffected by Charles's reactions. She was too busy making plans.

Ann Dramm from Stamford, was coming to spend a few days with Tess and Dempsey in January. Dempsey was looking forward to this guest, but had learned early in life to hide what she cared about, thought about, or reacted to. In the fourth-grade Dempsey had a pocket-sized black book in which she wrote prayers she made up. One recess three girls in her class somehow had gotten her personal "prayer book" (she attended Catholic school) and they were reading it aloud. She snatched the small black book from them, took her beloved "prayer book" home after school, bent its black covers back until they touched with pages jutting out, while she used scissors to savagely cut out and shred every page she'd written. No eyes would ever again read her deep thoughts. She learned to hide much. She learned to hide her religious interest from others.

Tess and Dempsey shared the pleasure of a volunteer, Dorothy from the church, who began bringing communion (Eucharist) weekly. Dorothy fit beautifully into their simple but busy routine. She chatted with them a bit, then read something inspirational, gave them communion hosts followed by the Lord's Prayer and Hail Mary, and bade them farewell.

There was a sense of busyness to their routine with chemo and other medical activities. Friends and former colleagues sent flowers to Tess so that their apartment was filled with scents and colors, which meant Dempsey had to keep up with the cut arrangements and potted plants or they became unsightly, and she was keenly aware of not letting that happen for Tess so loved the attractive, the beautiful. Tess did not need to see sick plants.

Dempsey tried to respond to whatever turned up, aware that her love for Tess pushed her into flexibility, adaptability, spontaneous responsibility, decision-making capability. Dempsey could feel the changes inside herself. Lifetime love for her aunt allowed Dempsey to be stretched and then stretched some more. And just then a new turn of events unfolded.

CHAPTER SIXTEEN

Zack

The telephone rang and a deep male voice said, "This is Zack Kendrick, father of Cynthia and Charles and I would like to speak with Mister or someone who could speak for Mister." "I am Mister's agent," Dempsey replied, surprising herself with her quick wit, not so different from Tess's cleverness in her healthy days.

The male laughed and went on to explain the children wished to invite Mister and his family to come to Christmas dinner. Dempsey thanked him for the kind offer and said Mister's family included herself and her aunt.

He said, "Yes, I know. Mrs. Arndt has shared details of your entire lives which she has extracted from you with skills she perfected as chief interrogator for the C.I.A., F.B.I., and K.G.B." Dempsey was amused with his wit, and replied, "Yes, Mrs. Arndt and I have talked a few times."

He continued, "Dear Mrs. Arndt is a sponge soaking up everything one says, and a sieve letting it all flow out telling another person. However, she is absolutely dependable with Cynthia and Charles, which is all that matters. Please think about Christmas dinner. We'd like Mister and his family to join us."

It was true. Mrs. Arndt told Dempsey the story of Mr. Kendrick and his children whose wife and mother died three years ago in bed asleep in the middle of the night at the age of 43 from an electrical malfunction of the heart; such a pity.

Tess said "yes" to Christmas dinner with the Kendrick family, so Dempsey telephoned Zack and a traditional menu was planned with Mister's family bringing side dishes. Dempsey offered dessert, but he said he'd ordered pumpkin and chocolate pies, but did they have another preference? Dempsey assured Zack that the pies he'd ordered would please them.

Then quickly, very quickly, for Christmas was just around the corner, Dempsey bought small gifts for Cynthia and Charles. She had already decorated the temporary apartment with a small lighted Christmas tree and a framed flat-sculptured faux ivory nativity scene brought from Stamford. A vigil candle lit up the nativity scene placed amongst selected flowers and plants which Tess's eye for beauty guided while Dempsey arranged them.

On Christmas Eve, traditional carols from a local radio station softly filled their apartment home away from home. Dempsey's parents telephoned, and both Tess and Dempsey spoke with them, and then Dempsey was busy preparing tomorrow's dishes for Christmas at the Kendricks.

Dempsey had learned she must depend on herself and not on Tess's feeble appetite to dictate a menu. Increasingly stumped about grocery shopping and meal planning, Dempsey had begun looking for ideas on the internet. She turned on TV cooking shows hoping Tess would watch and get interested in food. However, Tess fell asleep while the TV chefs created their delicacies.

Christmas Eve, finished in the kitchen, Dempsey joined Tess who began recalling childhood Christmas Eve memories with grandparents, aunts, uncles, cousins galore, all familiar to Dempsey. Tess recalled the magic, the glow, the warmth indoors on the fiercely cold nights in Terryton, with Christmas decorations, special foods.

CHAPTER SEVENTEEN

Christmas

Tess reminisced, "This was the dependable tradition I replaced with city life and opportunity. Growing up, I found the simple story of the manger, angels, shepherds, star and wisemen satisfying. In my turbulent thirties a new realtor in the office, a Catholic, asked me to go with her to classes at church on the Christmas story, which had a strange effect on me, for I learned there isn't just one Christmas story but two. Which means two of the gospels do not even mention his birth story. Something like that.

One gospel author wrote about the wisemen and the star, and a bible scholar claimed the wisemen (Magi) represented Gentiles while the new star also suggested Gentiles would see a new revelation on earth in Jesus. The other gospel author who has the manger, angels, and shepherds in his story is another way of telling the impact of the birth of Jesus.

"But the real challenge to my simple Christmas story, even if my now chemo-brain "facts" are not absolutely correct, was a bible scholar's insight that the gospels with Jesus' birth stories in them were written about fifty years after Jesus' death and thus the birth stories were written with considerable hindsight. When I learned this, it felt to me like details of his birth were "stretched" in a conniving way to fill out who Jesus was. I didn't know anything about metaphor or symbol at the time and I wanted the Christmas story to be straightforward and unreflective, like the one I knew as a child.

"One of my husbands said I was too much of a straight-line thinker, which I resented, and told him that at least I was able to think! I do wish I could be more elaborate and complex in my understanding, but ideas, circumstances, have always seemed obvious to me: either black or white, yes or no, which has brought me both success and failure." Tess fell silent in a painful way.

Dempsey found herself hurting for Tess, while at the same time being amazed that Tess's usual chemo-brain these days had spun with clarity the Nativity and a remark by one of her husbands. In Dempsey's amazement and anxiety, she began to blurt out how some of her earliest memories of Tess were about them having fun together. And then how, as Dempsey got older, she fondly remembered not only the fun Tess brought but that Tess became Dempsey's role model. "I wanted to be like you, and one thing I so lacked was your clear-headed focus, which maybe is straight-line thinking, but all I saw and still see is independence and courage in a woman who knows her own mind and implements what she wants."

Dempsey choked with tears relating her life-long star-struck adoration for her aunt. Tess began crying because Dempsey was crying and then they were laughing about their crying. It was a memorable Christmas Eve in Sandshell, as Tess made fun of herself being bundled up in an afghan and wearing a turban in warm Florida. She had always known how to laugh at herself.

These days she wore a scarf or turban, even to bed, for warmth and comfort, and told Dempsey of the turban she'd wear to the Christmas meal the next day at one o'clock with the Kendrick family, when Cynthia and Charles would first come to the apartment to take Mister and prepared dishes to their condo while Dempsey would follow with Tess steadied by Dempsey's arm.

The short walk to the Kendrick apartment was somewhat convoluted, for while Tess and Dempsey lived on the top floor of the back building, the Kendrick apartment was on the ground floor of the shorter front building, which meant a short trek outside from the back building to the front building. Dempsey suggested they use the wheelchair but Tess insisted she walk, though she typically declined walking outside with Dempsey and Mister.

Christmas day, Tess was dressed in a turban of muted colors, wearing black flats, black trousers, burgundy-colored caftan with ivory light-weight shawl, and a just-right slight touch of make-up which made her look more robust than she was. The shawl helped hide her somewhat too-large clothes because of weight loss. Though Tess looked good and felt invigorated for the occasion, Dempsey knew to expect Tess would want to return to their apartment after the meal, ready to rest, relax in quiet, sleep.

And so, two female adults, a dog, and two children carrying dishes of food and gifts, made for a happy group on their way to the children's apartment. When the door to the apartment opened, the father was wearing a Christmas tree design apron and a Santa hat and was the same male who offered to help Dempsey unload the SUV on arrival day. He did not seem to recognize Dempsey.

Mrs. Arndt who stayed with the children after school had told Dempsey the children's father was maintenance manager of this and another apartment complex, which provided him with free rent on the ground floor, which was without a good view or balcony, but was roomy with two bedrooms and two baths. On this Christmas day Dempsey did not mention meeting Zack at the back of the SUV.

The Kendrick apartment was filled with welcoming smells of food Tess and Dempsey verbally acknowledged, which Zach attributed to a grocery store deli. Cynthia immediately gave Mister his gifts and began unwrapping them for him. Some wrappings from Santa gifts earlier that morning remained strewn under the lighted Christmas tree.

While Cynthia was busy with Mister, Charles pointedly and knowingly widened his eyes at the guests, then looked out the corner of his eye at his sister as he showed his "Santa Claus" (wink, wink) video game gift he opened this morning; his exaggerated eye movements keeping Santa alive for his little sister who was listening. Thereupon she demonstrated the camera she got from Santa by trying to take a picture of Mister, who was frisky, running about. Children and dog provided plenty of energy for the occasion.

The table had already been set. Dempsey offered to help with food in the kitchen, and buttered dinner rolls hot from the oven, then filled glasses with tea. Shortly, everyone was seated at the table. The father and children did a routine "grace," each being grateful for current good fortune: their guests, the food, Mister, their presents, for Christmas itself. Mister waited under the table for crumbs to drop but did not beg, and Dempsey was grateful for that.

Mealtime talk included information that the Kendricks usually had Christmas with another family who left town this year to be with relatives. Charles gave more detailed aspects of his new video game he and his dad had been playing that morning and who'd been winning. His father added his own commentary about their competitive ventures. Cynthia recited each gift she got from whom, and asked if, after the meal, they could open their gifts from Mister.

Dempsey noticed her own self-conscious lack of spontaneity at the table and realized she still wanted Tess to provide wit and charm, which Tess could now scarcely do. Mostly Tess smiled at the table conversation and seemed genuinely amused when the children described Dempsey's basketball and bicycle skills to her.

Dempsey was more natural around the children outside than here with their father present. She said little and felt grateful when others filled the air with talk. Lively Christmas music playing in the background helped make the atmosphere amiable and loose as did Cynthia's question about whether everyone could go for a walk on the beach after the meal, as she wanted to take a picture of Mister on the beach.

CHAPTER EIGHTEEN

Beach Storm

Dempsey told of doggles (dog goggles) Mister had to keep sand out of his eyes, a gift from one of Tess's friends when they were coming to Florida and the beach, though Mister had not yet been to the beach. Cynthia was excited about Mister's doggles and could hardly wait to see him in them. Her enthusiasm was tempered when her father reminded the group they would first need to finish the meal, clear the table and load the dishwasher before heading to the beach. The question was: should dessert be after the meal or after the beach. Dessert after the beach won the vote.

Then, Cynthia asked if it was time to open a gift for each child "from Mister." It was time. Mister started playing and fighting with the wrapping paper falling to the floor and offered entertainment as Cynthia and Charles unwrapped their golden wrapped box adorned with red and green ribbon and found wrapped gifts inside. Charles commented it was amazing how well Mister could wrap, but maybe it was because of his four paws compared to two human hands. Everyone agreed with Charles's astute paw-observation.

The inside gifts were golden wrapped bags of microwaveable popcorn and golden wrapped packets of candy to add weight to the real gift which was a gift card in another gold wrapped box buried at the bottom of the main box. All that unwrapping had been exciting for the children and Mister who entertained with his antics in the paper on the floor.

With a walk to the beach on their minds, the children automatically started picking-up the wrapping paper and ribbon strewn about by Mister who seemed to have worn himself out. Tess said she wouldn't be going to the beach. Dempsey mentioned having to find Mister's doggles in the apartment.

Zack said everyone would need a jacket at the beach. Cynthia wanted Mister to stay with her while Dempsey went to find the doggles, but Mister's frantic barking when the door closed behind Dempsey meant Dempsey had to take him with her.

In the apartment Dempsey easily found Mister's doggles while Tess readied herself for an afternoon nap. Once Tess was comfortably in bed, Dempsey returned to the Kendrick apartment where the others were waiting, and Cynthia had spasms of laughter and delight about Mister's doggles.

Dempsey carried Mister while the four of them walked several blocks to the public entrance of the beach. Mister's legs were too short and he stopped and sniffed too often for them to move quickly. Clouds were forming and they may not have much time to enjoy the beach.

Once on the sand, Cynthia took pictures of bedoggled Mister. She squatted for a close- up of him and dictated to the rest of them what they were to do while she took a beach photo of each. Her daddy took pictures of Cynthia holding bedoggled Mister, and walking him on the leash.

And then, father and son walked on ahead with plans to launch a Christmas-present kite on a dock extending over the water. Dempsey held the camera while Cynthia walked bedoggled Mister with the leash and hunted for sea shells. Cynthia regretted they hadn't brought a sack or shovel, and stuffed shells into her pockets, "but they sometimes get broken and grind up in your pocket when you walk," she explained.

Cynthia complained about it not being warmer so she could walk in the water, or at least walk barefoot in the sand. She said more sun was needed for them to really enjoy the beach, knowing Dempsey was new to the area. Cynthia explained further that this wasn't a good beach day and that's why so few people were there. She alternated between interest in Mister, showing Dempsey treasures she was finding, checking on the now distant location of her father and brother, looking at the sky and predicting it was about to rain.

Indeed, the sky was grey, wind coolish, seaside mostly deserted. Only a few weeks ago Dempsey and Tess were still in Stamford, the Kendrick family unknown to them, and now Dempsey was with the family on a cloudy beach, when she and Tess had come for a sun-filled Christmas. *We know so little of the future*, Dempsey thought to herself. The future was as unpredictable as the wind which had begun blowing sand about, increasing the feel of an impending storm.

Before long, blowing sand was stinging Cynthia's bare lower legs in walking shorts, which a northerner like Dempsey would never wear in December. Dempsey's long pants shielded her from the sand's stings as they steadily increased. Cynthia was brave at first, but then was about to cry. Dempsey had Cynthia stand in front of her to shield the little body somewhat from the determined south wind, as Dempsey took off her windbreaker, tied its sleeves around Cynthia's waist in front, thus shielding the backs of her legs from the pelting pesky sand. Cynthia's legs were now protected and otherwise she was warm in her hooded sweatshirt.

Dempsey, though warm in her fleece jacket now felt sand attacking her head which was no longer protected by the windbreaker hood. Holding Mister in one arm and Cynthia's hand with the other, they started walking briskly north toward the beach exit which couldn't come soon enough, as the howling wind and blowing sand grew fierce, making it impossible to turn around and see where her father and brother were, which greatly troubled Cynthia.

Dempsey reassured Cynthia her father and Charles would come to the beach exit. And finally, after Cynthia's continued crying from fear rather than pain, there was Zack's voice, carried by the wind, though his words could not be understood.

Cynthia was relieved. They heard his voice again and shortly thereafter the father and son arrived breathing heavily from running. Zack shielded the back of Dempsey's head with what was left of the kite, as she was the only one unhooded. Charles took Cynthia's hand.

They arrived at the beach exit, where, slightly shielded by bushes Zack discarded the broken kite into a trash can, returned Dempsey's hooded windbreaker to her, "We have to walk facing into the wind now."

Charles held Mister while Dempsey put on her windbreaker tying the hood tight. Dempsey took Mister from Charles. Zack lifted Cynthia up, her arms around his neck, head on his shoulder, her legs around his waist inside his mostly unzipped hoodie, his arms around her rump, telling Charles to hold Dempsey's hand, "So we can go as fast as we can." Charles and Dempsey entwined fingers.

Concentrated on staying close behind Zack, they heard his commands: "curb–stop–car coming–let's go–turning left" and so on. Finally, there was not as much blowing sand in the east direction streets, yet there was still some grit whirling in the howling wind as they walked a few more blocks in the uncomfortable gusts, finally arriving at their gated community, where Zack put Cynthia down, input the gate numbers, everyone ran to the apartment building where Charles put in the code, held open the door, and the group was out of the storm.

Now safe, they looked at each other. Zack thanked Dempsey profusely for taking care of Cynthia, for sharing her windbreaker. Cynthia told how scared she was that her daddy and brother were lost, and Charles showed his reddened legs, describing their ongoing stinging, burning sensation and how the wind might have blown him off the dock when he and his dad were running, if not for holding onto his dad's hand.

Zack said they had lotion in the apartment that would help Charles's legs. Cynthia talked to Mister about the scary sand storm and how his doggles helped him. She wanted to know if Mister could come to their apartment for awhile–and Dempsey, too, who said she needed to check on Tess.

Cynthia begged Dempsey and Mister to come back to the Kendrick apartment after checking on Tess, because, "The beach wasn't fun; we didn't get to have a good time because of the sand storm." Charles said they could play the board game they got for Christmas, which works better with four players than three. Dempsey said she'd telephone them later. The group was in the throes of an adrenalin rush. Mister was panting in Dempsey's arms.

As Dempsey turned to go out the door Zack said he'd walk them to their building, for the wind was still blowing slightly. Dempsey assured him she could make it, however he speed-walked with them to their building entrance where, under the canopy, Dempsey input the security code, Zack again thanked her for taking care of Cynthia, she and Mister disappeared safely into the building.

CHAPTER NINETEEN

Matchmaking

The Kendrick family spent the evening in the apartment of Tess and Dempsey, where there were finger-foods, soft drinks for the children, wine for Dempsey and Zack, and Perrier sparkling water for Tess, who in pre-chemo days would never have passed up a glass of wine. Dempsey felt a dash of joy mixed with foreboding, not daring to think what Christmas next year might be.

Low background Christmas music added ambience, as did the paper holiday plates and napkins purchased to help Christmas be Christmassy, just as Dempsey also bought appropriate tableware for the coming New Year holiday. Tess's sense of whimsy and artful attention in these matters entered Dempsey's life, though when younger her mother did similar things. However, immature Dempsey at the time felt sullen and stubborn toward her mother's efforts, which Dempsey now wished she could have appreciated.

After a while, a board game began at the table: Charles and Dempsey were partners against Cynthia and her father. Munchies remained on the bar embellished by the light of candles. Tess retreated to the recliner. A soft, lightweight afghan covered her and Mister made himself comfortable beside her. The room was cozy with a lighted vigil candle on the small table with snacks next to the recliner, Mister's curious nose sniffing the food. A strand of tiny white lights graced one of the larger potted plants someone had sent Tess.

Despite the loveliness of the evening, Dempsey was thinking about the tragic loss of Roxanne, wife and mother in the Kendrick family. Thinking of that woman's sudden death Dempsey wondered why she herself couldn't practice the power of positive thinking; developing the habit of assuming Tess was going to beat liver cancer. *"Why can't I do this?"*

Dempsey knew the answer to her question. Positive thinking felt too much like wishful thinking. Dempsey knew the slim odds of surviving liver cancer long-term. Was positive thinking different from having faith? Was faith mere positive attitude? What did it take for cancer to go into remission; for Tess's immune system to triumph?

During the board game Dempsey learned the Kendrick family would drive north tomorrow to the Florida Panhandle and the home of the children's grandparents, their mother's parents. They would be back by New Year's Eve. "And we'll have another party with you just like tonight," Cynthia announced, which made everyone laugh, and her father remark, "Cynthia tends to be subtle."

Between Christmas and the New Year, Tess visited the doctor. Her numbers were good; chemo seemed to be working. Fatigue was simply the price that must be paid for a possible remission.

The Kendrick family was to arrive home later that day from visiting grandparents. Tess suggested the Kendricks be invited for New Year's Eve so Cynthia needn't ask. "We can order pizza in. If they've made other plans, we'll still order pizza for us and celebrate the arrival of another year with television celebrations around the globe, though I'll likely be snoozing before midnight."

Tess seemed enthused about the New Year's Eve gathering, imagining Cynthia's delight of Mister in a party hat; surely, she'd bring her camera. A favorable weather forecast indicated a good evening to watch the sun set. There would be hors d'oeuvres when the guests arrived and later pizzas would be ordered. There was something to be said for timing an event, Tess believed. She knew how to host an event.

Tess's enthusiasm mystified Dempsey. What could explain Tess's mood? Was it the encouraging medical numbers she received from the doctor? Was it the energy the children would bring tomorrow evening? Was it simply the joy of having people in on New Year's Eve? Was it a combination of all these? Intuitively, Tess guessed Dempsey's wondering and said simply, "I want you and Zack to get to know each other better."

Dempsey's forehead wrinkled in surprise. Tess boldly continued, "Yes, I'm matchmaking. Never was good at it for myself, but testing my hand at it for you. Don't you think he's good-looking? You like the kids, and the kids like you. I found him interesting Christmas evening. He was a CPA before this job – did you know? Perhaps you and the kids had gone outside for a potty walk with Mister when he told me. It would be super if the two of you were mutually attracted. He needs a wife. You need a husband. Even my chemo-brain knows this."

Dempsey responded, "I'd say he's handsome," which caused Tess to clap her hands, which made Mister bark, and Dempsey laughed at the chain reaction, including her laughter. The apartment was filled with enthusiasm for the impending New Year's Eve party.

CHAPTER TWENTY

Seeing Purple

New Year's Eve and the Kendrick family arrived; Charles with two new board games, which were gifts received at relatives' homes in the Panhandle. Dempsey began hoping she would not be Dull Dempsey, the only one who wouldn't know how to play, when Charles said they hadn't yet played the games. Dempsey felt encouraged.

The hors d'oeuvres seemed to please. Conversation was easy about the Kendrick trip, their relatives, more gifts. Cynthia asked about what was "new" with Dempsey and Tess. Immediately, Tess told of her good numbers from the doctor, a friend, Ann, was coming to visit soon, and then Dempsey's parents would later arrive, explaining that Tess's brother was Dempsey's father, which Cynthia first questioned and then understood.

The Kendrick family would be spending the next day, New Year's Day afternoon, playing miniature-golf with the family they usually had Christmas with, Cynthia explained while attempting to corral Mister.

Charles was in charge of instructions about the board game which he and his dad had obviously reviewed beforehand. Charles explained game rules backed-up with clarification from Zack when needed. Cynthia asked to sit so she could monitor the setting sun. Tess almost said "yes" to participating in the game, but then chose instead listening to the gamers from her beloved recliner where Mister would curl up with her.

At what seemed the "right time," Dempsey telephoned-in the pizza order. The evening had its own lovely pace. Party hats were issued. Zack took pictures of the others in their festive hats. Cynthia tended to Mister who kept removing his hat.

The evening meshed in a lovely way. Conversation, togetherness, hors d'oeuvres, pizza, drinks were enjoyed, as were the board games, sunset, candles and lighted Christmas tree.

A bit past 10:00, Cynthia abruptly left the game to go to the couch and fall asleep. She did not announce her departure. Zack and Charles said she does that at home, too. Shortly thereafter, the Kendrick family left. It had been a remarkably fine evening.

A week later, Ann Dramm arrived in Sandshell with the gift of her personality and a song about a beach, a seashore. The song had a plethora of meaning for Ann, which she was eager to share with Tess and Dempsey. She had background information: "The song was composed in 1979 by Cesareo Gabarain (1936-1991) a Spanish priest. In Spanish the title is *Pescador de Hombres* – (Fisher of Men.) It's on YouTube.

Ann explained, "The lyrics speak to me in terms of my life story: my soul lost in depression, from which Mel so lovingly helped me find relief with the support of a wise therapist swimming with me in the turbulence of things I had not been conscious of. My therapist kept me from drowning in painful family dynamics."

They listened to the song again and again during Ann's three-day visit. Tess likened the music to life-review therapy. She said, "I'm not ready to die, though this is likely just around the corner for me." Ann's commonsense gentleness reminded, "It's eventually around the corner for all of us–if we can just remember this."

Ann's visit heightened the tender spiritual side of Tess while reminding her also of the blessings of her free-spirited daring. The two went hand-in-hand. Overall, the seashore song brought meaningful conversation about life, living, big questions about existence and what matters.

Ann spoke of the color purple which she sometimes "saw" in deep prayer. Though each episode was different, what she "saw" tended to be inexpressibly beautiful and soothing as ultraviolet and infrared colors mixed together with intermittent flashes or bursts and blends of dazzling light; flecks, specks, infinitesimally tiny misting luminosity gently folding and enfolding raw, stark, gentle purples, burgundies, crimsons, entrancingly endless; sometimes embellished with hints of geometric blurbs of other colors; an expanding threshold of soothing beauty. The more the color purple reigned, the greater the beauty.

Ann had an analogy to share. The deep prayer experience reminded her of barnacles on the bottom of a ship. As if her personality, when experiencing absorption in the color purple was being freed of negative energies (barnacles) which sucked energy out of her, just as barnacles on the bottom of a ship slow the ship. For her, deep prayer made anxieties and apprehensions fade. Not all anxieties were old barnacles. Some were current concerns; some, her concern for others. Ann said relief comes to her in this cocoon of purple beauty. She did not find absolute stillness in purple beauty, but felt she was immersed in quiet beauty, whatever that means.

CHAPTER TWENTY-ONE

Dempsey's Parents

Dempsey's parents arrived two weeks later in Sandshell. The song Ann had brought was shared with them, which seemed to fascinate Dempsey's mother while her dad found it mildly interesting. He was hard to read; so utterly male, Dempsey concluded. She'd been gone from her parents only a matter of months yet she now had a distance with which to view them, "My father leads and my mother accommodates."

It was clear to Dempsey that Tess in her prime played out her leadership abilities but was unable to accommodate except when she needed to make a business deal. However, Dempsey now realized, *How much Tess cares for me for she surely had to accommodate me and Mister when we moved in with her. She has been very accommodating in the best sense.*

Mister was bonded with Dempsey's parents, remembering them from Connecticut. On this visit they took him on walks. Dempsey's dad played on the floor with Mister in the apartment. Her parents repeatedly complimented her cooking and how well she looked. Weight-loss, a different hair style, attractive eyewear, caring about her appearance was not lost on her parents. Dempsey realized that family sharing, even the heartbreak of illness, could be beautiful. During her parents' visit Dempsey came to appreciate her parents more as she gained adult perspective about her childhood resistance to her father's competitive personality.

Dempsey reflected to herself, *Stubbornness developed in me against my father's expectations for me. He and his friends all had a male cockiness about them when they were together, as if they were all hewn from the same stone, drank the same potion of getting ahead of each other.*

I noticed at an early age when they came to the house to work on a car, play cards, watch sports on TV, their body language, voice tone, and laughter parroted each other. I believe they were caught in some kind of male immaturity. My parents would probably have been better off if they'd moved from Terryton upon marriage.

My dad didn't go to college. He married young, stayed too close to home, around high school friends, and remained in high school dynamics. Though he was a good father in most ways, he simply didn't mature as he might had his world been larger. My mother, being accommodating, did not offset his immature tendencies. These were some of Dempsey's perspectives as her parents visited in Florida.

Saturday afternoon, knowing the Kendrick family was playing in the green area below, Dempsey took her parents down to meet the children and Zack, for they knew holiday time had been spent with the Kendricks. Mister and the children were, of course, deliriously happy to be with each other. The adult conversation was pleasant and brief, having interrupted the Kendrick basketball game, so Dempsey's group did not linger.

The next Saturday afternoon after her parents left, another sunny day in Florida, taking Mister for a walk around the building, Dempsey encountered the Kendrick family; children hitting golf balls and Zack sitting in Mrs. Arndt's usual place, staring into an electronic screen he was holding.

He immediately explained, "I'm reading Great Courses material. You know, where you buy a course taught by a professor and read or listen whenever possible. I'm a fanatic. Roxanne gave me my first course. I haven't counted how many I've gone through. Sometimes they are a lifeline to sanity for me."

Dempsey remarked, "I've always been intrigued by them but haven't ordered any." Zack was very real. "I feel better when I am mentally stimulated. I believe part of my father's anger was lack of intellectual stimulation. I was an only child. At meals my father ranted and raved about his job. He was a well-regarded handy-man of the community; made good money with a large clientele willing to wait for him to come fix what needed fixing, but his brain needed to have gone to college.

"He fussed and fumed about the people who were seeking his help; how difficult they'd been in the past; he knew they felt he overcharged them, which would then send his mind to a recent job difficulty, and then another and another. I remember as a young kid I wondered why these people were asking him to work for them again if they so disapproved of him.

"He never acted like this around other people so far as I could tell, but with mother and myself as his audience at the mealtime table he unloaded all of his frustrations. After the meal he was in his easy-chair taking a nap, while I was in turmoil. I have no memory of pleasant conversation during meals while growing-up. Any and every topic devolved into something about his job which he acted like he hated. Yet on the weekends, he was in the garage tinkering, fixing things for his customers.

"He seemed content in the garage. Mother seemed to accept the situation as normal, but I dreaded mealtime and feel as if I never had a conversation with my father. Mostly, I listened to him complain, until not long before his death from stomach cancer, when he seemed capable of listening and conversing without complaining. My mother died a year or so after my dad. They left a monetary stash, so he had to have done financially well with his job. I did not understand my father."

Zack apologized, "Sorry to rattle on." She apologized, "Mister and I are sorry to have interrupted your reading. We're off to see if Tess has awakened." She wanted to add, *I don't understand my dad, either, though I've discovered I love him anyway. Maybe dads are not understandable.* She wanted to say this.

CHAPTER TWENTY-TWO

Getting Acquainted

The next week Dempsey learned from Mrs. Arndt that Zack and Roxanne met in college, where he was an accounting major and she was in interior design. Mrs. Arndt added her own impressions. She believed Zack's wife had an eye for beautiful things, but he would rather have had money in the bank than beautiful things, which was always an edgy part of their relationship, but not a serious problem. Mrs. Arndt "guessed" these things, she admitted.

Mrs. Arndt said she occasionally looked after the children for a few hours on Saturday or Sunday so Zack could play golf, as well as after school during the week. She knew that Zack left his career as a certified public accountant to do work with more time flexibility so as to be available for Charles and Cynthia, and so he took this maintenance manager position, probably because it included rent-free quarters, Mrs. Arndt concluded. She always added her opinions.

She explained his time flexibility: he could drive to the kids' school or home if needed during the workday without having to inform an office manager because he was his own boss on a daily basis so long as he hired and supervised plumbers, carpenters, painters, heating and air-conditioner people to do what needed doing. "And Zack himself is handy with things like replacing light bulbs, tightening screws and pounding a nail when he needs to." Mrs. Arndt was a nosey but dependable person.

Mrs. Arndt interrogated Dempsey: Had she gone to college? Her career? What about marriage? Her aunt's illness, career, whether married, children? When Dempsey said Tess had been married three times, Mrs. Arndt suggested, "Your aunt should have asked me, I could have told her one marriage is more than enough."

Dempsey began to feel Mrs. Arndt should have been a journalist interviewing people to write human interest stories. Yet Dempsey endured her inquisitive nature so that Mister and the children could delight in each other's company. Besides, she talked about Zack. Dempsey was interested in learning about Zack.

The next Saturday, Zack and children were in the green space behind the building hitting golf balls, as Mister and Dempsey approached. Their recreation stopped while the children and Mister interacted. Zack asked if Dempsey played golf. "No," she answered.

He questioned, "How can anyone live a normal life without golf?"

"Goodness, I don't claim normality or normalcy," she confessed.

"But you must have a hobby, don't you?"

"I enjoy reading."

"Medieval stories? Mrs. Arndt tells me you have a degree in medieval literature," he smiled.

"Dear Mrs. Arndt. Yes, I have such a degree."

"Mrs. Arndt knows all and tells all. But she is good with the kids, and her husband is as well. He plays cards and chess with them, and I'm grateful for the family atmosphere and stability the Arndts provide. And so back to you—you read medieval stories and go to Mass."

"What," Dempsey exclaimed in bewilderment, "What are you talking about?"

Zack admitted, "I'm being weird. The Sunday morning you and your parents were getting into the car and the kids and I were coming here to play, I asked if there was anything I could do for Tess while you were gone. You said you wouldn't be gone long and she'd be fine, but if I wanted to telephone Tess and tell her I was available if she needed me, she would appreciate that. And so, I telephoned Tess. She thanked me, said Mass would last about an hour and then you'd be home, and she felt she'd be OK, but it felt good to know I was nearby. Mrs. Arndt and I have our ways of gathering information."

Dempsey laughed.

He reiterated, "And so you read medieval literature and go to Mass."

"Well, that doesn't exactly define me," she amiably informed him.

He laughed, stood up and said he was ready to challenge Dempsey and the children in a soccer game. She said she was not a soccer player. He suggested she be the goalie for Charles and Cynthia's team. She tethered Mister to the bench, and became a member of three against Zach, which was altogether hilarious. Dempsey's efforts were clumsy but surprisingly comical to her.

After copious antics and laughter, the "game" ended, the kids were folding the soccer goals, and waiting on them, Zack held the soccer ball, golf clubs and commented. "OK, and so now I know you are a soccer goalie in addition to reading old stores and going to Mass."

Dempsey responded, "Now you know everything," and added, "You are a good one-man team."

"Average, very average player overall," he said with mocking bravado. "But I need to know more about you if we're going to get to know each other."

Dempsey was surprisingly candid, "I didn't know we were getting to know each other."

"Time is short before you leave. Time is of the essence," he feigned seriousness. Or was he serious? Cynthia and Charles joined them with soccer goals in hand, saying what fun the soccer game had been. Positively delighted Dempsey, carrying Mister, opened the door to their apartment building while the Kendricks walked their short distance home.

Dempsey's abundant joy from Zack's comments about time being of the essence in getting to know each other was clouded by the other reality in Dempsey's life.

CHAPTER TWENTY-THREE

Tess Dies

Tess wasn't doing well. Perhaps the visits of Ann Dramm and Dempsey's parents were too exhausting as much as she enjoyed having them. Tess began talking about stopping chemotherapy. She was tired of doctors and chemo; maybe she should return to the doctors in Stamford, yet the drive seemed ominous, though a medical flight was a possibility.

In contrast, Tess found comfort in the sunny days, the sunroom, the recliner, which made her talk about extending their stay. And what would Dempsey do if Tess died in Florida? Tess was restless; she was fretting non-stop.

And then, Tess's health was in a downward spiral. She was hospitalized for pneumonia and though the pneumonia was clearing-up, her body in general was overwhelmed. Dempsey spent all day every day at the hospital except for short trips to the apartment to take Mister for a walk. Some evenings Mister and Dempsey ate with Zack and the children. Cynthia said the group was like a family.

Dempsey was with Tess when she died peacefully in the hospital having received the sacrament of the anointing of the sick a few days prior, at which time Tess's appearance became calm, peaceful, and remained so. Arrangements for cremation had already been made by Tess no matter where she died. Dempsey knew Tess wanted a funeral Mass in Terryton so family could gather, and there would be no need to rush, as Tess wanted the possibility of pleasant weather in the Spring for the family gathering.

Not much time was left on the Florida apartment contract. Then, Dempsey would take the cremains back to Stamford, having informed family, friends and acquaintances, legal and business contacts of her death. Dempsey laundered Tess's clothes and gave them to charity. She gave vases from the many floral arrangements to a second-hand store and decided to keep potted plants at Zack's suggestion, whereupon he planted them in a barren shaded spot outside.

Dempsey listened to Ann's seashore song and wept. It was a crying time when Mister and Dempsey walked to the beach and watched the sunset. Dempsey sat in Tess's recliner weeping, reflecting.

Zack telephoned offering to help however he could. This had to bring back memories of his wife's death, Dempsey supposed. Dempsey's parents offered to come be with her either in Florida or Stamford. Part of her tears were about leaving Zack and the children, as well as the apartment that embodied quality time with Tess.

On that Saturday Mister and Dempsey were to start the drive back to Stamford after farewells with Zack and the children standing next to the packed SUV. With the children, Dempsey found words and embraces comfortable though sad. This was even more true of the embrace between Dempsey and Zack.

Zack had occasionally hugged Dempsey during Tess's final days and since. Hugs of sympathy, empathy. Dempsey wondered if this was merely compassion borne out of his wife's death. In the vulnerability of grief Dempsey seemed to know how to hug and be hugged. But actually, during her parents' visit she noticed she was better able to hug and be hugged. The months with Aunt Teresa lessened her extreme tendency to be an overly self-conscious private-person. The hugs between Zack and Dempsey had been the most comforting, soothing source of well-being of her adult life. Dempsey shockingly realized this.

When Mister and Dempsey were finally situated in the SUV for the drive to Stamford, Zack closed her car door, said "have a safe trip," and tapped the top of the vehicle twice with his fingers, which seemed a caring gesture of sending them on their way.

This blue-eyed, self-proclaimed average guy was more than average in Dempsey's eyes. With his light brown no-part thick hair, slightly taller than average lean athletic build, he was far more than average-appealing to her. He was clever—and caring, so far as Dempsey could tell. She did not want to leave him, the children he obviously cherished, or the Florida seashore.

CHAPTER TWENTY-FOUR

Dog Mister is Run Over

The road trip for Dempsey and Mister was uneventful: hours to think, remember, plan and wonder about the future. Dempsey would need to get a job, but not immediately, for she'd need to keep up with estate concerns with lawyers; the death certificate would be arriving, copies made and distributed as required to lawyers and other entities.

The brownstone would be sold because taxes were too high, as Tess had schooled Dempsey. With Tess alive her niece understood and felt capable, but without her aunt's assistance, energy, and acumen, how able would Dempsey be with finances? Tess was her buffer.

Dempsey thought of the initial trip south to Florida without a clue that she and Mister would be driving north with Tess's ashes. Winter was not yet gone in Stamford. There would be cold, gray days ahead. Some stretches of the trip the hum of the tires on the interstate captured Dempsey's attention and the sound felt ominous.

Finally, Mister and Dempsey arrived in Stamford on a cold, grey day. She drove by the brownstone, which looked fine, to the end of the street, turned in the alley to the middle of the block, clicked the garage door opener, her car was there.

Once parked, she clicked close the garage door, put the leash on Mister who was panting with excitement, apparently knowing they were home. She opened the back car door, picked up the urn of the cremains in a special wooden box on the car floor, closed the car door, opened the garage door to the yard and somehow in the process, Mister yanked the leash from her grasp, racing out the garage door into the yard, the urn in the box crashed to the cement floor. Dempsey saw the yard gate next to the house was open. Mister bounded towards it and through it, she ran after him crazy with fear, screaming for him to come back as he continued into the street where a car was coming from the left.

Dempsey was too late. Mister was run over in the street in front of the brownstone. The car stopped. Mister was dead in the street. People got out of the car. They comforted her. Others gathered. Dempsey was in shock. Everything happened at once, as in slow motion.

A person appeared with a shovel and a plastic yard bag saying he would clear the street, keep Mister's body, and talk with Dempsey later. She pointed to where she lived. Another person walked Dempsey up the front steps of the brownstone where Dempsey had a terrible time retrieving the keys in her purse to the outer glass door and the inner door.

The person said she would stay with Dempsey. On automatic pilot, Dempsey thanked the person but said she would telephone someone to come. Then, in the house, alone, without Mister, she telephoned Ann Dramm who said she'd be right over. Dempsey sat on the sofa. She was numb.

Had she left the gate open the day they left for Florida when she checked the outside faucet at the side of the house to be sure its winterizing was intact? The yardman left a tool in the backyard before they left; did he retrieve the tool and forget to close the gate? One of Tess's realtor friends was caring for plants in the house in their absence; did she leave the gate open? Did neighboring kids come for a ball kicked over the fence and forget to close the gate?

In her jumbled state, Dempsey realized her precious Mister would be cremated. She remembered Tess's cremation box slamming to the floor in the garage and wondered about the state it was in. Finally, she heard a car door close in front of the house. It was Ann. Dempsey opened the front door. They hugged.

After a bit, Ann and Dempsey unloaded the car in the garage. Tess's cremation box had a chipped corner from hitting the concrete garage floor, which was just one more horror of the day. Ann suggested a funeral home would have a larger box in which to place this box and all would be well, which brought relief to Dempsey.

Dempsey came to realize without Mister to start the days she would want to stay in bed in the mornings until she felt mentally and physically awful; a pre-Mister habit she detested but couldn't change. She knew she needed extra rest at this time. However, she also knew she must not allow herself to remain in her robe all day, or she would slip into sluggishness (depression). She prayed for the grace to attend daily late afternoon Mass, bringing discipline and the strength each day to put one foot in front of the other. At church she lit candles for Tess and Mister.

She prayed herself to sleep at night and continued to eat well; better than in pre-Tess days, for wholesome food did make her feel better all over. The telephone was now more her companion than she preferred, dealing with Tess's estate and friends. Even in death her aunt was helping Dempsey be more alive than she might have chosen on her own.

Her parents telephoned often, inviting her to return to Terryton. It was true that Stamford was a lonely place. Zack telephoned every day. Telling the children about Mister had been difficult. Cynthia cried when Dempsey spoke with her and Charles's voice cracked as he offered his condolences. Zack telephoned usually after the children were in bed. On the weekends the routine changed and she spoke with the children. She was always pleased to hear his voice. He urged her to return to Sandshell.

CHAPTER TWENTY-FIVE

Suspicions

Tess's death certificate arrived with the cause of death listed as cirrhosis and cancer of the liver. Cirrhosis! Dempsey hadn't known; not a clue. Yes, Tess did sip wine every evening beginning with the evening meal, until chemo began and she stopped the wine. Tess must have known about the cirrhosis diagnosis and was perhaps why she had so many fears about infirmity and old age even before cancer was mentioned. She'd had regrets about the past when she explicated the seashore song, kept the wine fridge in the basement well-stocked; repeatedly told how wine helped her sleep better than any meds.

Dempsey had the feeling of being indirectly betrayed. Yet, alcohol was Tess's secret to keep if she so chose. Dempsey decided to tell no one; not family or friends. Those working on the estate would know when Dempsey mailed them a copy of the death certificate. Dempsey's head was spinning again, but she was clear-headed enough to know as executor of Tess's estate she would not legally try to go poking through her medical records. Dempsey also knew cirrhosis could occur without excessive use of alcohol. But why hadn't Tess mentioned cirrhosis as part of her medical diagnosis?

One evening telephone conversation, she told Zack about Tess's cirrhosis. She had to tell someone. He was strangely silent, until he said he felt alcohol played a role in Roxanne's death. "She ignored her high blood pressure medicine's warnings to not mix with alcohol, and she, too, drank wine to sleep better. She was stressed, as a wife, mother, a perfectionist of sorts, gathering home design clientele who had high expectations. The pressure was great, and every evening she drank wine, disregarding the medicine's warnings.

"Her official cause of death was electrical malfunction of the heart. I have always suspected it was the mix of alcohol and the medicine. I carry that burden of feeling responsible. Should I have been more in her face about not mixing the two? I tried that, but she resisted. It was an issue between us."

Dempsey, feeling somewhat deceived or misled (no word was correct) by Tess, whom she so trusted, started feeling distrustful of everyone. Her suspiciousness became bizarre. What if Zack made up a story about Roxanne to match Dempsey's story about Tess; you know, strengthening the bond between them. What if his wanting her to come to Florida and his hints of marriage were his needing a nanny. Did he suspect Dempsey would have inheritance money knowing what Tess paid for renting the Florida apartment and seeing her luxury vehicle. Perhaps he knew the brownstone would be sold, though Dempsey never told him Tess had bequeathed it to her.

Dempsey retraced old conversations and felt sure she never talked money with him. She remembered he'd said his parents left him a stash of money; Mrs. Arndt surmised he'd rather had money in the bank than the beautiful things Roxanne purchased, and she said he snatched up his present job when he realized free apartment rent was part of the deal.

Dempsey's suspicious feelings made her feel even more alone. This was when people make mistakes, she told herself. Telephone chats with Zack changed. She dismissed his urgings that she move to Florida where she could complete Tess's estate details, sell the house from Florida, and fly from Florida to Connecticut for Tess's funeral in May. Dempsey felt he knew something was different in their conversations.

Yet, or maybe *because* he felt her distance, he told her he was attracted to her the day he saw her unloading the back of the SUV and asked if he could be of help, which she quickly declined. *So he did know on Christmas that had been Dempsey at the back of the SUV several weeks earlier, the day Tess and Dempsey arrived.*

Dempsey found his stated attraction to her hard to believe, not having had much experience of men being attracted to her. He suggested she get a one-bedroom apartment in the apartment building they'd been in or in the other complex some distance away if that felt more comfortable. He could get a rental discount for her. The current economy was good, and if she wanted temporary office work, he was sure such was available. He said he wanted her to move there so that "we can get to know each other better," which, of course, he'd said before.

Zack assumed she was miserable without Mister, and he was correct about that. She missed the sound of Mister's paws on the hard wood floors, his snorting, sneezing sounds, his spoiled insistence that she hold him whenever she sat down, his racing up and down the stair case, extended sniffings in the backyard for the few minutes he was there, always anxious to return inside. Mister and Dempsey had been co-dependent; joined at the hip, so to speak. The two who needed Dempsey most were gone in such a short time.

For a few days she entertained the possibility of sharing the brownstone with a renter to make a little money and have another person in the house some of the time. This quickly lost appeal. She didn't list the house for sale because she didn't know where she'd move. Perhaps she should list the house for sale so that she was forced to decide her future. And then a strange thing happened.

CHAPTER TWENTY-SIX

Stray Kitten

Dempsey, inside Tess's brownstone, heard a distressed animal sound outside. Perhaps it was a dying large bird in the alley she told herself, though she'd never heard or seen such. Looking out her upstairs bedroom windows, she saw no animals. She went downstairs to the almost-sunroom and saw no animals, though the sound was definitely closer. She opened the sunroom door to the outside and huddled in the corner where the steps connected to the house was a kitten, who did not run away when Dempsey bent down to get a better look.

Yes, it was a grey kitten, not tiny, tiny, but quite young. When Dempsey put her hand out to touch the cute creature, it began to move away, meowing in distress. She remembered hearing cautions about feeding cats unless one wanted them to stay permanently, but throwing caution to the wind, she brought a small bowl of milk to this lone delightful noisemaker until she could buy more proper food. Thus began a story; a relationship.

Dempsey had never had a cat and consulted with Ann Dramm who was an official authority with her own cats, Grrr and Cali. The kitten remained outside where Dempsey placed in the corner a plastic cage with restricted opening, lined with folded blanket, and checked to be sure the kitten had food and water. Still a kitten, it slept a lot. Dempsey did not attempt to touch it, but the kitten had begun to brush against her extended hand.

Within days Dempsey brought the kitten inside, as nights were chilly. First, the kitten was in the sunroom outfitted with litter box which she learned in two days. The kitten was given some of Mister's old toys which weren't quite satisfactory, and then a few days later the furry one was brought into the house out of concern for its loneliness.

The female kitten became "Sister" because Dempsey kept mistakenly calling her Mister, thus when misspoken the kitten perhaps couldn't distinguish "Mister" from "Sister." Sister was taken to a vet who said the kitten had healthy lungs and heart and was perhaps six weeks old. Dempsey made an appointment to have her spayed when older.

Ann gave Dempsey an authoritative book on cats. However, the most urgent questions weren't answered in the book: Was Sister a feral cat? Where did she come from? How did she end-up in the backyard? The book said all cats are born feral, though contact with mother cat and litter kittens makes them more ready for eventual human socializing.

However, the book continued, if human interaction does not happen soon enough, the cat may not become properly domesticated. Also, if a kitten is too young on its own, frightened and alone, it may become overly aggressive. This was likely the story of Sister as it unraveled and as the kitten unraveled Dempsey when she began destroying the house soon to be listed for sale.

Plants were Sister's first line of attack. The furniture in general was fair game, and she especially engaged in trying to climb the Belgian lace curtains. Sister was pesky for Dempsey to hold, as scratches on hands and arms testified. Yet, Dempsey didn't want the fast-growing kitten outside fearing for her safety. Sister wasn't yet spayed, and without her precise age it couldn't be predicted when she'd be ready for romance, and Dempsey certainly didn't want another litter of kittens.

Dempsey bought more elaborate toys for Sister in the basement with a second litter box, and put a pheromone collar round her little neck to help calm her, yet she meowed incessantly when put in the basement for even short periods of time. Mostly the feline seemed to enjoy attacking plants, climbing and jumping onto any and all furnishings in the main part of the house and upstairs. After two months, Dempsey was defeated by the uncontrollable young cat.

Dempsey felt she failed with Sister and the story ended with taking Sister to a no-kill animal shelter where a donation was made to cover spaying expenses plus more; gladly leaving the accumulated cat paraphernalia, with Dempsey crying as she drove home feeling she was abandoning the cat, not knowing if the cat had already been abandoned before she found Dempsey.

However, with the tears there was also relief, for when Dempsey walked into the house, she felt a wrecking ball had been removed; she was no longer on edge. Dempsey had said a prayer that the right people adopt Sister, as she signed papers surrendering the cat to the shelter. But this wasn't the end of the story of Sister. The story had a strange twist to it.

CHAPTER TWENTY-SEVEN

Dempsey Becomes Dee

Sister the kitten, had triggered a strange mental image inside Dempsey, in her mind's eye, as soon as she came into Dempsey's world. The mental image of Sister included an aura. The image-aura covered the entire underside of the cat's body going up a bit on the sides of her body bathed in the color purple—a medium shade of violet. Even after surrendering Sister to the shelter Dempsey could bring the image-aura to mind. Also, on rare occasions when Sister had let Dempsey gently pick her up with her two hands supporting the feline underside for stability, Dempsey felt soothing tenderness in her hands from the underside of the cat, as if Dempsey was touching an exquisite softness of the cat's interior.

Dempsey would like to have held the cat lovingly to her chest, though Sister wouldn't allow this. Even after Sister had been taken to the shelter, Dempsey could feel the extraordinary soft gentle energy from the cat and Dempsey still wanted to tenderly hold wild Sister who had been taken to the animal shelter.

Nothing about the aura or feelings of tenderness seemed frightening, only perplexing. Was Dempsey putting feelings of vulnerability, tender loss of Tess and Mister onto Sister? How could this be? Dempsey spoke with Ann about the color purple, knowing Ann's mystical association with the color.

Ann suggested Dempsey get information about animals as totems. A few days later, Ann and Dempsey had lunch in the brownstone to discuss Dempsey's hallucinatory cat image experience which was still present when she chose to recall it. The purple aura cat reminded Dempsey of a summer event when she was perhaps twelve years of age, riding her bicycle on a bright, sunny day, when she had the distinct impression she could meet the sky, fly up to the sky, but was afraid to let that happen. She vividly remembered the long-forgotten vision.

The luncheon day with Ann, the two of them compiled a list about cat characteristics and their cat traits included: independent, curious, lands on its feet, a nocturnal animal, quickly reverts to being feral (wild) to survive, relates to humans in limited ways but is not companionable like a dog, patiently stalks prey until the right time to attack, said to have nine lives, is aloof, mysterious, adventurous, agile/flexible/coordinated/relaxed, with keen eyesight.

The questions became: in what ways did Dempsey have any of these cat-like qualities? Was her mental image (vision) a psychological reaction to what she needed to know about herself at this time? Did totem animals provide a kind of psychological vocabulary for indigenous peoples; a way to speak about, to describe the human personality. Today people still say so-and-so is like a bear (perhaps grumpy or angry), or cocky (like a rooster), or catty, or a snake (as in the Garden of Eden) which needs to be watched carefully because of devious, deceptive traits, or someone can be bull-headed (stubborn).

Indigenous cultures, intuitively enmeshed with animals in their natural habitat, were likely more symbiotically connected with animal characteristics than people today.

Ann and Dempsey returned again and again to the fact that Dempsey's personality produced a mental picture of a cat with a purple aura. What might Dempsey learn from this? Was she going mad? Despite dealing with grief and uncertainty about the future, Dempsey felt quite sane. The mental image was not frightening, but pleasantly mysterious or mysteriously pleasant.

Ann suggested Dempsey choose words she most related to from the list of cat-qualities the two women put together. Dempsey found she could not eliminate any on the list and began to chastise herself for her ineptitude. Dempsey knew how to chastise herself.

Ann suggested they share metaphoric possibilities between cat behaviors and human personality. Their conversation began about a cat having nine lives. Was Dempsey a strong "survivor" in terms of being a psychological survivor. Again and again, she had had to be a psychological survivor, but wasn't this true for everyone?

Next, Dempsey could not make much sense out of *stalking prey* until the suggestion was made about knowing how to be patient, to wait, until the right time for something to fall into place and then take advantage of it. This too, made psychological sense to Dempsey. She was often like that.

Then, the suggestion of *keen eyesight* did not fit, for Dempsey had had to wear eyeglasses since childhood. Again, she needed to think psychologically about being able to see people and situations clearly, and for the most part she could do this pretty well.

Reverts to being feral (wild) to survive. Well, Dempsey could become wildly indifferent to people and situations when necessary, and go her own way. *Land on one's feet.* Yes, she could stay pretty well grounded and not go belly-up when things went awry. A *nocturnal animal.* Yes, she could see enough to make her way even when pretty much in the dark about what was going on in a situation or with a person.

Not companionable like a dog. It was true, Dempsey was not profoundly a people person. Sometimes she turned inward, away from others; to ideas and spirituality more than people. *Independent, curious, aloof, mysterious, adventurous, agile/flexible/coordinated.* Dempsey had all of these tendencies in her inner psychological world and she knew they could be seen in her outer personality, sometimes to the bewilderment or annoyance of others.

When asked to name her strongest trait, Dempsey said, "Independence. Yes, I am an independent survivor who is fairly coordinated and adventurous exploring the inner world and life's big questions, though I don't necessarily or readily share this with others."

Then the suggestion was made that Dempsey look at the downside of her fierce independent aloofness. Was it sometimes too much? Like the kitten, did she lack relatability factors. Like the kitten, she didn't easily let others get close to her, embrace her psychologically or physically.

And just as Dempsey had the desire to hold the kitten close to her chest, there was also in Dempsey the strong psychological impulse to take into her heart, to fully embrace the truths wild feline Sister represented about Dempsey. The cat Sister was a kind of animal totem—a description of Dempsey's basic nature, including traits of wildness that made her give Sister away. There was something about the name Sister that resonated, brought Dempsey to tears remembering the tender underbelly of Sister.

Ann suggested: "Guts. Let's talk about psychological "guts," for you said the soothing tenderness felt in your hands from the underside of the cat's body were meaningful to you." Immediately the word "guts" translated for Dempsey into having the guts to make the decision about going to Florida, along with the heart (feelings) strong enough to do this; coupled with other feline traits like independence and curiosity to "handle" going to Florida not knowing how things would turn out. But that was not all Dempsey learned.

Simultaneously and more importantly, Dempsey knew "guts" had to do with her having the psychological guts to be the soft, flexible, loving and lovable person she naturally was, not having to be a "fighter" as she was slated to be with the name Dempsey. In the most heartfelt way, she realized how much she was not a competitor; she didn't have to be strident and persuasive. This was a deep truth about her personality which she needed to embrace, and could "handle" (the energy in her hands holding the cat) because she had the fierce inner independence to do so.

Conflicts in Dempsey's personality had come to the fore because Sister came into her life when she was grieving and psychologically vulnerable, and now these old inner battles could perhaps fade because of the therapeutic wisdom and friendship of Ann, and what they discovered together through metaphor. Dempsey was a fighter in her own way–in a fiercely independent way. She was being set free because of the truth uncovered with Ann. Jesus said truth can set one free.

Ann talked about the cat image's purple aura in several contexts. First she told about how humans learned to create purple dye. Then, she tied purple to ultraviolet energy with wavelengths too short for humans to see. She noted that purple is rare in nature and because it was costly to produce, became a symbol for royalty only. It is also a regal color symbolizing valor, as in the military Purple Heart for those wounded or killed in battle. Ann said purple often is thought to indicate highly evolved spirituality. In the Catholic and Anglican Mass purple tends to be the color of Lent and Advent. Colors are used in different churches in Orthodox Christianity in their sacramental symbolism and in some Protestant worship services. Artist Ann knew about colors.

That afternoon in the brownstone, Dempsey came to know much about herself, and more was on the horizon. She spontaneously began to think of herself as Dee, not Dempsey.

CHAPTER TWENTY-EIGHT

Dee and Zack Marry

Meanwhile, before, during and after the cat episode in Dee's life, there were many telephone conversations between her and the Kendricks in Sandshell. She was now referring to herself as Dee, and they easily switched to calling her Dee. The children begged her to come see them and while she missed Charles and Cynthia, she couldn't build a relationship with Zack solely on her fondness for the children.

Dee couldn't deny having a frighteningly deep, profound interest in Zack. Why frightening? Because what she felt was a scary yearning and longing to be with him, rather than merely a profound interest in him. She knew such passion held potential for overwhelming psychological pain, which she would rather avoid.

In a recent telephone conversation Zack shared his philosophy of life, which he labeled "collapsing into." He explained that after Roxanne died, life was so difficult he wanted to give up, but having the children kept him plugging on. He found when he collapsed into duties, chores, details, the next thing and the next and the next, whatever came down the pike, he accepted what was required, engaged with what needed doing, participated and functioned without resistance to the moment, the event, the situation, he became an obedient robot to life's demands, then slowly, living became less difficult and burdensome. The passage of time was itself the necessary scaffold that supported his "collapse into" attitude.

"Life as a robot was easier. Bible phrases roamed around in me, being raised in a fundamental bible church, and these bible quotes added up to the idea that if you do the right thing so far as you can, situations turn out OK because you become capable of dealing with what needs managing. And so, I collapsed into day-by-day events; giving of myself. Day by day I was an obedient robot to life's requirements, existence became more livable, more manageable for the kids and me. And things have worked out reasonably well. For the most part I try to cooperate with what presents itself, not wasting time or energy resisting, while also judging priorities; the importance of this over that. This is my "collapse into" way of life. Actually, I think it's called maturing, becoming a mature person, but I like the drama of it being a kind of flamboyant giving-in."

He continued, "I have collapsed into the possibility of making a fool of myself feeling you are who I want to be with, but realize I probably have not given enough room for your feelings, your point of view. Yet overall, we may not know each other very well. So, am I a fool to say this to you, or am I mature enough to tell you my feelings?"

Dee's reply came from her newfound feline independence and the ability to strike at the right moment. She said, "Speaking as a maturing person myself, I want to come to Florida." He asked, "Then, why don't you do that?" She answered, "I am. I'm going to do that." And thus her decision to go to Florida happened gradually and kind of all at once.

In Stamford, house furnishings were appraised and became part of the asking price for the brownstone. Dee donated her old car to charity. Tess's belongings were given to charities; a few cherished items sent to relatives. Dee informed lawyers and real estate people of her impending Florida move. There were many details to tend to, but Dee was not overwhelmed, as Dempsey might have been.

Meanwhile, Zack secured a small apartment for Dee in another residential complex, so the children wouldn't be able to access her so easily. And then, finally, she was on the road to Florida with two urns of cremains; overwhelmed recalling the first trip to Florida, less than a year ago, as a living threesome.

Close to her destination, she telephoned Zack telling him she was near Sandshell. He said he'd be waiting for her outside the familiar apartment. And indeed, he was standing outside his truck with a remote control to open the gate. She parked in the same space she'd parked the first time. Momentarily, he was at the SUV window; she lowered the window a bit, and with teasing terse blandness, asked, "Yes?" as if to say "What do you want?"

He answered, "I'd like to help unload your car." She responded, "Can I trust you?" This replay of their first encounter had them laughing as he opened the SUV door, she was outside the car, and there was an epic embrace; a grand, spectacular, tender, enduring, physical and emotional embrace. The world-axis surely tilted with that embrace, she told herself. Her personal world certainly tilted toward wanting a life with Zack.

She loved being with Zack, helping him and the children; his wisdom of knowing she would need distance from the demanding energies of the children while the adults came to know each other better. She easily, comfortably acclimated to the Kendrick family.

Telling him she wanted to fill her day, and how could she be of help to him. His request came in the form of searching for a house to buy, for he said the children needed their own yard and neighborhood; the family had outgrown the condo whether or not Dee chose to become part of the family. Therefore, if she would do the initial looking with a realtor and develop a short list he could check out, this would be enormously helpful.

Dee saw how organized Zack was. He already had a realtor, a price range, a chosen area of town based on schools. She asked, "Are you always this organized?" He answered: "I can't stop collapsing into the requirements of the moment."

Dee and Zack married, moved with Charles and Cynthia into a house realtor Monique found for them, where the ashes of Mister were then buried in the back yard. Monique was dubbed "Unique Monique" by Zack who was certain she couldn't possibly breathe while talking as much as she did with a strong French accent, for she'd come years earlier to Florida from France, with Algerian ancestry. Dee and Monique remained friends long after the purchase of the house, duplicating what Dee had seen between Tess and Ann Dramm.

One Saturday, the Kendrick family came home from an animal shelter with a puppy of mixed heritage who became known as "Lucky" because the children decided they were lucky to have him and he was so lucky to have a yard to run, play and be safe, and a family to love him.

On their visit to the animal shelter Dee saw a kitten who kept coming to mind, though she tried to ignore the urgings. She put the question to Zack, "If dealing with a puppy, then why not also a kitten, thus giving me a chance to redeem my failure with Sister, the kitten in Stamford." Zack said, "Why not." Thus, a grey tabby kitten who came to be named Totem, joined the household. Lucky and Totem added their personalities to the family.

Each day Dee awakened to a world filled with the requirements of maintaining a home, children, pets, and a marriage relationship. Her financial inheritance from aunt Tess helped them pay cash for the house. Dee came to live a life she never thought possible.

However, tragically, though she didn't expect Ann Dramm to live forever, she couldn't accept that Ann's life ended by hitting her head falling on an icy sidewalk outside her high-rise condo in Stamford. Peaceful, wise Ann who'd been a primary change-agent for Dee, guiding her through metaphoric discernment to the truth of her own soul based on Dee's extraordinary experience of a purple aura and the tender touch of "guts" involving Sister, the feral cat. Metaphoric discernment's revelation, with Ann's help, led Dee back to Florida, to Zach and the children.

At Ann's funeral Dee met Beth from Austin, only survivor of the original foursome: Matti, Gabby, Beth and Ann. Also at the funeral, Dee met from Clarksdale KS, Julia Montel, Matti's biological daughter, and retired psychiatrist Lenore with whom Ann went on an ancestral pilgrimage in Kansas. Dee would become intimately involved with Julia and Lenore in unforeseeable ways.

Not long after Ann Dramm's funeral, Dee's father died. On the day of Dee's father's funeral, Dee learned from older relatives that when Dee's father was five years old, his little sister Agnes, two years younger, died from birth defects after living her short time on earth in the home of a married aunt who had no children and thus was able to devote herself full-time to caring for this child with special needs. The parents of Agnes, Dee's grandparents, must have helped bury the tragedy of Agnes's life and death by giving no mention of her to their other children. Why had Dee's father or Tess never mentioned Agnes?

Perhaps Dee's father needed children who were fighters because of weak Agnes who died, which may also have been Tess's motivation to be tough, strong, and not want children.

As for the Kendrick children, Charles easily accepted Dee into the family. Not so with Cynthia who wanted Dee as part of the family, but not have Dee living in the same house, sharing the bedroom with Zack, seeing his affection for Dee. This was not easy for Cynthia who sometimes treated Dee as an imposter. Charles created an affectionate name for Dee, Mum-Dee to go along with his pet-name for his dad, Dad-Zack. However, for Cynthia, Dee would remain "Dee."

Late one Saturday morning several months after the wedding, the Kendrick family set out on bicycles to an athletic park with a lengthy bike trail around its perimeter. Zack and Charles left the bike trail to toss a baseball back and forth. Cynthia and Dee continued in a leisurely way on the trail. Cynthia was leading the way when she crashed to the ground. Dee was not far behind, saw Cynthia's tumble, and was terrified about her head being hurt, after the fall that killed Ann Dramm.

Cynthia was crying hard and tangled in the bicycle when Dee reached her momentarily. Dee kept asking about her head though covered by a helmet. "Did you hit your head?" She was sobbing, "No." Yet Dee needed to be sure, "Are you sure you didn't hit your head?" Sobbing, she emphatically replied, "Deeee, my helmet didn't hit the ground. It's my legs." "Don't try to stand up," Dee cautioned, waving her arms, calling out to Zack.

Cynthia's legs did not look broken; but scraped and scratched. Dee realized Cynthia had thrown "Deeee" at her, but excused the voice tone considering the accident. Dee and Zack had on various occasions talked about this aspect of Cynthia's behavior and decided it best to ignore the icy attitude.

Zack and Charles arrived quickly. Cynthia's crying increased as Zack knelt, looked at her leg scrapes, lifted the bicycle off of her, helped her stand, hugged her while Charles handed him a tube from the first aid kit attached to his bicycle with an ointment that eased the pain of abrasions.

Zack applied the pain relief gel while suggesting, "Charles and I will ride home, bring the truck back for the bicycles and you two." Cynthia protested, "No, I can ride. I'm OK. Can we go for ice cream as usual?" And that's what they did.

Cynthia had a plucky personality; easily spoke her mind. Often, it was hard to understand Cynthia's reactions.

During the first year of marriage at an evening meal Charles told the family about "This mouthy mean kid Neal at school who picks on Riley, a small shy guy in our class. Today Neal was calling Riley "homo, gay guy." Dimitri said to Neal, 'Why are you calling him that?' Neal said, 'You can tell how he looks he's a fag and my dad says God hates fags.' So I said, 'My mom doesn't say God hates anybody and she knows about religion."' Charles looked at Zack for validation and asked, "She goes to church every week, right?" Zack answered, "Yes, she does." Charles continued his story: "Neal said to me, 'Your mom doesn't know anything." And I said to him, 'Why are you so mean?' and he walked away."

Zack told Charles, "You were brave to stand up with Dimitri and help Riley against Neal. That takes courage." Zack and Charles exchanged a high-five across the table, while Cynthia smiled in a strange way, giving the impression of a scoff or sneer. What part of Charles's story brought that reaction in Cynthia?

How might one read Cynthia's smile? Was it ludicrous that Charles could be brave? That Charles related to Dee as "mom?" The comment of Dee knowing what is religious? Neal's comment that Dee doesn't know anything was satisfying to Cynthia? Or perhaps Cynthia found the story humorous, or she was proud of her brother, or for altogether other reasons. Dee hid her discomfort with Cynthia at times like this.

CHAPTER TWENTY-NINE

Dee's Inheritance

There was ordinary sibling bickering between Cynthia and Charles, which escalated as they grew into adolescence. Charles had his own teen conundrums while there seemed to be pervasive angry-sadness in Cynthia. Dee was patient with both children, and only slowly stopped feeling like an outsider. Certainly, she related more easily with Charles while Cynthia's personality was harder to understand.

Sometimes Dee felt Zack teased the children too much, as her dad had done with her and Max. She wished Zach would be simpler with Charles and Cynthia. She mentioned this to Zack and he said, "Roxanne routinely told me I teased too much, but I don't think that changed anything. I only tease people I care about. I wish my dad had known how to tease. He was too straight, too serious. I would have felt we were more connected, and I wanted that. I never saw him tease my mother with some kind of lighthearted playfulness between them. I only tease people I like." That put a new spin on the subject for Dee.

In the early years of marriage, Dee felt she should have a career, though financially, because of inheritance from Tess, they were comfortable. She had no idea what career appealed to her. Zack was very wrapped-up in his job at Sandshell City Hall, which he began shortly after they married. He was supervisor of maintenance for City Hall and its grounds, a job that suited him, but it was here Zack would come to know trauma.

In the back of Dee's mind, she always wondered if Zack married her for her inheritance. He knew the cost of the apartment she and aunt Tess lived in. It was the most expensive apartment on the property because of the view of the Gulf. Zack saw the luxury SUV Dee and Tess arrived in. He was aware of how long they were staying in the apartment and how much that cost.

Zack brought money to the marriage, inheritance from his parents, profit selling the home he and Roxanne had, insurance money from Roxanne's death. As a former accountant, he seemed to know how to invest money. He was frugal and hard-working. He reminded Dee how much money they would save for the children's college and the overall financial security they'd have through the years by having been able to pay cash for their home. He often voiced his gratitude for the role her inheritance played in the purchase.

Dee tried to stop her money suspicions about Zack and her inheritance and felt on one hand she was overly suspicious and on the other hand she was naive. Why couldn't she simply be wise? She knew her limitations and often recited in her head Mother Mary Catholic prayers.

"Hail Mary" and "*Memorare*," very old prayers, were favorites of Dee. She intuitively knew she needed the feminine side of God to balance her father's overly-masculine expectations that had their influence on her. It was as if these two feminine prayers were companions imprinted on her being.

> Hail Mary (*Ave Maria*): Hail Mary full of Grace, the Lord is with thee. Blessed art thou amongst women and blessed is the fruit of thy womb Jesus. Holy Mary mother of God, pray for us sinners now and at the hour of our death. Amen.
>
> *Memorare (Remember)*

> Remember, O most gracious Virgin Mary, that never was it known that anyone who fled to thy protection, implored thy help, or sought thy intercession was left unaided. Inspired with this confidence, I fly unto thee, O Virgin of Virgins, my Mother; to thee do I come; before thee I stand, sinful and sorrowful. O Mother of the Word Incarnate, despise not my petitions, but in thy mercy hear and answer me. Amen.

Dee said the prayers with thee, thy, and thou, as she had learned them in elementary school. She embraced the prayers most when she was stressed.

As a newlywed, Dee had plunged into furnishing and decorating their new home. She increased pressure on herself by remembering that Zack's wife Roxanne had a career in interior design. Aunt Tess had a knack for that, and so too, Dee's mother created appealing living spaces. Dee, in what she now recognized as her identity gender confusion conflict resisted what she might have appreciated in her mother. Now, in this new home she found herself eager to school herself in creating a beautiful home interior. Now dealing with marriage, children, household, she was embarrassed how critical and sullen she had been of her mother.

Dee was overwhelmed at times but also swept-up, scarcely believing her new life, finding herself furniture shopping, seeking out people who could help with colors and styles, searching the internet, interested in magazines related to making the new home beautiful. She enjoyed developing this side of herself. There were former times when she would have judged such information frivolous and unworthy; which she came to see as a cheap snobbery born out of her conflicted confusion, being unknowingly trapped, dominated in masculine energy, so to speak.

She now admitted to herself she was energized, informed, elated by what she was doing with the house. Pockets of enthusiasm she never knew came alive in her as she planned, implemented, enjoyed the five-sense world of realtor Monique, who became a permanent friend.

The spacious split-bedroom Kendrick home came increasingly alive. Charles and Cynthia made choices for their rooms. Dee's usual reading fare stopped as she was consumed by the creativity she experienced developing and refining the sensate side of her personality. She was grateful she and Zack had the money to design the interior, not lavishly but well, with quality furniture and furnishings.

And then, besides Monique the realtor, another female friend entered Dee's world.

CHAPTER THIRTY

Golf and Friends

Zack loved golf—a lot. Dee learned this almost as soon as they met. He enjoyed the camaraderie as much as the game—especially Reggie. It was some time before Dee met Reggie, and Zack never mentioned Reggie was African-American. Dee was shocked Zack hadn't mentioned that immediately. Was Zack hiding the fact? Dee couldn't imagine the color of Reggie's skin was irrelevant to Zack. In this, Dee met her own racism and was ashamed.

When Dee met Reggie's exceptional wife, Estelle, and learned she was an ex-nun, this was beyond Dee's comprehension—she had never experienced a black-American nun. Dee realized how limited her world in Terryton had been. She had only rarely seen black-Americans at Mass, and now her world was about to be stretched by this extraordinary woman.

Estelle was attractive, stately in stature, well-dressed, exuding composure. She never seemed rushed or overwhelmed by being the mother of three boys older than Charles and Cynthia, a full-time high school counselor, involved with adult education at church. How could Estelle handle so much and remain calm? Dee would learn a great deal from Estelle, including why was she an "ex" nun.

As personalities, Estelle and realtor Monique were opposite types. Monique talked non-stop, telling everything. Monique's rapid-fire talk did not invite sharing, as she interrupted, finished sentences, came to conclusions, engaged in a rapidity of saying everything for herself and the other person as well, as if stuck on high-speed urgency, uttering aloud everything she thought.

In contrast, Estelle was reserved and only cautiously divulged her life. She was a listener. Friends of Dee, both Estelle and Monique brought countless richness to her; she had waited years for such companionship.

Monique was slightly older than Dee, with a daughter and son: Christiane and Justin. Besides being talkative, she was hard working, thoughtful, filled with real estate knowledge, all expressed with a strong French accent. Monique and husband Henri came to Florida years ago from France, their grandparents having emigrated separately to France from Algeria when Algeria was a French colony.

The young couple experienced racial prejudice in the U.S., due to their darker skin, and the strange English they spoke. Monique told how she came to understand the roots of racism are about survival: we trust those who are most like us and feel uncertain with those most different from us. Monique claimed to have risen above the pain of racial discrimination upon realizing this "similar to us" or "not like us" factor. Monique's active mind and ability to adapt matched her animated emotions.

Monique's husband Henri finally had his own company, tending to exquisite homes of wealthy owners who came to their regal beach homes only occasionally. Monique and Henri lived in this country years before he found this kind of situation worked for him. Monique had been the primary breadwinner before Henri found his niche. Monique was the stronger of the two. Her strength would be challenged again and yet again, and the Kendrick family would help her pick up the pieces.

Estelle was from New Orleans, Reggie from Sandshell, FL. They met in New Orleans after she left the convent, and he was visiting his ill mother in New Orleans; his father had already died. Reggie was raised by grandparents (his mother's parents) in Sandshell after his musician parents in New Orleans left him with the grandparents permanently when their jazz night life careers could not accommodate raising a child.

Eventually, Estelle shared with Dee she entered the convent for reasons that did not exactly fit "having a vocation." She made a bargain with God: she would become a nun and God's job was to see to it that her alcoholic father stopped drinking. After six years in the convent and her father was still drinking, she felt her bargain was ill-conceived. Being a nun did not fit who she was. She left the convent.

Estelle met Reggie, handsome with an athletic build, while dining out with her two biological sisters in a restaurant and Reggie was waiting for a buddy at a nearby table. A miscommunication with his friend meant the friend never came. A conversation began between the three sisters and the lone Reggie. He was attracted to Estelle and learning she was a high school counselor, diligently, relentlessly, eventually tracked her down and after a lengthy courtship, they married, had three sons, and some years later, Reggie became owner of a boat business in Sandshell. Reggie and Zack met and became steadfast friends on the golf course. Over the years, the Kendrick family sometimes sailed in one of Reggie's boats on the gulf waters with Reggie and Estelle, whose boys were already in college and beyond.

Former nun Estelle brought the Spiritual Exercises of St. Ignatius of Loyola alive for Dee who had heard about them but did not know what they had to offer as personal experience. As someone who learned the power of mental images through her purple aura cat with Ann Dramm, Dee easily related to what Spanish Ignatius (1491-1556) discovered about mental images while convalescing from battle wounds caused by a cannon ball. At one point in his lengthy recovery, he was in such turmoil trying to decide what to do with his life after recovery, he considered throwing himself into a cistern. Dee easily understood his turmoil.

CHAPTER THIRTY-ONE

Dee's Anger

After several years of marriage Dee was still searching for a career. Before marriage she'd had jobs but never a career. Zack was not eager for her to have either job or career outside the home, which would make the household more time-pressured. However, Dee admired aunt Tess as a realtor and Monique as well, and Estelle as a high school counselor. Dee's mother had worked daily in her husband's auto parts store. The exception on her list was Ann Dramm who had a partial career as a portrait artist and was a volunteer intensely involved in a maternity center in the community. Dee compared herself to these women.

She remembered a day several years into the marriage when her career dilemma boiled over. She began to feel angry towards Zack early in the afternoon, as if he should have answers for her, which she knew was ludicrous. She had begun to realize how easy it was to blame him for unresolved issues within herself. Yet she didn't want Zack to have her answers. That day in frustrated anger, her thoughts were racing: *he is not going to push me around, control my future, tell me what is best for me, try and influence me against myself.* She was furious with mighty determination; intractable stubbornness had grabbed hold of her. She had never before been outwardly furious with Zack (or maybe anyone) and didn't know how to navigate the situation, but was determined he would not run her over. Truthfully, he hadn't tried to run her over, simply made suggestions, yet even that was too much.

She would have to fake the hug when he came home from work. And so it was. Theirs was a perfunctory hug that day. He seemed all amiable and pleasant. She felt like a stone; wanted to be better but couldn't make that happen.

The chill remained through the evening meal into the evening. Once the children were in their rooms with homework or such, Zack queried, "OK, what's wrong? How could I possibly have offended you when I was at work?" There was silence on her part. He tried again, "Don't use the silent treatment. Just tell me what's wrong."

In her mind his words sounded as if he was saying: "I've been married before. I've seen this kind of behavior. Do it my way because I know best; I've had more experience." She knew she was thinking stupidly.

She blurted out, "I'm so angry. I don't want to be furious but I am. I feel you are trying to railroad me into a career of your making."

"We didn't even talk about career stuff today." Her fury continued, "Not today, but recently. You cannot tell me what to do about something that is not your decision to make."

Zack replied, "OK, I get that. I've been thinking about the future, too, and realized I may have over-stepped my bounds with my suggestions. I was trying to be helpful. Can't we talk about it and not be angry about it?"

She responded, "There is a part of bruised Dempsey that hears and fears suggestions as decrees."

He explained, "My concern is should something happen to me, that you and the children always have enough money. However, another concern is that as a family we don't live constantly time-stressed, which no amount of money can fix. So, I am comfortable how we are now. I don't think it is healthy to be constantly racing against time." Dee knew he felt Roxanne had been time-pressured.

She agreed, "I don't want us to be rushing—rushing about. I don't want to destroy what we have now. Yet I feel time might be passing me by and the day will come when it's too late for me to find what I want to do."

He recalled, "I remember we agreed before we were married that you would not pursue a career outside the home until the children were older. Am I correct about this? It seems we're borrowing trouble from the future which we don't need to be dealing with now."

He didn't understand, which increased her anger, "It's about time, the passage of time, running out of time." Then they were both quiet until she said, "And I have an urgency inside me that doesn't go away." She thought of what Estelle told her about Ignatius centuries ago, so desperate to know what to do with his life that he thought of ending it.

Zack broke the silence, "I am more inclined to think of you pursuing something that could make money, should that ever be necessary. It seems to me you are more about following your heart's desire even if you can't make much money with it, whatever that might be." This ignited Dee's old concerns about him marrying her for her inheritance.

She sidestepped that topic, "Taking care of aunt Tess made me know I much prefer working directly with an individual who needs me; perhaps hospice work in some capacity. I'm not sure."

Zack knew he wasn't going to point out how that would not be particularly lucrative. The room was quiet until she broke the silence, "You may be the target of some of the anger I've swallowed and haven't voiced in my lifetime. And I have to say it feels good to be outwardly angry, infuriated. Maybe for the first time in my life I am capable of vehemently expressing opposition, boldly defending myself against being disregarded, misunderstood. Maybe I have to be angry before I can be otherwise serious about finding a career. I feel as if an anger burden has been jarred-loose this evening."

Zack was perhaps the first person in her adult life with whom she'd been outwardly, expressively angry (that she remembered). She realized inner Dempsey didn't have to set her face in stone against everyone. Instead, she could express her anger and then continue the relationship with whom she'd felt anger. This was freeing for her. "Freeing for me and thee," she spouted congenially. He rhymed cleverly, "I see." Their poetic parody changed the dynamics of the evening and ignited romance.

Next morning, Zack was back from his early golf game, and the Saturday family breakfast reveled in cohesion and conversation. Cynthia, who readily evaluated situations said, "This is a really good day. I can tell, because the food tastes especially good, and Totem and Lucky were chasing each other in the yard a minute ago; playing. Some days are better than other days." Charles did not roll his eyes at her, which meant he likely agreed, or at least didn't disagree. Cynthia's observation that some days are better than other days, was to become excruciatingly evident.

CHAPTER THIRTY-TWO

Divorce and Powerlessness

Dee answered the telephone early one morning to hear a distressed Monique crying so that she could hardly speak in her strange English, "Henri is divorcing me. He has a woman, Merrick, her first or last name, I don't know. He throws our marriage out the window, our family. He said so in the night, left our house to go to her. I tell him he is crazy, we are together so long, since we are young, so much struggle the two of us, beautiful children we have, I work, work. He works, too, but me more. And now in his work he finds his Merrick woman with a mansion beach house he maintains. Oh god, I hurt like I could die."

As days unfolded, the reality remained: Henri wanted a divorce. Along the way, to appease Monique, he agreed to go to a marriage counselor, the way Americans do. In the one counseling session they attended Henri said, "Monique talks too much."

Monique later told Dee, "Can you believe that? I talk too much, but he commits adultery and kills the marriage, the family. He could not see the difference. I laughed. I had to laugh at his accusation. He divorces me for too much talk compared to his immorals. I still laugh at 'talking too much' when not crying that Henri does not want me, but instead takes Merrick, a wealthy widow with a beach mansion, older than him, from New York City."

In the aftermath of the divorce, Monique's daughter Christiane, just out of college, and Justin, beginning college, emotionally supported Monique but also were sometimes critical of her, which brought a response from her. Monique believed their criticisms were prompted by the pain they felt from the divorce. "They had to fling anguish someplace and knew as mother I could and would take it. But when I say the word "stepmother," they scream with offense. They do not see Henri at stepmother's house but meet him in a restaurant."

Dee knew her role in Monique chats. Monique was smart, had discretion, didn't want her real estate colleagues to know every detail of the marriage break-up. And since Monique seemed to process her thoughts aloud, she could do this safely with Dee. Monique said, "You should be a therapist." Dee took the suggestion seriously. Therapist? Hospice? She was still weighing all career possibilities.

Henri gave the house to Monique in the divorce. He just wanted "out." As a realtor, she knew how unusual this was. She concluded he was naïve, but accepted his naivete to compensate for abandoning the marriage. She would reminisce, "We were children, not yet twenty when we met, so in love, my parents and his parents not approving, for I was Catholic and his family had no religion. Together we planned and saved money to marry in secret in France and then come to this country." She would shake her head and tears would flow.

Henri re-married as quickly as he legally could. He married Merrick, "First name, last name, makes no difference, I can't care," Monique said, "A lot like the name Monique." After that, Monique never again said the name Merrick, calling the other woman, "new-wife."

Henri had indeed been naïve. Apparently, his new-marriage began crumbling after not much time passed. He and new-wife never made it to their first anniversary, for Henri shot himself in the night in a remote patch of swampy vegetation not far from the beach, south of Sandshell.

New-wife worked with authorities, told of Henri's last days, their fraying relationship. It was Monique who had the body cremated, arranged for a small gathering of people to acknowledge the life of Henri, as she summarized, "He was not a strong person; I was stronger. God give him rest."

Dee saw Zack's strength at that time of crisis. He, of course, had suffered the shock and loss of Roxanne and shielded his children as much as he could. He was very aware of what Monique, Christiane and Justin were going through, helped them immensely, and stopped referring to Monique as Unique Monique.

Henceforth, Monique, Christiane, Justin shared holidays, birthdays, and other special occasions with the Kendricks. They were two families without relatives in the area. Christiane, after college, was back living with Monique, starting a dance studio in Sandshell. Dance had long been her passion, which her exotic face and lithe, small body, epitomized. Her expressive brown eyes exuded calm intrigue. Charles had a forever crush on Christiane and both families knew it. When Cynthia felt the need to embarrass Charles, she would mention his obvious affections for Christiane who was six years older than Charles. Cynthia had a mean streak in her.

Sometimes, when the families were celebrating a special day together, the rug in the large Kendrick family room was rolled up, furniture pushed against walls, and Christiane would lead them in dance. Eventually, Zack joined such activity. He finally learned to dance and enjoy it.

One such evening, Cynthia had embarrassed Charles about Christiane and Monique boldly intervened, settling more than one issue, "After Henri divorced, Christiane and Justin criticized that I humiliate family, correcting one in front of others and why I didn't correct one-by-one privately, that is kinder, gentler. I thought and realized I felt powerless in France, not pure French, for generations an immigrant, second-class citizen. Powerlessness prompted me to reprimand in a way to augment my power by increasing shame for you when others hear and see my punishment on you.

"Self-reflection is not strong with me. I react. But when I see truth in me, I know it is so. Powerlessness makes this behavior in me. Cynthia, do you do this to Charles about Christiane from powerlessness? Think about it." After that, Cynthia did not like Monique, for Monique had embarrassed her in front of everyone! Was this the lesson Monique meant Cynthia to experience?

Cynthia was fighting her own battles, "Charles is bigger and older than me. I don't like being his "little" sister. And I don't like Monique because she thinks she can say anything to anybody at anytime."

CHAPTER THIRTY-THREE

Mobius Strip

More troubles would enter Monique's life, but also something quite fine came to pass after she facilitated the sale of a condo to Francine Tournier, a French-Canadian psychotherapist moving to Sandshell to be near her daughter and family. This was a plus for Monique for the two could speak French together which Monique found a soothing balm. After Henri left, she had no one with whom she could speak her mother tongue.

Dee became intrigued with Francine whose background and education were steeped in the humanities, especially medieval culture, alongside the field of psychology. Months after Francine's move to Sandshell from Montreal, at a meal on the Kendrick screened patio with large ceiling fan, the back yard filled with coreopsis, dahlia, amaryllis, pentas, evolvulus, gerber daisy, gloxinia, blue salvia, portulaca, lavender; the plants were Dee's companions, playmates, delightful wonders, joyful hobby.

Zack grilled seafood and vegetables. Monique brought a salad, Francine came with dessert, Dee provided other side-delicacies and special breads. Reggie and Estelle were engaged with their sons' young families and not at Kendrick patio parties. Christiane and Justin weren't there that evening when the topic turned to transgender issues in the news. Francine's observations regarding transgender issues reverberated in every inch of Dee's being.

Francine spoke about the bodies of men and women producing both male and female hormones in widely varying degrees. She mentioned the psychology of Swiss psychiatrist C.G. Jung (1875-1961) who named the feminine element in males *anima* and the masculine element in females *animus*, and declared that the major task in an individual's psychological life is to deal with maleness and femaleness within one's own personality.

The topic of the Chinese *Yin-Yang* image was discussed as a way to talk about personality extrapolated from nature where the sun shines and things are clearly seen, contrasted with shadows, which can illustrate ambiguity. The image suggests ambiguity vs. clarity, the difference between analytic vs. intuitive knowing, masculine energy vs. feminine energy, a very old way to express *complementarity,* a word from quantum physics. In the *Yin-Yang* image, the dot in each the dark and the light, can express androgyny. The "other" present in each side.

"Anatomy may also have influenced talk about feminine-masculine energies. Male genitals are mostly exterior, obvious, easily seen, as in the sunshine *Yang*. Female genitals are mostly interior, in the dark, ambiguous as in the *Yin* shadow image."

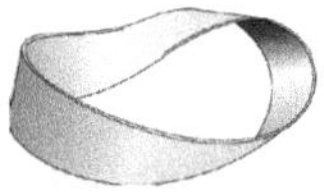

As the conversation flowed, Francine opened a large paper napkin, tore a strip, wrote on one side *feminine traits* and on the other side *masculine traits*. She gave the strip a twist, moistened the ends with wine from her glass and stuck the ends together, creating a moebius strip or band. She put the mobius strip on her wrist as a bracelet, and moved the paper bracelet in one direction demonstrating the unique feature of the mobius band, which is, bringing alternating sides to the surface, the top, into view, and then going out of sight momentarily until resurfacing into view as the band is moved in one direction.

Then, Francine unstuck the wine-joined corners, laid the strip out flat, wrote a few traditionally male and female traits on each side labeled thusly, and told how she facilitates workshops where participants do this.

She summarized, "The mobius band demonstrates androgynous characteristics as constants in the personality. The mobius strip embodies a crucial psychological dilemma these days for individuals now that strict genders roles continue to fade; the twisted band demonstrates contrasexuality, androgyny." She shared a pamphlet she'd written for clients.

Brain-Hemispheres and a Mobius-Strip
by
Francine Tourneau, Ph.D.
Psychotherapist

I have created a mobius band to wear on the wrist imprinted with words which heighten awareness of personality habits. Moving the mobius band on the wrist shows and hides words, which illustrates momentary shifts, back-and-forth approaches to dealing with everyday life.

Below, the words on the mobius band are shown side-by-side, matched by numbers that show the complementarity of opposite traits, and they suggest the possibility of developing both of the opposites. Otherwise, absolute rationality without intuition can become unreasonable. Likewise, intuition without rational clarity can be beside the point, scattered, too diffuse. Intuitive inspiration and rational rigor together are best.

I created these *yin-yang* lists and turned them into a moebius band on the assumption that awareness of the opposites helps develop more neural pathways in the brain. The lists below are not based on scientific findings, though brain-hemisphere (split-brain) research influences the lists. The two columns are a folksy way of relating to everyday experience which I've gathered from many clients in therapy over the years, and I've numbered for easy comparison. The lists are suggestions, not absolutes. If the columns are interpreted as knee-jerk rigidities, this is not my intention.

I suggest you add to what I present below, with your own complementary opposites.

Traditional *Yin* feminine, right brain-hemisphere	Traditional *Yang* masculine, left brain-hemisphere
1. Mother nature	1. Father time
2. Statue of liberty, representing the U.S.	2. Uncle Sam, representing the U. S.
3. Simultaneous comprehension	3. Sequential comprehension
4. Intuitive, all-at-once, associative	4. Logical, analytical, linear, step-by-step
5. "In touch" with one's own body	5. Detached somewhat from one's own body
6. Receptive, diffuse, "open" awareness	6. Focused, penetrating, controlled awareness
7. Metaphoric, symbolic, figurative world	7. Literal, five-sense, physical world
8. Appreciates ambiguity	8. Prefers "facts"
9. Unconscious oriented	9. "Ego" knowing
10. Grasps multi-faceted, non-quantifiable	10. Controls variables, replicates, quantifies
11. Life is a mystery to be lived	11. Life is a problem to be solved
12. Dream images, waking phantasies	12. Language, numbers
13. Left-side of body	13. Right-side of body
14. Synchronicity: extraordinary coincidence	14. Notices causality (this-causes-that)
15. Co-operative and process-oriented	15. Competitive and goal-oriented
16. Notices hints, clues, allusions	16. Depends on stark analysis
17. Values balance and harmony	17. Values progress, success
18. Values interdependence	18. Values independence
19. Seeks wisdom	19. Seeks knowledge, information
20. Inspiration	20. Insight
21. Subjective experience	21. Objective experience
22. Hands-on learning	22. Abstract learning

23. Paradox; "both/and" understanding	23. Prone to "either/or" understanding
24. Tender-minded	24. Tough-minded
25. Gentler approach	25. More forceful approach
26. Implicit	26. Explicit
27. Values beauty	27. Bigger is better
28. Pliable, flexible understanding	28. Rigid, static understanding
29. Probable, improbable	29. Possible/impossible
30. Values simply "playing the game"	30. Winning/losing is everything
31. Includes grey areas in judgments	31. Black/white judgments
32. Adaptable	32. Ruled, regulated
33. Informed by beauty	33. Practical, pragmatic
34. *Kairos* (timing) favorable/unfavorable time	34. *Chronos* chronological time
35. Imaginative	35. Introspective
36. Processes the amorphous	36. Seeks the clearly definable
37. Open to the eternal	37. Uses one's own will
38. Values effective over efficient	38. Values efficient over effective
39. Dedicated, devoted	39. Disciplined
40. Experiential reality	40. Theoretical possibility

CHAPTER THIRTY-FOUR

Androgyny and Dreams

Francine told her own story of how an elementary school classmate cruelly said Francine looked like an "owl" and other kids laughed in agreement. Upset, Francine went home and told her mother about the incident. Her mother shared that owls are said to be wise. The next day at school Francine learned about a famous man who was said to be "wise." Her young mind connected wisdom with maleness. She laughed, saying there were other factors that also played into her own masculine-feminine development.

Dee listened carefully, for growing-up she felt more boyish than girlish. Francine continued, "I believe with the growth of science and technology too much of life collapsed into physical, concrete objectivity, which doesn't mean we should abandon science or technology but rather recognize that science is limited in dealing with layered meanings in life's complexities; with the plethora of subjective experience; potential self-knowledge. We are masters in science and technology, but mere apprentices at discerning the inner world, its wants and needs.

"Transgender issues today remind me of when I was a young psychology student in college and took the personality test, MMPI, the Minnesota Multiphasic Personality Inventory. It turned out I was a high scorer in typically masculine interests. This confirmed what I already knew about myself; I did not have traditional feminine interests, and indeed, my life has proved this. I was interested in non-traditional specialties not typical for women in my day; luckily, I managed not to smother the psychological and cultural implications with simplistic biological bias and certitude. I knew this was more about psychology than biology, however much they are connected.

"As a psychologist, my job is to help personalities relate to their psychologically androgynous nature, and not make the mistake of solving psychological androgyny in physical ways. Prior generations did not have the dilemma of role choice, for division of labor and other cultural customs contained, constricted and obscured androgyny. Today we both enjoy and are plagued by our increasingly acknowledged androgyny."

Francine was uncomfortable talking this much and became quiet, unaware of how welcome her ideas were to Dee whose struggle as Dempsey had been enormous. Francine brought more delicious psychological gems to the meals that followed on the Kendrick's screened patio. Dee expressed gratitude. Francine appreciated these relaxing evenings set in an uncommonly lovely backyard with people she enjoyed, enlarging her social circle beyond her daughter and family in her new life in Florida.

That summer, Charles, home from university, ripe with curiosity from the stimulation of classes, joined in family patio dinners with Monique and Francine. He was fascinated with Francine's wisdom—which he would find critically helpful. Cynthia too, listened and learned.

During the evening patio meals, Charles internalized Francine's words borrowed from others, about being a "wounded healer." Francine told of a recurring dream she had that dove-tailed with her college psychological test results she'd shared which indicated her non-traditional gender interests. "This recurring dream was going on when I was newly married, having graduated from college, aware of the changing role of women in culture, however, unknowingly I was still entrenched in the traditional female's place in the scheme of things.

"In my recurring dream I would re-find my car, a Volkswagen "bug," which I had in waking life before I married. The re-found car was always in good shape and I was very happy to have it back. That was the crux of the dream. Though happy in the dream, upon awakening, I would feel disquieted, agitated, at odds with myself.

"I knew little about dreams at the time and thought I was having a wish fulfillment dream, desiring my former freedom (car, "wheels", means of transport) now that I was married. The dream kept coming. Though the setting of the dream differed, the theme was the same.

"One day, I had a breakthrough, an insight. I realized the dream was telling me I would be happier when I re-found my "drive," which was still in good shape. After understanding the dream in this way, it never returned. The dream was important because I had always been a rather "driven" person with goals and projects. Getting married, I went into a kind of limbo no longer pursuing, inwardly or outwardly, what I wanted to accomplish. This persistent little dream encouraged me to re-find my drive and these many years later, I'm glad I did. My life would surely be different and less satisfying if I hadn't re-found my drive. I subsequently went to graduate school, earned my doctorate, and became a psychotherapist."

That evening, Monique coaxed Francine to tell them more about how to deal with dreams. Monique was intrigued with information about the inner world though she didn't seem to apply the techniques or methods in her own life. At the next patio dinner, Francine shared a pamphlet she'd written for her clients.

Relating to Your Dreams
by
Francine Tourneau, Ph.D.
Psychotherapist

My reason for writing this is to give you the nuts and bolts of getting close to your dreams. Humans have approximately five dreams a night, based on sleeping an average of eight hours, for we dream about every ninety minutes while asleep. Daytime naps often yield dreams as valuable as nighttime dreams. Dream-recall

is a habit, just as not remembering dreams is a habit. It is prudent to regard dreams as personal status reports, which tell us about our personality as nothing else can. We need a supple attitude to catch onto dreams, for they have a life of their own.

Befriend your dreams, which means putting paper and pen by your bed which alerts the dreamer in you know you want to recall your dreams. Don't try to fool yourself. It won't work. If you don't intend to write down your dreams, just putting the writing materials by your bed won't enhance dream recall.

However, if you are sincere, your dreams will show off for you, becoming quite vivid. Or likely, your dreams aren't showing off, you're just paying attention. You, the audience, have changed your attitude. Let's say that though the actors on stage have been performing fully, now the audience is watching and the actors know it. In short, when one begins remembering dreams, it's as if a fresh connection has been made within your being.

You may prefer writing a word-for-word story of your dreams. But remember that dreams are more images (mental pictures) than words, so don't choose the written story approach because it seems the most thorough. You can draw sketches if you prefer, and also add words to the sketches.

It may be that "a picture is worth a thousand words," the question is how to find which thousand words might apply to a dream. Dreams do speak though we must unravel what they are "saying." One way to do this is using *figurative speech* to discern psychological meaning.

One of my dreams about a soccer game made me realize I was kicking competing ideas around, back-and-forth, with the goal of scoring points toward trying to understand or resolve something I was dealing with in waking life.

A young adult male who had lots of "windows" in his dreams came to realize windows can relate to one's "outlook," speaking psychologically, metaphorically.

A client dreamed about a government social security check which helped put her in touch with feeling insecure about her social-skills in waking life. She also dreamed about wearing clothes too large for her, or trying on over-sized clothes or looking through racks of clothes too large, which seemed to be saying she need not "put on" so much for others to see. In waking life she was an introverted person trying too hard to develop more extraversion.

An aspiring writer dreamed about an old-fashioned typewriter, thus bringing her to the realization of the type-of-writer she was, her writing style.

A young male had an intense dream about the game of lacrosse, which led him to realize his competing views about "the cross" (Christianity).

Besides thinking metaphorically about dreams, below are seven ways to interact with dreams:

(1) When awake, in your mind change the dream in any way you want to make the dream feel more satisfactory or complete. You may want to confront, extend or enlarge aspects of the dream, delete or change whatever. Do what feels best; make yourself peaceful.

(2) With pen and paper draw the dream as it was and also redraw it as you would like it to be. Artistic talent is not important doing this.

(3) Match words with parts of the dream. If you dream of New York City, what words describe New York City to you? What associations do you make?

(4) Write poetry about your dream. You may want to scribble write, which means connect words without spaces, don't dot "i"(s) or cross "t"(s) and leave out letters. It's true you won't be able to read this later, but neither can anyone else, which means scribbling gives maximum privacy, great freedom to express anything and everything while keeping the mind focused on the task at hand.

(5) Write a dialogue between you and your dream or a particular dream image.

(6) Write a monologue—*you become* the dream image and speak as the dream image.

(7) **Pay attention to anything unnatural in a dream, such as oranges growing on a tree in a snow scene, and reflect on what that may be indicating psychologically.**

~~~~

Francine shared: "I have had many recurring dreams in which males, often past boyfriends, choose other females instead of me. I have come to understand this as my masculine attitude *forsaking, devaluing* the feminine within me. This dream-theme has changed over the years and continues to evolve as a lifetime task too lengthy to discuss here. For those beginning to pay attention to their dreams, regarding dreams as metaphorical statements is reliable, as seen in these comments," handing each a sheet with five memorable quotes on dreams and metaphor:

> Learning to see metaphorical forms in literal images is essential for dreamwork.[1]

> We have to learn about the metaphorical nature of the dream communication…you have to get closer to the dream by addressing the images and learning how to look at them metaphorically…there are metaphorical overtones that go beyond any literal meaning the events may have for us.[2]

> The most interesting feature of our dream life, to my way of thinking, is the way that significant information is encoded in highly personal and often ingeniously crafted metaphors. Our dream life becomes manifest to us figuratively through the use of the visual metaphor…Our dreams may be thought of as metaphors in motion.[3]

---

[1] Robert Bosnak, *A Little Course in Dreams: A Basic Handbook of Jungian Dreamwork* (Boston MA: Shambhala, 1988), p. 90.

[2] Montague Ullman, Nan Zimmerman, *Working With Dreams* (Los Angeles CA: Jeremy P. Tarcher, 1979), p. 101.

[3] Montague Ullman, Stanley Krippner, Alan Vaughan, *Dream Telepathy: Experiments in Nocturnal ESP*, 2nd edition (Jefferson NC: McFarland & Company, Inc., 1989), p. 220.
~~~~

The unconscious reveals itself in symbols or metaphors…metaphors are more likely than a purely intellectual statement to touch a human chord and arouse our emotions, and thus give us a feeling for what is meant.[4]

Taking advantage of the same metaphor-making abilities we use in daily thinking, the brain creates visual images and actions in dreams to express our emotions and preoccupations.[5]

---

[4] Bruno Bettelheim, *Freud and Man's Soul* (New York NY: Vintage Books, 1982), pp. 37-38.

[5] Andrea Rock, *The Mind at Night: The New Science of How and Why We Dream*, (New York NY: Basic Books, 2004), p. 66.

CHAPTER THIRTY-FIVE

Brunch Sharing

There came a time in the Kendrick marriage when Dee was isolated from friends. Her loneliness became such that she had the courage to invite Francine, Monique and Estelle to brunch, remembering with aching nostalgia the rich patio evening dinners contrasted with the bleak time she was now going through.

It was at brunch that Francine mentioned her mother was a beautiful woman, whereas Francine looked like her father who had an angular face, hawkish nose, stern-looking eyes, and she'd heard since her earliest days that she looked like her father. This situation had all kinds of implications, and made impressions on Francine, which was something she'd never spoken of with anyone but a therapist during her psychological training. It was her stern eyes which likely made her young classmates say she looked like an owl.

She said, "It has taken a long time for me to realize I wasn't an ugly child but I did look like my father. I didn't have the beautiful face of my older sister who looked like our attractive mother."

Monthly brunches expanded to the homes of Francine, Monique, and Estelle. Harmony was mostly, but not always, the prevalent atmosphere at the brunches. For instance, there was the time when Francine and Monique had an encounter. That day Monique shared too much about a fellow currently looking to buy a home, checking out home prices, considering a move to Sandshell after leaving an academic position in the Midwest because a student assistant stumbled across porn on the professor's office computer. Disturbed by the porn, the assistant went to a higher authority at the institution and Monique's client lost his position and eventually his wife when his claim of researching porn as information for class use wasn't convincing. He was now relocating to Florida to start a new life.

Francine was increasingly uneasy as Monique gave details of this man's story, finally saying, "Monique, you're telling too much about this person." Monique defended herself, "He's not coming here, prices too high he decided." Francine inserted, "What if he changes his mind?" Monique defended again, "I don't give a name." Francine corrected, "You don't need to. You said enough to be able to identify him. Sandshell isn't such a large place, and his story is somewhat unusual."

Monique was irritated, "In years of work I have no such troubles. I know what is discreet." France shared, "In my early days as a psychotherapist I once gave too many obscure details that nearly led to revealing a client's identity. It was a lesson I never forgot. I know that's why I'm having this reaction now." Monique saw Francine's distress, "*Ma chere*, I say thank you for your lesson. I overexcite, I know—which is my weakness."

Monique had so easily accepted correction, or was she playing with Francine? The brunch table was momentarily silent. Monique laughed, "I talk sometimes too much. You are correct. Henri said so." Monique hadn't mentioned Henri in some time, "Why do I bring up Henri? This fellow is a little like Henri to me. I see that. Life is crazy. Me too." And gave a dismissive hand gesture. "I can do better."

The clash brought greater intimacy to the foursome. Having dealt with confidentiality in the group it seemed as if Estelle found it easier to share her increasing trials with Reggie, recently retired. In the middle of the night, he was mixing dreams with waking reality, getting out of bed, going to the closet to dress, readying to go to a meeting, his business, or deal with some situation. Reggie was beginning to suffer with Sundowner's syndrome, or some such.

When he was confused like this Estelle would say, "You're having a dream," and recently he'd begun answering with agitation, "Stop saying that." Re-told, the incidents were amusing, but actually, they weren't. Not at all.

He often talked at length in his sleep, and there were instances of sleepwalking, which meant Estelle's sleep wasn't sound, for she was vigilant. Three times he'd opened a door to the outside in the middle of the night saying he was going to a meeting, to play golf, pick up something from "Ed," whoever that might have been. Estelle had alarms installed on all outside doors.

She was in the midst of setting up home health care for him, and for her to learn how to better deal with him. Reggie had always had kinks in his personality. Raised by his grandparents, who doted on him, abandoned by his musician parents, his grandparents did everything for him. Estelle told Dee she nearly divorced Reggie when their three boys were still young.

Back then, she was working as a school counselor, while Reggie was a bank teller who acted as if that was his only job, while the household and the three sons were her concerns along with her counseling job. He left whiskers and toothpaste in the bathroom sink, clothes beside the laundry basket rather than in it, when he was in charge of the boys she came home to compounded disarray, as if an adult had not been supervising the boys. She was overworked, overwhelmed, at the end of her rope, after many attempts to improve the situation she told Reggie of her plan move to New Orleans with the boys and divorce him.

This did catch his attention. He changed jobs, became a salesman working on commission at the boat business he would one day own. His selling talent was such they were able to hire ample household help. The marriage was salvaged.

Estelle came to realize her own psychological baggage. Growing up, Estelle's alcoholic father routinely wrecked order in their home, psychologically and physically. He would rummage through drawers and closets looking for booze he'd hidden. When on a binge he was unkempt and messy. Estelle's mother and the three daughters scrambled to keep order and run the family restaurant. Estelle's mother had had to work too hard. Reggie's disorderliness got under Estelle's skin. She did not want to repeat her mother's life.

Reggie never conquered his scattered ways, but they could afford enough household help to keep the household livable. There was an oppositional streak in Reggie. Though an exceptional salesman, it seemed to Estelle he never tended to his inner being; he was a stranger to himself.

He was all extravert, with little developed introversion. So it seemed to Estelle, as she wrestled with these issues daily. Despite these tensions, their marriage had worked-out fairly OK. Their three boys knew family stability. Occasionally, Estelle could stop hoping aspects of Reggie's personality would change, for he was dear in many ways, but she did so want him to improve aspects of himself. Perhaps this is just what wives do, she told herself.

The Kendrick marriage, though amazingly compatible, met an unexpected dead end at one point, which brought isolation and loneliness.

CHAPTER THIRTY-SIX

Panic Attack

The trouble began Thanksgiving evening when Charles was a senior in college and Cynthia a senior in high school. The coolish overcast day with no walk on the beach had gone well enough with Monique, Justin, and Christiane recently divorced, with her young son "J" sharing in the feast and leaving the Kendrick home early evening.

Later that evening the Kendrick four were in the family room when the topic of careers came up, as Charles recently started working part-time in the men's clothing department in a big-name department store, and mentioned he might continue fulltime with the company after graduation, at least for awhile.

Cynthia reminded him he was a history major, so why would he work retail? She went on to explain she was taking a class on careers where she learned retail wasn't lucrative, so not only would he not make much money, he also wouldn't be doing anything "important" to improve the world.

She told of learning in the class about an exceptional teacher, a unique woman of English ancestry, who developed a way of teaching indigenous Maori children in New Zealand when the British way of teaching these children to read didn't work. Cynthia emphasized the teacher's "new" approach along with the courage it took to do something others didn't understand or approve of. Cynthia was goading Charles.

Finally, Charles retaliated, "How can it be that Miss Senior High who has not yet been to college, or wrestled with settling on a major field of study, or ever had even a part-time job, is so smart about this stuff?"

Cynthia shot back, "I'm not saying I know everything, but I do know I don't want to be a loser." Charles returned the acidic talk, "You don't have enough experience to be able to define who is and is not a loser, which is a mean, ignorant label to pin on anyone anyway."

Cynthia was her usual impetuous, impulsive, spontaneous self. Charles was more quietly reflective, cautious, circumspect. She was impatient with him, and he tended to disregard her. Clearly, they annoyed each other. Zack tried to tease them away from the friction between them. Dee would, on rare occasion try re-phrasing, using different words, finding common ground, which sometimes helped, other times aggravated the tension.

Dee often felt trapped between being an imposter, an outsider trying to exert her influence with the two scrappers, and a full-member of the family reacting to family dynamics. The sparring between Cynthia and Charles was part of the unforgettable Thanksgiving evening Zack became ill.

The room was tense with sibling strife; Totem left the room, followed shortly by Lucky who was not in good health. The topic of a career hit Dee in a sore spot and though the children didn't know, Zack's career had recently taken a dive. His unhappy job experience was devastating to him.

Zack's "collapse into" work ethic worked well for him until it didn't. After marrying Dee, his managerial job in maintenance at city hall was most satisfying for more than a dozen years. Recently however, Zack was passed-over for a newly created position at city hall, which was filled by a younger person with more city-planning schooling but far less work experience, and Zack was devastated. His "collapse into" work ethic failed him; he was a failure. Co-workers and the general opinion at city hall believed Zack would get the position.

Not getting the job was gut-wrenching with the added dilemma of whether he could bear to continue his job at city hall having suffered such a rebuff. This was the question plaguing him that Thanksgiving evening of the nasty exchange between Charles and Cynthia about careers and being a loser.

That evening, Zack and Dee were in the dual recliner where they usually sat, when he slumped over moaning, gasping, in terrible distress. After a 911 call, an ambulance arrived, and shortly he was on the way to an emergency room, followed by Charles driving Dee and Cynthia, as his car was quickest to access, parked outside the garage.

Cynthia spoke the obvious in the car, "Surely he won't die, he's not old, he's healthy, doctors know how to treat heart attacks." Zack was kept for observation overnight in the hospital. The other three spent a fitful night trying to sleep in a household that was frightened, worried, after Dee explained to Charles and Cynthia the tale of Zack's stress from not getting the new job.

Next morning the diagnosis was "no heart attack," but a panic (anxiety) attack. Medications were prescribed, psychiatric referrals given. Dependable Zack had been stressed to the maximum not getting the job he and others expected was in his pocket.

The four Kendricks in the car on the way home from the hospital reviewed in detail every word the doctor said. Dee told Zack she'd explained his job situation to Cynthia and Charles. The four were aware of their love as a family while also aware of the stress Zack was under. Dee quietly knew it was best he not continue at City Hall.

In the following week with Charles back at college and Cynthia involved with school and friends, Dee and Zack together wrote his letter of resignation after privately discussing their financial situation as stable. He enjoyed being at City Hall and was too young to retire. However and foremost, the panic attack had cut deep into every cell of his body; into his memory bank.

Dee beat up on herself for not having a money-making job. It would be hard to explain quitting his job to the guys he played golf with. Zack stopped golf. Only with Reggie did he share the panic attack, who said immediately, "It must be time for you to do something else." For all of

Reggie's memory confusion, he could at times still be profound and encouraging to others.

What Zack did was become a recluse, fearing another episode yet refusing to seek counseling or psychiatric help. "Why go talk to someone about what I already know caused the attack," he reasoned. He was going down a path Dee knew was not healthy, yet he tried to reassure her he knew what he was doing. His reclusive response grew. Fear of another attack controlled him.

Weeks went by. Zack stayed home, didn't play golf. Dee's mother, brother Max and family were not coming to Florida for Christmas this year. Zack was not enthused to have Monique and family for Christmas. He was becoming a hermit.

Dee tried to keep Zack's fears away from Charles on campus and Cynthia involved with senior year activities and college plans. Christmas day did include Monique and family, but it was subdued, with no dancing led by Christiane, no walk on the beach, no spontaneous carols that ignited a group sing fest. Dee attended Christmas Mass by herself. It was a lonely holiday. Lucky the dog, recently died, which added to the grim atmosphere.

Dee missed her parents. Her mother planned to come to Sandshell for the month of February. Her father's death left a hole in her life and she found herself remembering the trip her parents, Zack, the children and she took to Scotland and the Orkney Islands.

At the time of the trip with Dee's parents, Cynthia was in middle school and Charles in high school. Zack had long wanted to play the Old Course at St. Andrews in Scotland and then travel to the Orkney Islands north of Scotland where he would participate in midnight golf on June 21, the longest day of the year, the summer solstice.

Kendricks planned their trip, and Dee's parents became interested in meeting them in New York and going with them, which happened. The six traveled together in what became an exceptional voyage with lasting consequences. Dee experienced her parents in a new light. Zack and Dee's father Harold went off and did golf, Cynthia and Dee's mother Paula became pals, while Dee and Charles went to archeological sites together.

Flying home over the Atlantic, Dee's parents were sitting ahead where she could see the back of her father's head and she remembered a Christmas season her parents spent in Florida where her father told how he was a poor student in elementary school, who had to be tutored on Saturday morning and how he hated that he had to go to school an additional day. He told how he was the only child in his large family that didn't go to college, which Dee hadn't realized. She saw hurdles that he had to try and jump over and she had increasing compassion for him.

On this trip Dee saw how adaptable her mother was with Cynthia, which Cynthia thoroughly enjoyed. That sublimating of self was her mother's strength and also a weakness. On one hand, Dee could imagine the personality dynamics of her young parents which were detrimental to her, and on the other hand she could understand some of the circumstances which shaped their personalities. It had taken years for Dee to arrive at this understanding, propelling her into greater forgiveness.

Dee realized anew the importance of female friendship, female conversation, being able to pour out one's troubles with someone who understands. The relationship between Estelle and Dee became cemented at this time and would prove vital in the future as Reggie deteriorated.

Reggie had grown-up in Sandshell, became a businessman and knew what was going on in town. After Zack's panic episode Reggie's mention of plans for an affordable housing project made a huge difference in Zack's re-entry into life. Reggie was a master at selling anything; boats or the idea of an affordable housing project to a man who needed such a project. Even in Reggie's diminishing state, he could still be persuasive—sometimes.

CHAPTER THIRTY-SEVEN

Myth is Real

Reggie knew Zack grew up in rural Georgia where as a boy with his father driving the truck down country roads, his father would make comments about homes in good repair and those needing repair. Zack had a keen awareness of the vast difference between how houses were maintained. His dad would say, "That's no way to live," or "Somebody in that house has the gumption to see to it they can live decent."

As an adult, Zack appreciated that the quality of life is greatly affected by whether the roof leaks or the plumbing doesn't work. His years of experience managing maintenance in the private sector and then at City Hall, reinforced his understanding that peoples' lives are greatly enhanced, their talents substantially aided, their futures brighter if they live in well-maintained places.

Reggie knew Zack's background, and intuitively knew mention of working on an affordable housing project would resonate with Zack and help bring back the confidence that he could contribute directly to the welfare of those struggling to live better.

In Estelle's present annoyance with Reggie's encroaching dementia, she needed to realize he did still have this intuitive knack for helping others though he couldn't improve himself; couldn't or wouldn't change his own habits, deal with his shortcomings. These were old aggravations she was dealing with, with herself.

Estelle never wanted Reggie to be a househusband, but surely he could pick-up after himself, close a cupboard door. He used to be a more sunshine personality but now he was mostly grumpy. Estelle increasingly felt trapped with Reggie's present deteriorating condition, though she realized it was he who was held captive by it.

Meanwhile, Zack became an integral part of a non-profit effort to organize an affordable housing project, which would need co-ordination with City Hall that Zack could provide, having resigned there on good terms.

The affordable housing project moved slowly, which was the pace Zack needed, and it was also a time he talked with Dee about his father's grumpy, fearful, angry attitude related to work, a job, and realized his own "collapse into" notion may include fears about work; afraid of not getting things done, not taken care of, not keeping up with ongoing necessities—basic survival skills reaching into the roots of human existence, one of humanity's great struggles. In Dee he had a partner who enjoyed pondering the imponderable, and the ever so practical. He learned about himself. Prior to the panic attack, he hadn't had a job, the job had him.

In conversation with Dee, Zack remembered an event involving his father, "I was home from college for Christmas vacation when my father heard someone on television use the phrase "the myth of Christianity," and since my dad understood the meaning of myth to be falsehood/untruth, he was incensed, a fury that lasted for several meals, a lovely way to spend my college vacation, and when I tried to feebly explain the definition of myth as I'd learned in a college class which I myself scarcely understood, he only became more agitated, and I became quiet so my mother wouldn't have to listen to his harangue, and there we were again at the table: one person fuming, two forced to endure."

Dee understood his father's upset, "Well yes, the word myth is used incorrectly today, as meaning something that is untrue, false. Actually, myth is a big story, an overarching explanation of life and living; a story that explains something about why we are born only to die after striving, struggling, suffering, sacrificing between birth and death with countless choices we must make, or choices that are somehow made for us which we must deal with. Myth is the human effort to make sense of the whole panorama of living and dying.

"The word myth has come to mean falsehood in recent centuries as science (itself a myth—a way to explain everything) became so dominant that any non-scientific understanding was thought to be of little value, thus untrue, not trustworthy, false. And so, when your father heard "the myth of Christianity," his ears heard, "the falseness of Christianity," whereas the speaker may have been saying "the grand story, the all-embracing understanding Christianity gives to being alive though one suffers, is sacrificed, crucified again and again by simply being alive, and how this story is the story of the Christ, the Messiah, the Anointed One who died only to live again and forever."

Dee continued, "I had a college professor who said there are two major myths and all other myths are versions or echoes of these two: the myth of the eternal return and the myth of the hero's journey. I came to realize in Christianity the Jesus story is certainly the myth of the hero, as he was an individual who made a new path, a new consciousness possible for those who follow, thus each can contribute to evolving creative consciousness on the earth, which was Jesus' Kingdom of God, where justice, mercy, fairness, opportunity, understanding, respect prevail. People noticed a heroic quality in humanity before Jesus was on earth, thus the myth of the hero (or heroine's) journey is pre-Christian.

"And, it seems to me Christianity also includes the myth of the eternal return, for Jesus lived beyond death (Easter), just as the seasons of the year change but come back again, the earth lives in a cycle, a daily 24 hour rhythm, a 28 day moon cycle. There is much repetition in life; we just keep on keeping on; there is the same ol' same ol'. The church calendar (liturgical year) recognizes there is ordinary time, yet there also are special times like Lent, the Easter Season, Advent and Christmas, feast days, holy days, year after year. People saw this rhythmic aspect of life even before Jesus was on earth. The myth of the eternal return is pre-Christian but solidified in Christ's death and resurrection which says that life continues beyond change, endures beyond death, keeps evolving. We live and die but leave a mark of our having been here; our body is returned (recycled) to earth as ashes or decaying corpse, yet our essence lives on."

By the end of Dee's lengthy explanation of the Christian myth, Zack was staring at her and said, "You're better than a Great Course. You are my in-house professor. You know a lot more than you usually reveal," whereupon he hugged her. Zack was beginning to hug again after his panic attack. He was healing.

Together, Dee and Zack dealt with the fact that he would make less money than before, but working on providing affordable housing in the community was his heart's desire he came to realize. Over the years, through realtor Monique, Zack and Dee had purchased two rental homes which brought cash flow and they had other investments. Charles was nearly finished with college and Cynthia's college money was secure. Satisfied they would make it financially, they asked themselves how much more money did they need—really.

It became clearer to them that the bitter defeat he experienced at City Hall led to something better for him, while his plunge into being a recluse made Dee realize she needed friends more than she'd known, and gave her the courage to invite Monique, Francine and Estelle every month or so for Saturday brunch. They came to call themselves the Brunch Bunch.

CHAPTER THIRTY-EIGHT

Enchantment

At about the same time, Charles was trying to figure out why he was attracted to the movie, *Of Gods and Men,* based on the true story of eight French Trappist monks living in a poor community in Algeria, having to decide during the Algerian Civil War under threat by fundamentalist terrorists, whether to stay in Algeria and possibly be killed or return to the safety of France. The movie stuck with Charles, who viewed it again and again.

What drew him to this film? What was its attraction? Some kind of spiritual impulse? Charles wasn't Catholic, not interested in becoming a monk or living a celibate life, or risking himself to help others by living in a dangerous area. Was it simply the idea of fierce commitment to an ideal? Did he connect to Monique and her family roots in Algeria? His crush on Christiane when he was younger?

From those patio dinner discussions with Francine he'd come to appreciate word-play when dealing with emotions. He approached his reactions, why the film "spoke" to him and played with words, "I'm attracted to it, it holds my interest, I'm intrigued, fascinated, captivated, enthralled. I'm enchanted by it." The word *enchanted* was the key that opened the door of his understanding.

The monks chanting in the film was his attraction to the movie. He began listening to recorded Christian chanting by monks and nuns, which he found soothing while also invigorating, overall feeling more put-together. This became his habit, sometimes chanting with the recordings.

He also had the habit of telephoning Zack often to check on him, as the panic attack left its jarring impression. Charles always asked about Dee when telephoning with his dad, but somehow felt she knew how to take care of herself for he saw her strength at the time of his dad's attack; she was steady, level-headed, realistic.

Charles remembered a conversation with Dee shortly after the panic scare in which she talked about beauty and her intrigue with beauty, the colorful backyard with its feast of flora and fauna which helped her realize the beautiful emotions of peace and joy.

After graduation, Charles moved to Tampa with a job in men's retail with the same nation-wide department store where he'd been working. He became reasonably satisfied there socially with a group of guys attending sporting events, going to the beach, dating. His roommate was seldom in their apartment, having a job in which he traveled. It was ideal; an absentee roommate who paid half the rent and utilities. Charles chanted with recordings whenever he wanted.

The Brunch Bunch was vital to Dee, and to Estelle at this time of increasing difficulty in her life when she confided again to the group that she'd looked forward to travel when she and Reggie were both retired. Now that they were retired, travel was an impossibility, and Estelle was disappointed. Such irony: Zack was coming to life with the help of Reggie who was regressing and turned-over the boat business to their son, Lee, who had been working there since college and saw his father's decline. At a glance, others might not notice, but eventually Reggie's increasing mental fog was apparent to their other two sons, Webb, a supervisor in off-shore drilling and Ross, a CPA. Though Estelle had the full support of the sons and their families, she bore the bulk of dealing with Reggie.

The Brunch Bunch was valued by Monique who always had more than her share of stress. Daughter Christiane became pregnant not long after marriage, and the newborn baby boy Jameson was found to be severely hearing impaired. The baby's father, James, left Christiane within months, saying parenting wasn't for him. He paid child support but had no contact with Jameson or Christiane. Monique grieved over this situation while Christiane and Jameson moved in with her, and she shared with Christiane the medical decision of a cochlear implant for the young boy.

And then Justin, Monique's son, tried his hand with commercial real estate during a time when the economy dipped. He hadn't the patience to persevere despite Monique's financial help and reassurance, and he left real estate, which was a disappointment to Monique. She worried Justin might have some of Henri's instabilities, and asked Francine about generational psychological influence.

Francine related a generational story of one of her clients in Canada, saying not to make too much of it regarding Justin, however, Francine had been fascinated by what she learned through the client.

"The person who came to therapy was an obese female in her thirties, suffering with chronic depression, desperate to get her food-intake under control, she hoped hypnosis might help, and I was certified in hypnotherapy. We proceeded, and what came to pass was information the client was able to research and confirm.

"In her mother's family tree, a Scotsman (a white slave) arrived in Canada in the mid-1600s after his family lost their land in Scotland being on the wrong side of political Protestant-Catholic conflicts at the time. He nearly starved to death first in Scotland, then Ireland, eventually arriving in Canada. Surprisingly, the horrors of near-starvation remained in his descendant, the young woman, generations later. She could not control her food intake."

Francine shared, "Her body shook uncontrollably as this truth was uncovered, as if cells themselves were crying out in fear, rage, sorrow. Over time, her insatiable hunger diminished as she researched what she knew from family tales and public records of his arrival in Canada. Yes, this white-slave ancestor was part of who she was.

"I wouldn't say Justin would benefit from hypnotherapy or needs to do family research. However, I believe all parents do well to pray for their own ancestors as well as the other side of their children's ancestry so generational woundedness can be healed, talents and giftedness developed."

With the Brunch Bunch, Francine shared she was considering cutting back on the number of hours she worked, saying she felt it was time she step-back from the intensities clients bring, though she didn't want to languish in retirement. Nor did she want to become dependent on her daughter and family to fill her need for non-work human contact. Francine enjoyed being part of the Brunch Bunch as extended family.

Clearly, the Brunch Bunch needed each other, and Dee needed a project to work on.

CHAPTER THIRTY-NINE

Dee and Julia in Austin

Dee became interested in the parables of Jesus and began the long-term project of explicating his parables in memory of Aunt Tess who said Jesus' parables often did not make much sense to her. Dee used the revised fourfold medieval format uncovered and revised by Gabby and Matti, which she made her own.

Dee found another project in the Kendrick back yard—the St. Francis statue, part of their yard art. Originally, it was young Cynthia's insistence the family buy the statue of St. Francis with a bird in his hands when she saw the concrete piece at a plant nursery shortly after the family moved into the house.

Cynthia had questions about the statue. What else was there about Francis other than he loved nature, which is why people put his statue in their yards. Dee didn't know a lot about the Italian saint but told Cynthia she'd sometimes taken her dog Mister to church to be blessed on October 4, Francis's feast day, for St. Francis loved animals. Dee began researching St. Francis of Assisi, a medieval personality. Meanwhile, there was another lovely happening.

Julia Montel from Clarksdale KS, re-entered Dee's life, not that they'd ever lost contact, but they hadn't talked for a while. Julia telephoned asking Dee to meet in Austin TX for a visit with Beth, who at age 92, recently moved into an independent living facility, still clear in mind, but no longer wanting to deal with her large home in which Julia met her biological father, Cal. Dee met Beth and Julia at Ann Dramm's funeral.

And thus it came to pass that Dee and Julia hugged at the airport in Austin TX, thrilled to see each other. Each looked at the other thinking she had changed little and realizing the magnitude of pure enjoyment of being together again. Each had only hints of grey in her hair, and Julia's blondish hair mostly hid her grey. Julia complimented Dee's Florida tan.

The memory of Matti, Gabby, Ann and Beth was alive this day in Austin, and Dee tenderly remembered the friendship between aunt Teresa and Ann Dramm who came to see Tess in Sandshell. Ann came to Tess's funeral and Dee's wedding in Connecticut. Dee would never forget Ann guiding her metaphorically through discerning the purple aura cat image.

In Austin, the cab arrived at Beth's well-landscaped, upscale senior residence facility where Dee and Julia easily found Beth in her fourth-floor apartment. Beth still had a twinkle in her eye, a ready smile on her lips, an older version of herself no longer a chemical blonde, but with snow white hair, more wrinkles but quite intact, opening her door to them, her arms immediately ready for hugs. Her apartment overlooked a lovely courtyard which made one forget how hot it was this summer day in Austin.

They talked as they sipped homemade lemonade. Spry Beth had made the drink and now served her friends, not using her cane in the apartment. How easy and enjoyable the conversation when roots of friendship stretch way back.

The conversation in Beth's apartment was about Lenore whose husband Logan died, and Lenore was now in an independent senior facility in southeastern Kansas. Lenore and Logan had had nine exceptionally fine years together.

Logan left his mark in Clarksdale in the miniature wood carvings his surgeon's hands carved in his glass hut; carvings still in use in Julia's activity "Tiny Things" at Golden Acres. Julia remained closely connected to Lenore who assembled the purple leather binder with documents from Matti's computer as a gift to Julia, who at the time was still bitter with her birth mother.

Julia explained to Beth and Dee, "Lenore's purple leather binder has borne fruit with Benjamin, our eldest, just now finishing his residency in psychiatry who may one day come back to our local behavioral treatment facility. He is acquainted with "allusion confusion" and "metaphoric discernment" as paradigms for understanding and treating some disorders."

Julia shared further, "Daughter Kendal is a beginning lawyer in St. Louis, Patrick is about to graduate from college prepared to be a high school basketball coach, health education teacher. No one is coming back to Clarksdale to work with Marc in Montel Furniture."

Just then, Beth's daughter Susan arrived with plans for the group. Tomorrow mid-morning, they were scheduled to visit Beth's former home with the Texas-shaped swimming pool. Susan arranged this, with her mother wanting to see the place "one more time." Dee was secretly elated for she wanted to see the pool. Julia felt calm about this site where she met biological dad Cal, now re-married, continuing to live in Santa Fe. Julia and Cal kept in contact.

Tomorrow's plan was that after the house tour the four of them would go to the Tex-Mex restaurant the original foursome used to frequent.

Next morning, Susan took her mother and guests to the longtime family home with its unique swimming pool, amiably greeted by the lovely youngish wife/mother who now lived there. Beth and Susan were obviously enthralled with the young woman and "her" home. Julia and Dee were silent partners in this exciting escapade for Beth and Susan. The swimming pool the shape of Texas was in fine form, and Julia remembered exactly where she and Cal talked; her children then so young.

Now grown, none of the Montel children had followed Marc into the furniture store business. Who would one day take over Grandpa Montel's store? Would the store be sold after three generations? How hard would it be to sell the place when furniture franchises and online buying were now huge?

Montel furniture had its niche in the confidence and affection of the people of Clarksdale and surrounding rural area. Would another owner know how to keep the relationship with local residents alive? This was Marc's concern. Had the intensive retail hours he'd worked been off-putting for his children so that they chose different careers? His children did not fully appreciate the cash cow the store had been for them. However, they might one day weary of the struggle of making a living and return to Clarksdale and the store. Yet, he wanted them to go forth with their plans in other careers, other places.

Julia was acutely aware of Marc's anxieties about the store—the future. Even she had never been his partner in running the store. *The store is the goose that laid the golden egg, and also an albatross around the neck,* Julia thought this moment in Beth's former home, now someone else's home. The passage of time was vividly apparent at the moment.

Later, lunch in the Tex-Mex restaurant felt as if time stood still in this place that looked, smelled, seemed old, seasoned, perhaps generational, including the menu and Mexican music pouring from ceiling speakers. Julia read the restaurant's history on the menu: yes, it was a three-generation enterprise, as was the Montel furniture store. Julia returned to the present conversation, having not the faintest notion that something enormous would come from this trip with Dee Kendrick.

CHAPTER FORTY

Pink Palace

Months later, an evening in Tampa, after a busy retail day for Charles Kendrick, who was home alone with nothing special going on in his social life when a telephone call entered his world.

The call was from Kendal Montel lawyer in St. Louis, daughter of Julia Montel, who had been speaking with her mother about her recent trip to Austin with Dee Kendrick, whereupon Kendal learned Charles lived in Tampa, and Kendal would soon be traveling to Tampa on business. Julia got Charles's telephone number from Dee for Kendal.

Answering his telephone, for a split-second Charles did not register with the name Kendal Montel. She helped him, "We've met. We know each other. Our mothers know each other, Julia and Dee—they were not long ago together in Austin, TX. Our families know each other. We met each other as kids."

Charles laughed in recognition. "Kendal, yes, of course. Sorry the brain wasn't working there for a second. You have two brothers."

"Correct. Benjamin and Patrick," and told what they were now doing. Kendal explained she'd be in Tampa next week for only one night and would like to take him out to eat if that was possible. Charles checked his work schedule and he was free. He'd pick her up at the hotel. She made it simple, "I'll be out in front of the hotel." He described his car.

Her mother Julia had encouraged Kendal contacting Charles, "Why be alone in a new city when you know someone and can turn a work assignment into a social opportunity. Julia at times missed living in a large city. Growing up in Kansas City she wanted her children to return to Clarksdale someday but she also wanted them to enjoy the best of city life.

Julia felt guilty about not working at the furniture store with Marc though volunteer work with Golden Acres and other town activities was her heart's desire. Julia knew she needed to someday talk with Marc about her guilt over not working at Montel Furniture.

The day of Kendal in Tampa arrived. It was early evening when Charles drove to the hotel, having given Kendal a description of his older car. His impression of the Montels was they had money and probably never drove cars the age of his, but he decided not to be concerned about this.

Their families had been together more than once, he remembered. He and Kendal were probably not far apart in age. As a kid, she was blonde and she and Cynthia spent their time together doing their own thing. Younger brother Patrick had often been with the girls, while he mostly did stuff with older brother Benjamin. All that was long ago.

In the front of the hotel were people, cabs, luggage. Kendal spotted him, waved, walked to the car, where Charles had popped open the door for her and she immediately said, "You look like yourself." He replied, "And you look like your grown-up you."

"Guess neither of us has had to change our identity," Kendal concluded lightheartedly.

"Not yet," Charles replied, and barely away from the hotel, asked, "What would you think about going to St. Petersburg?" Kendal quipped, "Russia?" "Why not," Charles countered.

Kendal guessed, "The Pink Hotel? My family has been there and I've always wanted to go back." Charles replied, "Yes, the Pink Palace." Kendal dramatized, "My fantasyland." To deflate her thrill, he condescendingly replied, "Most tourists love the place." She caught his intent, "Not only tourists but also hard-working legal experts like myself." It was easy banter born of family knowing family.

Driving over the bridge from Tampa to St. Petersburg, the two in super-casual attire with sunglasses, on the way to St. Pete Beach, found the hot and humid early evening enjoyable. The motherly instinct of Julia had been correct; going to the Pink Palace with its white sands felt much better than eating by oneself at the hotel. This evening Kendal could forget about the stress connected with the work she'd be doing tomorrow.

There was the expanse of water, open sky, easy talk about family, jobs, particulars relating to her reason for being in Florida. The forty-five-minute drive was altogether comfortable and enjoyable, and after a brief walk on the beach, they were seated outside amidst the luxurious tropical blossoms with a crowd dressed in the relaxed chic casual atmosphere of the pink hotel where they enjoyed an appetizer with their beverage of choice: she had rum with a mix, and he had an imported beer, which was the total of their alcoholic intake for he was driving and she had to be alert for tomorrow's work.

Charles noticed he over-emphasized his interest in managerial training that evening to impress her. Kendal was aware she highlighted living in St. Louis, no longer a small-town Clarksdale girl, to impress him. They talked about their parents and what they were doing. She mentioned Montel furniture and how her dad was now the only Montel who worked in the store. Kendal talked in an offhand serious way about how she probably should have gotten a degree in business and gone back to Clarksdale and worked with her father, and she might one day go work there, but not yet, and then she was quiet.

Charles said he loved Sandshell but for some reason had never felt he wanted to live there permanently. "Maybe life was simpler when people didn't have so many choices," he added with philosophical gravity. "Sometimes I wish I lived in medieval Europe where I imagine people lived with fewer choices, yet I know life was harsh, brutal, short-lived. No, I really wouldn't have liked that. I'm satisfied with now."

Kendal said, "Sometimes when I look at the pastures and farmland around Clarksdale I imagine life in a simpler time, with Native Americans in small groups, and I went through a phase of reading about the Plains Indians. Their life wasn't easy, though in ways it appealed to me, their relationship with the earth, nature, the sun. Now, we just seem busy; always busy. I recently realized the word business is also busyness." She spelled out the words, slightly shook her head as she looked down at her plate. Charles didn't understand the gesture.

But he appreciated what she'd said, her body language of concern, and he commented, "We are clock-bound creatures, no doubt about that," he reflected, reminded of a recent video in which it was stated the modern era began when clock towers were built in medieval cities and then people began to be more organized. They needn't look at the sun for their sense of time, but only at a mechanical clock. In a way, they were building their lives around a machine." Kendal seemed interested.

He continued, "Dee, who knows a lot of literature, gives me quotes from time to time. Here's one by Charles Dickens, reaching into his wallet and handing a piece of paper to Kendal, which Dee had given him.

Charles Dickens, *Little Dorrit* (written 1855-1857)

Rattle me out of bed early, set me going, give me as short a time as you like to bolt my meals in, and keep me at it. Keep me always at it, and I'll keep you always at it, you keep somebody else always at it. There you are with the Whole Duty of Man in a commercial country.

Kendal did a sort of exhale laugh, "Dickens got this right." She read the quote herself, "I need to remind myself of this regularly." And then added, "A consequence of the duty of man in a commercial country is chronic stress." Charles followed her line of thinking with something he'd recently read about humans in our stressful concern of using time for maximum production and profit became unaware of the earth on which our existence depends and began exploiting and destroying the planet.

Kendal responded thoughtfully, "Humans are ruining themselves and the planet. I've thought of specializing in environmental law. I still have much to learn," and her voice indicated resignation about this formidable task.

For some reason, Charles remembered a quote of Martin Luther King, Jr., which gave him comfort when he was berating himself for not making a bigger mark in life, for not having a more spectacular career, and in this pause in the conversation, Charles said, "We live in such a competitive society I like to recall something Martin Luther King, Jr. said, 'If a person sweeps streets for a living, he should sweep streets as Michelangelo painted, Beethoven composed music, Shakespeare wrote poetry. He should sweep streets so well it can be said here lived a great street sweeper who did his job well.'"

Kendal understood, "Those sound like words of relief on days of inner turmoil. My dad, not usually a philosophical person, said a lot of stress has to do with time—how we relate with time. He said a downside of capitalism is the idea that "time is money," and explained, "While that is true in a certain sense, it's not an ultimate truth about time, for there is also timelessness. Time is like a conveyor belt that never stops, and in that sense, time feels burdensome, hurried, even frantic. He said some people fish, others play golf, as he does when he has time, or just looking at the sky can throw off the shackles of conveyor-belt-time and invite a sense of timelessness. My dad spends so much time at the furniture store I'm sure he feels time-stressed a lot of the time." She laughed, unable to avoid using the word "time."

Charles joined her word-play, "It may be *time* for us to leave this magical place so you can get back to the hotel and ready yourself for tomorrow." And so they left the pink palace after an evening of easy, rich, enjoyable conversation. However, an unforeseen snag took some of the magic of the evening away.

CHAPTER FORTY-ONE

Trapped on a Bridge

On the bridge over the bay back to Tampa, traffic slowed and then stopped. Charles immediately regretted having planned the evening at St. Pete Beach and apologized, "I should have thought of this possibility knowing you didn't want to be out late. Depending on what has happened, traffic can be stopped for quite some time. Trapped on a bridge there's nothing to do but wait. Sorry. So sorry. Do you want to put the seat back and try to nap?"

Kendal was amused, "If we are still sitting here at midnight I might try to sleep, but no, I'm fine."

"Midnight!? No, that's unlikely; that won't happen," Charles reassured. Windows open with a slight warm breeze, not too humid, the light of a half-moon on the water, cars behind them, onlooker slowdown on the westbound lanes, but at least those cars were moving, Charles reiterated, "I didn't think to think about this possibility."

"Well, neither did I," said Kendal, matter-of-fact. "But you don't live here," Charles clarified unnecessarily. She explained, "Living in St. Louis with the Mississippi and Missouri Rivers I frequently hear about bridge stoppages. Besides, returning to the Pink Palace is worth losing sleep even on a work night."

Charles felt relieved, "My job has become routine and I now don't feel like I'm on a slippery steep-slope like I did when I first started and was stressed-out all the time."

She remembered, "Your Charles Dickens quote about getting rattled out of bed early, eating lunch quickly, all in service to job, career, money, getting-ahead. That's what I'm trying to get a perspective on now. And then I think of my dad, and he's done that for years at the furniture store—he puts in long hours every week. The only thing is, he hasn't had to deal with traffic. A lot of time and energy is spent dealing with traffic."

"Even at this very moment," Charles observed pointedly, "Even at this very moment," Kendal smiled and added playfully, "As mommy Julia often says, 'This isn't a catastrophe, merely an inconvenience.'" He relaxed and said, "That's true."

He pushed his bucket seat back as far as it would go, and tilted it back, as if settling in to sleep. She did the same, laughing when she was left sitting several inches ahead of him. Her two brothers caused her to know how guys are crafty in their humor sometimes, as Charles inquired, "So other than bridge stoppages in St. Louis, how is life in St. Louis?"

"I expected it to be better, but that has nothing to do with the city. My closest friend ever, Lily, I met my freshman year at the university, is from St. Louis. Through all our college days we depended on each other, through every difficulty we helped each other. I accepted my job in St. Louis because she was to be living there, planning to marry someone she knew only slightly in high school who'd gone to college elsewhere, they re-met during Christmas vacation through mutual friends our senior year in college.

"Eric is his name and he is a control freak. I was in the bridal party. The little I'd been around him I liked him OK though he was taking my dearest friend away, but I figured we would all be friends in St. Louis. Wrong. Lily is his prisoner as I see it. Maybe I'm just jealous, but Lily and I don't do much together, and when we are together it's as if she seems tense, he's constantly texting her, I'm feeling annoyed. Not a happy situation.

"My mom says a new marriage can be stressful and since I've never been married, I can't know that. I told my mom that she and my dad are so comfortable together and she told me, 'Just believe me when I say a new marriage can have its own complications.' So, my life in St. Louis has a hole in it because of Ick Eric. That's what I call him but not around Lily of course. So, do you have any troubles in your life due to chronically unpleasant people?"

"No, not because of other people. My predicaments are mostly inside me. And we don't have enough time for me to give you those details. Though this might be such an opportunity, for people often tell their stories to others while waiting for the next thing to happen, on airplanes passing time until the destination arrives, on bridges waiting until traffic starts moving."

With this clever ending, Kendal laughed. "Passing time, waiting, we're back to the topic of time, and I live a time-pressured existence. How can it be that growing up in a small town I was time-pressured even then? I think it had to do with the hours my dad put in at the store. This is why I rushed through college, going to summer school, always wanting him to work less paying for college. I wanted to get out of school and start paying for myself."

Finally, their wait on the bridge was over. Engines started and the race to get Kendal to the hotel for a full night of sleep was accomplished.

CHAPTER FORTY-TWO

Romance

Time passed in Tampa. Charles's birthday was on the horizon. What was he to do with his life? The question had become his constant companion. He recalled Francine that summer of dinners on the Kendrick patio talking about being-in-love as "displaced spirituality," a misplaced search for answers to the mystery of one's own existence, one's personality, which can be satisfied only in the search for what is sacred, ultimate, infinite.

Francine explained the notion of romance becoming widespread in Western culture during the 12th century by which time the Christian experience of God had been diluted and the human pursuit for divine fulfillment was siphoned off into romantic novels about chivalrous knights pining for unattainable ladies, and is at the core of our fascination with romantic stories, movies, poetry, music which reinforces the belief that with romance we will live happily ever after, though daily life (and our divorce rate) says otherwise.

Charles didn't have a burning career passion. He liked retail OK. He knew he'd never make much money and didn't want to be caught in a money-trap. He was in a mild malaise about his future when Kendal telephoned and was again coming to town as part of the same legal case which initially brought her to Tampa. Kendal and Charles planned another evening together that would not include any destination which involved a river bridge, a viaduct, an overpass, a railroad bridge, or trestle. Their humor meshed.

Charles and Kendal told their mothers about the two times Kendal came to Tampa. They did not immediately tell anybody about the many telephone calls between them after the second Tampa date. Charles was smitten with Kendal's keen mind, quick humor, olive Italian skin, brown eyes, blondish hair, and pert little nose. Kendal found Charles attractive, appealing, easy to be with, wonderfully comfortable to talk to.

It took months of airline flights between Tampa and St. Louis—Charles and Kendal taking turns doing the traveling to be with each other, before the two talked about marriage. But where would they live? They did not want to rush into anything. They simply enjoyed being together.

Since Charles and Kendal had no need to meet the other's family, they didn't overtell their parents about their relationship. Both had had the experience of romances evaporating, and this time with the families knowing each other—well, that carried its own perils.

Charles and Kendal became engaged at the Pink Palace with just the two of them. They didn't want an engagement party. After that, the Montels in Clarksdale and Kendricks in Sandshell were included in plans as they unfolded between the soon-to-be-married couple.

The wedding took place in the Catholic Church in Clarksdale in June. Charles became a Catholic, which was an easy decision since he already chanted with Catholic monks and nuns on recordings and was comfortable with the Catholicism he'd gathered from Dee. The newlyweds would live in St. Louis, as her position held much potential and Charles was able to transfer to a store there. Things worked out well in St. Louis until they didn't.

CHAPTER FORTY-THREE

Octagonal House in Clarksdale

Making the trip to the Kansas wedding were Monique, Francine, Estelle without Reggie, as travel was something he could no longer do. Dee's family from Connecticut came. Cynthia was a bridesmaid.

The sacrament of matrimony took place, followed by a lovely reception with dancing in the country club located on the golf course. The June Kansas sky was clear, crisp, wheat harvest a short time away. Kendal's blondish medium-length hair caressed her naturally lovely face, brown eyes glowing, she was attired in a traditional white gown and veil. Kendal took Charles' family name, as she was amused with the likeness of her two names now: Kendal Kendrick.

Her father Marc with bits of gray in his black hair, intense dark eyes, looked the role of a successful man of the town, and Julia erect posture, graying blondish hair, blue eyes, dressed regally for the day, accompanied Kendal up the aisle to the altar where Charles with Zack and Dee on either side of him waited as the two families were united in this wedding ceremony, this marriage.

Charles, a dashing spectacle in a black suit, not a tuxedo, was in a joking, jovial mood that day, as was his habit in times of high tension. Zack and Dee, used to casual Florida clothing, this day labored to wear traditional appropriate wedding attire. The Montel and Kendrick families had a fine day celebrating the good fortune that their two families were now one. Cupid had worked in a lovely way.

Life for the newlyweds in St. Louis was satisfactory until, as time passed, they realized they no longer wanted to live in an apartment and began looking at houses for sale. They wanted a house with a yard, as were the homes of their youth and where their parents still lived. Houses they were interested in were pricey, they found.

Traffic to and from work wasted time they would rather spend in other ways. Kendal's friend Lily, though her maid-of-honor, remained under the thumb of husband Eric, and this was disheartening as Kendal thought surely the two couples would spend time together, but that never happened. Eric controlled Lily.

The newlyweds wrestled with options. It was Charles who surprisingly said, "We could move to Clarksdale, I could work at the furniture store, you could practice law. Now is that a crazy idea?" Shocked to the core, Kendal confessed, "I've thought of that but assumed it was too strange to say aloud. Moving to Clarksdale would relieve my guilt for not working at the store." They stared at each other in disbelief at what each had uttered. Once spoken, the idea did not go away.

Neither of them had grown-up in large cities and didn't feel the city was where they ideally would like to raise children. There was more than one law firm in Clarksdale and whether Kendal could find employment with one would need to be pursued. The prominence of the Montel family would help her with that. Was selling furniture the same as Charles selling men's wear? What if Kendal's dad Marc didn't embrace the idea? How awkward would that be, and how might they approach the possibility of their move to Clarksdale with Kendal's parents?

As if synchronicity, fate, destiny, Spirit, was working overtime, Kendal's mother telephoned Kendal one Saturday and said the unique custom-home Lenore and first husband Dennis built was for sale. "I've always loved that place and told your dad we need to buy it so no one else has it because I've regretted someone else living in it ever since Lenore sold it after Logan died. We could buy it and then decide what to do with it. There's enough acreage to turn it into a spiritual retreat center someday, perhaps."

Kendal said nothing, but could scarcely believe what she'd just heard and waited with high excitement for Charles to be home, while she went online and found the house listed with all pertinent details and pictures. It was the most unusual house in Clarksdale.

Kendal and Charles were in shock with what was happening. Later that evening, they telephoned Kendal's parents and told of them considering a move to Clarksdale before learning Lenore's house was for sale. No one replied, "Did you hear what we said?" Kendal asked. Marc answered, "Yes, we heard and both fainted." Julia added, "I wasn't expecting to ever hear what you just said, but your dad and I have talked about how wonderful that would be, never expecting it to happen, of course."

Do things like this really happen so easily, so naturally, each in their own way questioned. Charles and Marc were both just home from work that Saturday evening—long retail hours. That's how it would be in Clarksdale for Charles at the furniture store, but short distance and little traffic would lessen travel time.

The unsaid question was, did Kendal *want* to live in Clarksdale, or was she acquiescing to the needs of Montel Furniture? The store both gave and took away, that was no secret in the Montel family. It gave financial stability and took the time, energy, efforts of the family, now just her father, to keep it going. Aren't those the dynamics of any enterprise? Kendal tossed all of this around in her head.

The following weekend Kendal and Charles took a flight to Kansas City, rented a car and drove to Clarksdale to look at the custom home Lenore and Dennis built, on which Julia had already paid earnest money to secure the house against being sold to someone else.

Once in Clarksdale, Charles and Kendal drove to the house where a realtor was waiting. The driveway wound gently upward from the road at the edge of town into a yard of cedar trees and ivy just as Kendal remembered, this octagon shaped glass house with a thatched-looking metal roof, and an amazing mandorla-shaped front door. It was all as Kendal remembered. To Charles the place looked like a medieval hut or chapel, and he fell in love with the outside, the setting of the place.

Inside the home was as Kendal remembered: Stepping into the house one could see straight through to the out-of-doors on the other side with a stone floor patio, where water gently flowed out of a native stone wall, and disappeared below stones, recycling back again while ivy enhanced the gentle wall of water. Everything looked well cared for.

The center of the house was flooded with light from a skylight. There were two bedrooms and two baths on the main floor and another bedroom and bath downstairs with an open area and an igloo-type fireplace exactly like the one on the main floor, which Kendal liked as a child. At the bottom of stairs a door opened to the double garage dug into the side of the hill with easy access to a tornado shelter. On the main floor, in addition to the bedrooms and bathrooms, there was a small library alcove, dining area and kitchen and the open den with its igloo fireplace. Kendal had been in the house perhaps only two or three times.

Glass doors lead outside onto the inviting patio with stone floor and trickling water stone wall. A slightly treed back yard, more trees than Kendal remembered, moved gently upward beyond the patio to open grassland beyond and a boundless horizon and sky.

At the top of the inclined yard, slightly to the left, within trees, was a small, fanciful glass hut, a greenhouse perhaps. Kendal hadn't remembered this building. The realtor had information that someone who once occupied the property did wood carvings and had the hut built as a place for his carving hobby. This, of course, was Logan. Charles was thrilled with the tiny, uncommon glass structure.

CHAPTER FORTY-FOUR

Clarksdale Community

That evening, the four of them, Marc and Julia, Kendal and Charles ate together in the home where Kendal grew-up—such cozy familiarity—and they talked about the feasibility of a return to Clarksdale: the reality of the store, its future potential, what would await Charles as a newcomer.

Marc talked about the role of the store in the community, to the downtown area, and the privilege of serving the customers. People who depended on helpful advice, honest prices yet realized a business can't keep the doors open without making a profit. He spoke of Annette who worked at the store for years, knew how to listen to people, what they wanted, or helped them decide what they needed, which was sometimes the case. There was no hard-sell at Montel Furniture, rather patient, informed assistance which came from dedicated, informed assistants.

If changing times, online shopping, changing demographics were to make the store obsolete, buying the house Lenore and Dennis built with its six acres might provide financial security, for the land could be divided into lots and sold for other homes. It was not uncommon for farmers who retired to then move to town. Clarksdale was a thriving community, a hub that served the farmers that surrounded it.

A community college, the regional hospital with its behavioral center, Golden Acres home for the aged and infirm. These added layers of stability to the town with a population of a little over 7,000. The country club and golf course were mainstays, as were the churches, Marc observed.

Kendal was intrigued hearing her father's overview of the town which gave her a new perspective on the place, an adult perspective on the town and on her father, his position in town and the economic realities of the area, which were apparently part of his daily awareness which she never thought about.

Julia was thinking about how Lenore would react if Kendal and Charles bought the house she and Dennis built, that she lived in with Logan, which she could now revisit if she wanted to, and of course she'd want to. The place where she'd secretly assembled the leather binder with Matti's computer writings for Julia. Julia would be forever grateful for that.

Charles was overwhelmed listening to Marc, realizing what he'd have to learn about the day-to-day operations of Montel Furniture, the community at large, the mentality and expectations of the local population, the lack of anonymity. Clarksdale was much smaller than Sandshell. Would he like that?

What he did like was the curious glass hut amongst the trees. Julia knew Logan had the unique structure built for his carving hobby. The small structure charmed Charles: natural stone foundation rising two or three feet, glass with metal framing going up more than eight feet, with a steep roof made of what looked like dark plexiglass material giving the appearance of a thatched roof. Glass areas that opened and were screened for no-bug ventilation. Inside shelves at various places attached to metal supports. A sliding glass door. A remote-control heating-air unit. A flat-stone floor. He loved the little place. An extraordinary feature of the property. His favorite.

Kendal was engrossed with feelings about Clarksdale. She'd sensed at times over the years her mother's restlessness coming to this smallish town after growing up in Kansas City. Would Kendal feel trapped here?

Would she be moving back here out of duty? If so, is duty a bad thing? She was bonded to this place, the streets, her former classmates, teachers, the school plays she'd been in, basketball and volleyball, guys she dated, female friends, though in Lily from college she'd found her best friend, yet the way that worked out was painful.

Kendal would never have returned to Clarksdale to live if she wasn't married. She would *not* have wanted to live here unmarried. But now that she was married maybe it was time to settle here where everything was familiar: rolling hills, huge sky, gorgeous sunsets, where she knew lots of people and was known by many. And her parents were here. There would be frequent contact with them. Now that would be beautiful.

She thought of Lenore's house, the furniture they would need and how the store would make that easy. It was the most unusual house in town and didn't catch the fancy of many in the community but she liked the idea of it being out of the ordinary. It wasn't very large and would perhaps need to be built onto, but would that ruin it? She wouldn't think that far into the future.

Being a lawyer in town, once she learned the workings of the firm, she could perhaps work at home, using the lower-level bedroom for her office, or the library, depending on how much space she'd need. The first thing she'd need to do is pursue contacts with law firms and see if she might join one. Or should they buy Lenore's house first? Or another house? Surely they ought to look at other houses for sale. What if the store wouldn't work out for Charles, or Charles wouldn't be a match for the store? What if, what if . . .

By the time the four went to bed that night, much had been discussed, thought about, imagined, speculated, assumed. Charles felt certain that if they bought Lenore's house, and if he could use the enchanting glass house outside the main house for himself, he would use it for chanting. Though Kendal knew about his practice, would she agree to his using the little edifice for a chant-house joining his voice with recorded chanters of sacred music? There were so many decisions to be made, options to be weighed.

CHAPTER FORTY-FIVE

Estelle's Nude Vision

The move of Charles and Kendal to Clarksdale was not stress-free and they saw each other under pressure for the first time. Buying the house was tense—considering all angles of their move, taking on debt—but no, it was an investment. Both sets of parents contributed to a generous down-payment.

Charles realized how far he would now be from dad-Zack, mum-Dee and Cynthia, a beach, with the nearest airport over an hour's drive from Clarksdale. Had Dee suffered moving to Florida, so far from her family in Connecticut? Charles asked her on the telephone.

Dee reminded Charles she was much older when she moved to Florida than he was now. Dee didn't mention how Dempsey at the time didn't consciously know how much she ached to be liberated into Dee. How Zack and the children had done that for her, though aunt Tess certainly helped start the process—and Ann Dramm metabolized the process with metaphors connected to the cat purple aura image. Dee didn't tell Charles she needed to leave her hometown to grow, develop, transform.

Meanwhile in Sandshell, Dee and Zack frequently went to spend an evening with Estelle and Reggie. The two couples would share a meal the Kendricks picked-up on the way, or Estelle fixed food augmented by what Dee brought. After the meal, Reggie and Zack watched TV sports, which was a way to share with little talk required, as Reggie's cognitive abilities continued to decline along with his physical abilities. Home Health Care was a tremendous help for Estelle as Reggie seemed to enjoy the attention he received from the nurse, speech therapist and physical therapist, all females.

One evening after the meal, Reggie and Zack retreated to the family room to watch sports while the women remained seated at the kitchen table talking, when the topic of Charles in Clarksdale arose, the many changes he was experiencing. Estelle talked about her move from New Orleans to Sandshell when she married, and then there was something she had never told anyone.

She began, "Maleness has been a mystery to me. Growing up, I didn't feel I knew my father because of the alcoholism whereas my mother and two sisters were my windows to the world and then in the convent males were distant authority figures, priests, bishops and so on. After my female-dominated world, along came Reggie, and then three sons.

"A strange thing started happening to me when the boys were still young. During Mass, just as communion was being prepared, I would have a graphic mental image of nude Jesus on the cross, a full-frontal view. I was shocked, feeling some sort of devilish thing was going on but not knowing what, I mentally brushed it away. Then it happened again and again, a few Sundays in a row. I was troubled enough to quiet myself one day, and to write about the graphic mental image after praying in my most powerful way to be kept safe as I proceeded with uncovering the spontaneous picture.

"One might think my experience with Ignatius's Spiritual Exercises, praying the gospels would cause me to catch on quickly, but the nudity kept me far away from thinking about gospel stories. Finally, I began to dialogue with Jesus on the cross.

"The crux of what I learned is that, first, I had a stunted, repressed, incomplete view of maleness. Second, I needed to realize I had not created masculinity in the universe and was not responsible for it, which greatly surprised me. Did I ever feel I was responsible for maleness? Yes, I'd always wanted to change my father's drinking and I wanted to change Reggie; his unkempt habits around the house, and I tried to corral the rambunctiousness of three little boys.

"It has taken years to disentangle what is and is not my responsibility in these matters, and remains even today, though I now recognize the struggle and do not blindly get caught up in it. Rather, I sometimes step-back from, surrender control of, don't try to solve, provide clarity if I feel I have any to offer, and in general, discern what is and is not mine to deal with."

Estelle fell silent, but was obviously still thinking, "That shocking, uninvited mental image brought much practical help to me." Silent again, she then confided, "My powerful prayer the day I dealt with the mental image, and what is still my most powerful prayer, is ancient, raw, primal. I don't know when or where I first heard the prayer, *'I plead the most precious blood of Jesus over (blank),'* which might be a person or a situation. The words are embarrassingly intimate. As if they say everything that can be said. I believe the mystery imbedded in the prayer is too great to be articulated or even turned into an image, though there is traditionally pictured the sacred heart of Jesus. For me, the most precious blood of Jesus can only be experienced and known intuitively.

"I do also, sometimes mentally picture the *light of Christ* surrounding and infusing individuals, healing, bringing comfort to them, being part of a situation. And so, the primal blood of the human Jesus mixed with the en*light*enment of the Christ, form a way I pray; it's the human and divine mix in Christianity.

"And I pray for maleness when it seems overblown, out of control, testosterone toxic. Just as femaleness also has its healthy and unhealthy versions. But I need to pray specifically for Reggie when he has annoyed me most with his grumpy ingratitude. This I must do more often.

"I believe his generation of men still have an incorrect view of women as helpmates, perhaps excluding Zack," she said slyly. The term helpmate acknowledges their need for help, which women traditionally were to obediently supply. Surely our sons do better, though only their wives really know. Now that two-income households are a necessity and women have become educated beyond house and home, men must change.

"Reggie doesn't understand my retirement, only his own. This is not an easy time. I've often wondered why Reggie doesn't seek a religious outlook. He's gone along with what I've offered, but nothing seems to penetrate his skin. It's like he is afflicted with some sort of spiritual lethargy, he's blocked, trapped in the outer-world and cannot go to the inner world. So it seems to me.

"The image of naked Jesus took me to grappling with maleness but not specifically with Reggie. He is my albatross at the moment, and I wish that wasn't' the case. I really wish this wasn't my reaction to much of his demented behavior."

"Would Jesus have automatically healed my impatient attitude when he was on earth? I don't believe anyone ever came up to him and said they needed their impatience exorcised. Well, I've prayed for help in this area and I can be patient for awhile, however, I begin to be resentful feeling like I'm a doormat. This is tricky business, because Reggie would like to be waited on hand-and-foot, to borrow an old phrase.

"We are living longer than most people did in Jesus' day, and some of us must take care of those who can no longer care for themselves. But people have always had to do this. Do I judge Reggie unfairly when I say he seems spiritually lethargic? Maybe. However, deep down I feel that is the situation. Does that mean he's going to hell? I think he's living in hell now. I believe he would enjoy life more if he wasn't confined to limited-ego; that dreadful goldfish mentality saturated with every form of fear because it's too small to deal with life by itself, which it actually knows but can't open up to what is greater. There's some kind of psychological blockage. Alcoholics Anonymous would say for me to "detach" and let the Higher Power take over. I do that until I get caught in my own efforts again.

"I know you are comfortable with Jesus being considered a shaman after reading the book *The Life of a Galilean Shaman: Jesus of Nazareth in An Anthropological-Historical Perspective* by Pieter Craffert (2008). Recently I watched a video on healing, how many today try to access psychological-spiritual dimensions to receive different kinds of healing for themselves or others.

"I believe Jesus was in touch with everything secular culture is today trying to get in touch with. His immediate disciples knew how to heal, but then, later generations largely forgot the shamanic dimension and Jesus became a moralist, an ethicist, rather than a healer for body and soul. Christians retained the belief that Jesus could heal but they lost the ability to access and pass to others the healing spirit which was a large part of who he was.

"I pray for lessening Reggie's dementia and my anger, basically for the grace to be decent in my dealings with Reggie, while he is often confused though sure he's right, he's morose when actually he has ever so much to be grateful for. Oh, his bathroom issues. We have plenty of help, but he complains he doesn't like having others around. When people telephone to say "hi" he gives details about situations that are nowhere close to correct. I hope they can tell what he says is gnarled, convoluted, wrong, wrong, wrong."

Estelle spilled her anguish for the moment. Meanwhile, something else was stirring.

CHAPTER FORTY-SIX

Paris

Reggie had rare clarity with Zach that evening in the family room watching sports, volume turned low. Reggie said Estelle was worn-out caring for him and she needed a vacation with the Brunch Bunch. He had amazing momentary lucidity, almost as if he was entrusting his thoughts with Zach to bring the idea to fruition.

Driving home that evening, Zach shared this with Dee who later suggested to the Brunch Bunch that the four women take a trip together, never revealing it was Reggie's idea, feeling it somehow less complicated without that piece of information. The four friends agreed they needed to go someplace together, which they'd never done. But where?

Monique immediately said, "Paris." Though none of the others had considered such a grand trip, no other place was mentioned. With Monique and Francine both French-speaking, the women didn't need be part of a tour.

Monique had cousins not far from Paris, Francine had distant cousins in Paris and beyond, while Estelle had long wanted to see the Cathedral of Notre Dame, (This was before the fire April, 2019). Dee, even in college, wanted to be on French soil when she read the most popular and influential of all medieval romance literature, an allegory, *The Romance of the Rose*, with characters such as False Seeming, Constrained Abstinence,

Evil Tongue, Largess, Old Woman, Fair Welcome. She fondly remembered this allegorical tale.

And thus, the Brunch Bunch went to Paris and surrounding areas for ten days in early May before the dense tourist crowds arrived. Such satisfaction was theirs! Reggie's suggestion to Zach was the seed that grew into a most wonderful plant. Yes, Reggie, even in his depleted condition, planted an idea that grew to fruition for others.

One of the last evenings in Paris when Monique had her own plans, and Francine was also engaged elsewhere, Estelle and Dee were enjoying food and wine in a French restaurant not far from Notre Dame Cathedral, when Dee revealed it was Reggie's thoughtful suggestion that culminated in this uncommonly fine Brunch Bunch journey.

Estelle looked at Dee with puzzlement, "Reggie suggested a group trip to Zach?" She needed to absorb all that implied. So, Reggie *did* know her fatigue, her anguish, her moments of despair, which, if they lasted longer could reduce her to madness. Even more, he must have had some memory that after their retirements she wanted the two of them to travel, which was a major disappointment.

After considerable conversation with Dee, Estelle concluded, "I'm fortunate. Amidst my stress with Reggie, I am this moment in Paris at his suggestion. Think of the countless caregivers who get no relief; none. I will try and remember this. But then, of course, I'll forget and again be overwhelmed dealing with him. However, knowing he suggested a vacation for me with dearest friends, helps. It really does."

At the same time in Clarksdale KS, Kendal Kendrick was wondering if she would be content with life in Clarksdale after tasting life in a city? She wondered, yet some part of her had felt compelled to return to her home town. She liked buying the most unusual house in Clarksdale and Charles remained intrigued with the tiny glass hut built at just the right spot on the southeast side of the octagonal house in the trees. He so wanted the glass hut for his own use; chanting solitude, but had not yet mentioned his desire to use it for chanting, feeling the timing needed to be right.

He remembered the day they first looked at the property with the realtor. He and Kendal walked up the slight incline to the back end of the property, hand in hand, giddy, on the partially cloudy day with a pleasant warm breeze, noticing but not knowing this was the same wrought-iron bench Ann Dramm and Cal Hanover sat on under the big oak tree quite a number of years ago, spending an evening with Lenore and Logan.

Ann from CT and Cal from New Mexico in town to celebrate Julia's fiftieth birthday. Ann, staying with Lenore and Logan, Cal with Julia and Marc. Both having been intimately involved with Matti, Julia's birth mother.

Six acres. Kendal and Charles would own six acres, they realized as they hugged, excited with the prospect. And soon they were living in the house, furnishing it with lovely furniture at wholesale prices from Montel Furniture. Kendal was working with a law firm.

Charles was having to learn a lot. At his job in men's retail he didn't need to learn customers' names. Now, in the venerable Montel furniture store, recognizing names and faces was important. Montel Furniture was a big operation. Having his father-in-law as his boss was its own stress, though Marc reassured Charles, "Rome wasn't built in a day," meaning it would take time for Charles to learn everything.

Annette at the store, a seasoned employee, encouraged Charles, who so wanted to be a fast learner. Marc was patient, a good teacher, but he was running a business above all. Charles hoped his mother Roxanne's interior design talents were in him, as he realized customers asked for advice, wanted and needed suggestions. Just learning the inventory was a huge undertaking. Being a good listener was of great, perhaps greatest importance, Charles realized.

Charles went home exhausted which he tried to hide as best he could from Kendal, and this further exhausted him. He fell into bed fatigued which was not ideal for the young married couple.

The Kansas winter was arriving with near-daily cold wind and grey skies. Charles missed living with no beach nearby. His months in St. Louis gave him a taste of winter, but still this was different with more wind and cold. He knew himself well enough to know he needed the little glass hut for himself to help him with all these changes, yes, for chanting, which renewed him.

He was glad he'd discovered this chanting dimension in himself, certain the little glass house was the answer, but reluctant to ask Kendal for chanting rights to the place. One evening, sensing his exhaustion, she said, "Why don't you use the miniature hut as a chant-place." He realized he didn't need to have exclusive rights to the little glass house. It could be a multi-use space.

Lenore in an independent living facility, now knew "her house" had been purchased by Charles and Kendal. She was in her favorite chair at the senior facility when Julia told her on the telephone of their purchase and a shudder of emotion pierced Lenore's tiny body, whereupon she could only choke out the word, "Really?"

"I can't believe I can be in that house again. Surely Kendal and Charles would allow that wouldn't they?" Julia was able to answer, "Yes, they know I planned to tell you today and are eager for you to see the home, and for them to learn more about it from you."

The day came when fragile Lenore with her cane was in "her house." Her daughter and son were with their mother, anxious to see again the home their father designed after they were grown and gone from home. Lenore was overwhelmed at times that day, lingering to explain one and then another feature. Overall, she found the place "substantially unchanged," while memories of Dennis and Logan were everywhere.

The quaint glass hut in the trees was Logan's addition to carve in solitude. For Kendal and Charles, Lenore brought three of Logan's small carvings, unpainted: a young boy sticking out his tongue; a young girl with hair and dress flying in the wind; a young girl and boy hugging. Lenore explained, "He said the carvings depicted the two of us. I want them to come back here where they were born," Lenore explained, as she handed the carvings to Kendal.

In the library she talked about Dennis's books, which their children now had. She tenderly patted the shelves as she talked. Overall, it was an emotional day. At one point, Julia said to Lenore, "Thank you again for the time and effort you put into gathering Matti's computer writings into the leather purple binder for me, when I had such a shabby attitude toward Matti and her writings."

"I knew one day you'd want them, they'd be meaningful to you," Lenore replied. Julia acknowledged, "And you were right. I now prize them. I had to grow up and grow past my resentments of Matti."

Lenore reminisced, "I love Clarksdale, where I spent most of my life, actually. It's a good place, a very good place. Fine people, salt of the earth, enterprising people. I'll be buried here beside Dennis. I am a daughter of the Kansas earth to which I shall return. If it was a warmer day I'd walk the six acres, but these old bones don't want to do that in this cold wind." Lenore made an impression on Kendal and Charles. Her mind was clear, she left a powerful imprint on the young couple.

Charles began regularly to chant in the glass hut, which fortified him, gave him the strength to cope with the many changes in his life. He couldn't explain why chanting helped his energy level, but this was so. He simply felt more put together, while knowing much change or stress in one's life can make one become unglued, for Charles never forgot his dad's panic attack.

CHAPTER FORTY-SEVEN

James

Monique, back in Sandshell after an enjoyable time in France with the Brunch Bunch, was met with a significant challenge. Since daughter Christiane's divorce, Christiane never saw her ex-husband James or heard from him. Monthly child support payments were electronically wired to her bank account as if a phantom was sending them. Otherwise, James was fine in Miami so far as Christiane knew until she received a telephone call from him.

Months earlier, James was in a boating accident which killed Gwen, whom he was dating, and left him in a wheel chair paralyzed from the waist down. At first in the conversation, James said he was just wanting Christiane to know about the tragedy. Later in the conversation James said he was wanting to move to Sandshell so he could come to know his three-year-old son. He also said the boating accident was not his fault; he was awarded financial damages. In Sandshell he would continue working for the company where he was presently employed; technology made that possible.

Christiane was psychologically paralyzed with what James was saying. She'd survived his cruel departure and didn't want him back in her life, though he was her son's father, and a relationship between father and son may well be healthy and helpful. Christiane felt she was in limbo, numb, overwhelmed, dreading to tell her mother.

Monique immediately had an opinion: James needn't move to Sandshell, he could drive when he wanted to be with her grandson Jameson, and return just as swiftly to his home in Miami. His sudden desire to be a father to Jameson was born of desperation now that his own life was pitiful. Monique no longer called grandson Jameson by his name, but dubbed him "J," unable to bring herself to pronounce this darling boy "James's son" every time she said his name, so she began referring to him as "J," and increasingly the initial "J" was catching on with everyone except the boy's father, James.

Monique worried James would insert himself into Christiane's life which Christiane didn't need. Overall, Monique had never liked James, and her grandson was thriving without his father. Christiane and "J" were doing fine living with Monique, Christiane had her dance studio. They had Ingrid, a mature dependable babysitter for "J." A man in a wheelchair, like James, couldn't manage a toddler, not even for five minutes.

James was more persistent than Monique could imagine. He telephoned Monique, looking for a home to buy. Christiane was filled with anxiety. James was wanting to look at properties this coming weekend. Monique told him she would find another realtor to work with him, but he made it clear he wanted her. He said he trusted her.

Well, Monique didn't trust James, did not want to be part of his moving to Sandshell, did not want him upsetting, confusing, overwhelming Christiane. So Monique said "yes" to James. This would be her opportunity to tell him what she wanted to say to him—in person.

The weekend came, filled with increased anxiety for Christiane and with anger for Monique. "He thinks he can win me over, but he's a fool," Monique summarized. He insisted he pick her up at her office, "Wanting I notice how mobile in his converted-van, capable of caring for himself, so I expect he will not burden us."

Monique saw clearly, "Moving here, tying up Christiane's life, then, no room for another husband, if she wants. He's miserable, yes, regrettable. Plans to waltz back into Christiane's life. No stopping him. Conniving he is." She didn't want to find a property for him, but time with him did provide an opportunity to tell him face-to-face what she thought of his scheming. She wanted him to know she could see through his maneuvers. Monique had always found James superficial. He was good looking, charming, smart, self-assured and exterior. But there wasn't much inside him.

Meanwhile, Christiane's anxiety was multiple. She did not want "J" to form an attachment that might easily vanish, which was less likely if James moved to Sandshell instead of driving back and forth from Miami. She agreed with her mother that James might be an obstacle to Christiane finding a meaningful relationship with someone new, but this was not her concern at this time. Caring for "J" and having her beloved dance studio was all-consuming for Christiane.

She didn't dare tell her mother that James on the telephone seemed different from the former physically-whole, full-functioning James. She didn't tell her mother that James admitted he had been a shallow person, arrogant, cocksure, full of himself, probably incapable of loving anyone.

Monique had restless sleep the night before her day as James's realtor, but awakened not feeling as poorly as she expected. It was a lovely Florida day. He arrived in his converted-van at Monique's office, and she was impressed with how he manipulated the hand controls of the van, and when they arrived at a property how he maneuvered himself out of the driver's seat into the wheelchair behind the driver's seat, turning to the side door and the elevator which lowered him to the ground. With remote control he put the elevator back into the van, closed and locked the side door.

Monique was impressed with his skills and realized how much he'd had to learn, she saw the upper body strength he'd developed, realized what he'd been forced to accept about his limitations, his future. She'd done her homework on available wheelchair accessible properties, on those semi-accessible that could be readily renovated. The morning was all business, discussion of properties. James was pleasant, had many questions. This wasn't as hideous as Monique anticipated. But she didn't want the day to pass without saying what she wanted to say.

They had a late lunch together in a restaurant she knew was easily wheelchair accessible. After looking at the menu and ordering, James lost no time speaking frankly, "You probably wonder why I want to move to Sandshell. Well, I get so depressed I want to die. Dying would be welcome relief. Medicines and therapists help somewhat. If I didn't have them I likely would already have done myself in.

"I have no one to blame but myself. And that's the worst part. The boating accident wasn't my fault. But destroying the family I had was my fault. I may be incapable of love. Even with Gwen, there was the excitement of newness, but that's not love. I don't know what love is. I am crippled in more than one way. What I have prized is success, progress, getting ahead."

Monique was stunned with what seemed startling honesty. It was probably a rehearsed statement. She noticed James fiddling with arranging the napkin on his paralyzed legs, which gave a moment of relief, for he wasn't staring at her waiting for her to say something. But she did automatically say, "You've just said a lot."

James responded, "When you're in my shape, you cut through the crap. Excuse my speech."

"I appreciate your words," Monique didn't mean to sound so understanding. She was likely being duped. "So, you like your therapists?" she asked, implying he'd be giving them up if he moved to Sandshell.

He answered, "They're OK, but the future looks black. Endless black." His raw comment caught Monique off-guard again. She asked frivolously, "Do you sleep well?" He answered, "Fairly well. . . with pills, of course . . . but depression is there the moment I wake up . . . terrible heaviness . . . I try to go back to sleep. . . all I want is sleep."

James continued, "I don't know why I didn't die in the accident, death would have been better." He paused and then returned to the topic of his moving, "I believe in Sandshell I could learn to relate to Jameson, I could contribute to his life. I would have a reason to get up in the morning. I'll have a job. I don't have money problems. There was an insurance settlement from the accident, I have investments, I'll sell my house in Miami, I'm basically free of money worries. But I have no future, and no one can give me a future, no amount of money can buy me a future. I know that. I abandoned Jameson and Christiane. I don't want to be a burden on Christiane in any way; to jeopardize her future. The only ray of hope I see is I can be a father to Jameson."

Monique told James, "If you think money is parenting, you are mistaken. You send money each month. Keep that involvement, but don't move here. You do not have what it takes to parent. A man who leaves when hearing loss is found leaves a message. You left such message when you left.

"Don't expect a child to give a future to you. Children need and need and need. They must take and take until they care for themselves. You cannot tend a toddler. "J" doesn't know you. He is wild for his Uncle Justin and they enjoy together. Never touch Christiane's life again. She must remain free from you." She added, "You will need friends, and Sandshell may have none for you."

James reacted strangely to Monique's piercing comments, "We both know I can't walk out on anybody anymore." This puzzled Monique. Was he being funny? He has no choice about not walking out. Did he want her to believe desperation changed him? If this was humor, she wasn't laughing.

There was momentary quiet between them, until James said, "I'm asking all the time now, Why am I here? What can I do? My answers, I would say, are "You're here because you weren't lucky enough to die, and as to what you can do about it, nothing. Take your pills, go to work, do therapies, live your pitiful life and you will eventually die, as does everyone."

Monique countered his comments, "Those are the answers you give to yourself. It doesn't mean they are the only answers in the universe."

"What answers could the universe give me?"

Monique reacted, "I don't know. The answers would come to you, not me." Their lunch ended, James drove Monique to her office, she found herself complimenting his ease with the van, he thanked her for showing the properties. Pointing to the papers on the properties, he said, "I'll study these," which she wished he hadn't said. Monique did not want James in Sandshell.

CHAPTER FORTY-EIGHT

Francis of Assisi

At the same time, Dee was studying St. Francis of Assisi (1181/82-1226) who, it seemed to her, had much to learn about metaphoric discernment. She realized Francis was well-acquainted with descriptive metaphor but not metaphoric discernment. He was a literalist, as can be seen in how he understood a dream.

> In the dream it seemed to Francis that his whole house was filled with soldiers' armaments: saddles, shields, spears and other equipment. Though delighting for the most part, he silently wondered to himself about its meaning. For he was not accustomed to see such things in his house, but rather stacks of cloth to be sold [his father was a cloth merchant and this was his parents' home]. He was greatly bewildered at the sudden turn of events and the response that all these arms were to be for him and his soldiers. With a happy spirit he awoke the next morning.[6]

[6] *Francis of Assisi: The Saint*, Vol. I, edited by Regis J. Armstrong, J.A. Wayne Hellmann, William J. Short, (Hyde Park NY: New City Press, 1999), p. 186.

Francis's friend, Thomas of Celano, writes that in waking life Francis had been so impressed with a nobleman from Assisi who was gathering military weaponry getting ready for a military campaign in Apulia, that Francis also started gathering military necessities and was on the way to Apulia when he had the dream.

His friend Thomas comments that Francis "should have been able to see his interpretation of it [the dream] was mistaken."[7] Of course, Thomas wrote these words three years after Francis died and had the benefit of hindsight.

In Dee's metaphoric musing about Francis's dream, she speculated that "his whole house" was his father's house and might have represented his father's "frame of reference," "the constructs in which he lived" where Francis also lived psychologically; symbolizing an aspect of Francis's personality that was like his cloth-merchant father (who was apparently a "materialist" in more than one sense of the word).

In the dream, military arms instead of stacks of cloth (material–materialism) might have symbolized Francis's ability to fight against, combat, overcome, conquer materialistic tendencies in his own personality. If Francis had understood his dream in this way, he perhaps would not have had a broken relationship with his father, which is said to have happened. Instead, Francis would have been able to subjectively overcome his own materialism without externalizing it and breaking with his father.

Also, knowing how Francis's life turned out, we can wonder whether the dream was a statement about Francis's capacity for spiritual warfare, inner struggle. Dreams sometimes reveal potential which can take years to fully actualize.

It must be acknowledged that using Francis's dream said to have taken place eight-hundred years ago, reported by someone other than the dreamer, is problematic. However, as used here, it demonstrates metaphoric discernment, which is "reading" an event by metaphorically discerning it.

Thomas tells that Francis did not go to Apulia for his military pursuits because on his way there, asleep one night, he had an experience which changed everything. Since it is said he was asleep, he might have had a

---

[7] *Francis of Assisi: The Saint,* Vol. I, p. 186.

dream. This dream is reported as a conversation between Francis and "someone," which eventually became "the Lord," who told Francis to go back to where he was born and his dream would be fulfilled "in a spiritual way."[8] Francis went back to Assisi but remained rather literal in his understanding.

One day, praying inside the church of San Damiano, which was aging and in disrepair, while gazing at the crucifix, he heard "with his bodily ears a voice coming from that cross, telling him three times: 'Francis go and repair my house which, as you see, is all being destroyed.'" Francis immediately set about repairing the church of San Damiano, which was a worthwhile endeavor. However, it has been said that what Francis really helped rebuild was the Catholic church of his day which was in disrepair. Francis obeyed what he understood at the time, but this doesn't mean there wasn't a lot more to what he first understood. Only time and experience would reveal the fullness of what "rebuild my house" meant.

Another time, upon considering the gospel about Jesus sending his disciples out to preach with no silver, gold, wallet, staff, or shoes (Mt. 10:9-10/ Lk 9:2/Mk 6:12/Lk 1:47) Francis immediately took off his shoes, laid down his staff, and kept only one tunic. He proclaimed, "This is what I want, this is what I seek, this is what I desire with all my heart."[9] Franciscans still today wear sandals. It is, of course, possible that not wearing shoes was part of Francis's personal struggle against materialism and the alignment of himself with those too poor to have shoes. This is possible. However, if Francis did literally take off his shoes, as Thomas says, is this more profound than understanding shoes metaphorically and symbolically? Not really.

Shoes are human-made coverings to protect our feet. We stand on our feet. Metaphorically, feet allude to our under-standing, which is what stands under (is the foundation) of what we know and believe. The exhortation to not wear shoes could mean we are not to cover our understanding with human contrivances to protect our limited views and beliefs. Rather, our understanding is to rest on humility. The word humility

---

[8] *Francis of Assisi: The Founder,* Vol. II, edited by Regis J. Armstrong, J.A. Wayne Hellmann, William J. Short, (Hyde Park NY: New City Press, 2000), p. 245.

[9] *Francis of Assisi: The Saint,* Vol I, edited by Regis J. Armstrong, J.A. Wayne Hellmann, William J. Short, (Hyde Park NY: New City Press, 1999), pp. 201-202

comes from humus, the soil, the earth. Metaphorically, shoes (human-made understanding) can separate us from being "down to earth," from being real, genuine, honest and truthful, about who we are and what we do. Quite simply, human "understanding" (shoes) can keep us from being "grounded" in the Spirit of Truth, the Holy Spirit. Francis certainly did not live by human standards. All of these symbolic shoe implications were in the Rule which was to govern his brotherhood.

In Francis's Rule, the brothers were to live material poverty, having only the bare necessities of clothing, eating whatever food was set before them, accepting no money or coins but instead receiving sustenance for the body from their work, having ownership of no thing.

They were to live interior poverty, which is humility and means being down to earth, real, genuine, transparent. Francis often spoke of the heart in the biblical sense as the symbol of the depths of the human person, the center of one's being that can become hardened, capricious, vulnerable, but also, paradoxically, is one's greatest strength.[10]

The brothers are to live moral poverty, which is compassion, and means to "suffer with." They are to be united in the solidarity and welfare of all the brothers, and to live peaceably and non-judgmentally with everyone else. The biblical concept of *misericordia* (mercy, or a heart sensitive to misery) is what Francis advocated for his brothers.

The brothers are to live spiritual poverty, totally serving God in poverty and humility, which brings the Kingdom of Heaven, the fullness of life. Francis accepted all things as free gifts from an utterly good God, and he freely returned everything to God through praise.

Thomas wrote about Francis, "He prayed with all his heart that the eternal and true God guide his way and teach him to do His will. He endured great suffering in his soul, and he was not able to rest until he accomplished in action what he had conceived in his heart."[11]

Dee knew the crux, core and essence of human will and intention is to seek to do God's intention and will. Something like that.

---

[10] Regis J. Armstrong, "If My Words Remain in You," in *Francis of Assisi: History, Hagiography and Hermeneutics in the Early Documents*, edited by Jay M. Hammond, (Hyde Park NY: New City Press, 2004), p. 75.

[11] *Francis of Assisi: The Saint*, Vol. I, edited by Regis J. Armstrong, J.A. Wayne Hellmann, William J. Short, (Hyde Park NY: New City Press, 1999), p. 187.

CHAPTER FORTY-NINE

St. Francis Changing

Dee believed part of what Francis suffered was to grow from understanding literally to comprehending figuratively, with nuance and subtlety. Francis kept his simplicity of heart while growing into complexity of understanding, which the following stories show.

There is a story that a Dominican, who was a doctor of Sacred Theology, asked Francis, who had little education, to explain the words of Ezekiel to him: "If you do not warn the wicked man about his wickedness, I will hold you responsible for his soul" (Ezk 2:17-21). Reluctant Francis replied:

> If that passage is supposed to be understood in a universal sense, then I understand it to mean that a servant of God should be burning with life and holiness so brightly, that by the light of example and the tongue of his conduct, he will rebuke all the wicked. In that way, I say, the brightness of his life and the fragrance of his reputation will proclaim their wickedness to all of them.[12]

---

[12] *Francis of Assisi: The Founder,* Vol. II, edited by Regis J. Armstrong, J.A. Wayne Hellmann, William J. Short, (Hyde Park NY: New City Press, 2000), p. 140.

Francis takes the word "warn" to penetrating dimensions and interprets the bible passage with doubled-edged subtlety, placing responsibility back on the one who is doing the warning. Francis discerns the word "warn" is more profound than its usual, surface, literal meaning.

He implies that our personality, our morals and spiritual development serve as "warnings" to others, not as threats, but as healthy examples. And he uses metaphoric phrases to get his point across: "the light of example" "the tongue of his conduct" "the brightness of his life" and "the fragrance of his reputation." This story shows Francis both discerning and describing with metaphor.

Another story shows Francis's growing ability to discern metaphorically. The story tells that Francis had been tormented by a temptation for more than two years. One day while praying in a church, he heard in spirit the words of scripture: "If you have faith like a mustard seed, and you tell that mountain to move from its place and move to another place, it will happen." Francis replied: "What is that mountain?" He was told: "That mountain is your temptation." "In that case, Lord, be it done to me as you have said!" And he was set free.[13]

The story shows Francis knowing the mountain is a symbolic mountain which is why he asks "What is that mountain?" He doesn't ask where the mountain is so he can find it in the external world.

Two stories from the end of his life show a struggle Francis was having. This problem was the question about body/flesh. How should one deal with physical bodily needs? This question is complicated by the word *flesh*, a biblical term meaning the attitudes or tendencies in the personality whereby one lives by human, natural strengths alone, (the goldfish-ego) without the creative wisdom of God's grace. Francis seems to have the two words body and flesh enmeshed and was still dealing with this at the end of his life.

Dee understood that in medieval religious devotion there was the tendency to control, discipline, even torture the body, not so much to reject physicality but to elevate physicality into the divine. Today we have our own body conundrums.

We eat "comfort foods," or starve ourselves for psycho-spiritual reasons, or we crave the effects of mind/emotion changing drugs, or have

---

[13] *Francis of Assisi: The Founder,* Vol. II, p. 165 // Vol. II, p. 324// Vol. III, p. 43.

sexual encounters to ease loneliness, boredom, meaninglessness. Or in the case of pedophilia, do not know that childish, childhood or childlike issues or other child-related dynamics need attention and healing.

Today we diet for cosmetic reasons rather than fast for spiritual reasons as medieval people did. We manipulate body chemicals with psychoactive drugs like "ecstasy" while medieval people sought spiritual ecstasy through ascetical practices. They flagellated their bodies. We get body piercings, tattoos, cosmetic surgeries for our own reasons. We are sleep-deprived because we are too busy to sleep while they stayed awake to pray and to spiritually discipline their bodies. Though we strive to be healthy, we do not always live comfortably and wisely with our bodies.

Dee's reading of Francis is that he had a serious dilemma between how to treat the material body, with medieval asceticism on one side, and the Incarnation on the other side. And Francis left nothing in writing about the stigmata he is said to have received. We are left to wonder whether the stigmata moderated his medieval asceticism or reinforced it, believing that austerities invited the stigmata.

We are also left to wonder whether his painful and prolonged illnesses changed his ideas about the body. Though we don't have clear answers to these questions, the two stories which follow seem to show that Francis was changing his view about the body shortly before his death.

The first story is that near the end of his life Francis is reported to have "jokingly" said to his body: "Cheer up Brother Body, and forgive me; for I will now gladly do as you please, and gladly hurry to relieve your complaints!"[14] This "joking" comment took place when medical remedies were being smeared on his body and he sought a brother's opinion about their use, because Francis's conscience was bothering him about the matter.

After the brother's advice to care for the body which had served Francis so well, Francis jokingly asks the body's forgiveness for his having been reluctant about using the medical remedies. If Francis could "joke" about something related to the body does this show a new attitude

---

[14] *Francis of Assisi: The Founder,* Vol. II, edited by Regis J. Armstrong, J.A. Wayne Hellmann, William J. Short, (Hyde Park NY: New City Press, 2000), p. 383.

about the body, a practicality that had been absent, or was it merely a way to relieve the tension of reluctantly acquiescing to the medical remedies?[15]

One thing seemed clear to Dee: Francis was conflicted, his conscience was bothering him about how to treat his body.

In the second story, Francis is reported to have "confessed on his death bed that he had greatly sinned against 'Brother Body.'" Was this death bed "confession" a mere apology? Was Francis saying it was unfortunately necessary that his body be harshly subdued for the sake of sanctity? If this was true, would the phrase "he had greatly sinned" been used? It seems likely this story shows Francis had a change of heart; a wiser, more practical attitude about how to treat the body.

In general, Francis had to grow, develop, to expand his understanding and experience of everything and to fall-in-love with Life in the broadest, most exalted sense. Francis seems to have known being-in-love. At the end of his life, blind, very ill, in painful crisis from the tension between the original form of life envisioned by him and opposing viewpoints and developments in the brotherhood, Francis was depleted in every way. He was used up, humbled, humiliated. He "hit bottom," as the metaphorical phrase is used in AA. He was at the end of his rope, (another metaphor).

In this empty state (*kenosis*, in Greek) Francis wrote *The Canticle of the Creatures*, which praises God through creation. Today we might call this a coping mechanism. He accessed a truth larger than the truth of his situation, which brought him relief.

Francis seems to have developed the habit of praising God when he was powerless, when everything was going wrong. He was in-love with something greater than the difficulties of the moment and praising Creator/Creation catapulted him further into Love.[16]

---

15 *Francis of Assisi: The Founder,* Vol. II, p. 382.

16 Chapters on St. Francis are reproduced here with permission by New City Press, Hyde Park, New York, from Marilyn Hammond's article "Saint Francis as Struggling Hermeneut" in the 2004 book *Francis of Assisi: History, Hagiography and Hermeneutics in the Early Documents* edited by Jay M. Hammond.

CHAPTER FIFTY

No Baby, No Career

The Brunch Bunch was to meet mid-morning, when earlier that morning Charles and Kendal telephoned Zach and Dee to tell of Kendal's pregnancy. Dee's friends were congratulating the soon-to-be grandmother, who could not grasp that reality. Though elated, Dee had not yet absorbed her grandmother role, but was filled with the joy she heard in the telephone voices of Charles and Kendal announcing the pregnancy.

She commented to her Brunch friends, "You have all had the experience of giving birth to babies and careers, but I haven't. No babies, and I'm still waiting to give birth to the plan Life has for me as a career." Dee regretted her words. She burned emotionally. Why had she blurted this poor-pitiful-me statement? Her face was red with embarrassment, as she said aloud, "Now why did I say that?"

Only Dee felt her "no baby, no career" comment tasteless. Puzzlement registered on the faces of Monique, Estelle, Francine, as they exchanged bewildered glances. How could Dee not know what she birthed in her insights into the personality of St. Francis, into her giving birth to the Brunch Bunch itself. Did she not see her unique contributions?

Monique, forehead wrinkled in sincerity, earnestly intoned, "You know not what you give to me, dear friend. After you did St. Francis, his dream, the meanings of shoes, I had a shoe dream. Important, and because of you, I say."

Francine, head slightly bent, intense eyes looking at Dee, said softly, "You make a contribution with your hermeneutic talent; even as a grain of sand helps make a beach. Your interpretive insights are gifts that impact those around you. I have never forgotten the parables of the salt and fig tree you explicated exponentially, which I find helpful and brilliant."

Estelle, tenderly touched the top of Dee's hand on the table, "You follow your inspirations, make your contributions. Don't sell yourself short."

Just then in a most unusual gesture, Totem the cat at her advanced age came out of her chosen spot of seclusion in another part of the house, sauntered into the Kendrick kitchen going under the table, rubbing slowly, dramatically against Dee's legs which all four women noticed. They were stunned by the timing; the conversation and the cat.

Then, Totem came out from under the table, looked back at the women and slowly left the room the same way she'd arrived. Comments flew, "How strange! Uncanny. What *was* that about? Wouldn't believe it if I hadn't seen it. Totem was marking you as her own. She must have been listening to us. She could feel your emotion, Dee. She always stays hidden when others are here. She was affirming you. A synchronicity. A moment of special Grace. What *do* animals know?"

After the Brunch Bunch left, Dee quietly reflected on her own psychological gender-healing. She remembered being unable to sort out what was going on with her feeling alienated, removed, distanced from her body, from female breasts, other body parts, menstruation as a body function that seemed like an alien imposter. She long identified with maleness: strength, durability, what, in her mind, men could accomplish.

She had not been able to relate to most female conversation, which she found unworthy of consequence, and was surprised when women had anything profound to contribute. She had wanted to talk ideas. In college she'd had a sprinkling of female professors she admired, but those were isolated cases, she decided. For years she had been unable to find her way to who she was or needed to be and was beaten down by internal conflict.

But why now, today, learning Kendal and Charles were to become parents, Dee a grandmother-to-be, this onslaught of gender-confusion remembrance and Totem's behavior? What was going on? There was fear, some kind of fear caused her to say what she did about never birthing a child or a career.

After her Brunch Bunch friends were gone, Dee walked outside to the flower garden for solace. She heard Totem meow in the house, walked back, opened the door for the cat and sat with Totem on the patio reflecting on the fear that had gripped her. Dee knew Totem would not live much longer, and this came to be so. The house was then void of pets.

With Kendal pregnant, Dee was concerned about her own lack of experience with young babies, though she'd been a babysitter to many cousins. Her relatives did not leave their babies with a young adolescent babysitter. Her aunts were mothers who felt only an adult could tend to the very young. Dee's embarrassing comment to the Brunch Bunch came out of her fear of newborns; Kendal's pregnancy.

Not long after realizing this, Dee went through the process of becoming a baby cuddler at the hospital, and found holding, hugging, talking to, humming, singing to the swaddled tiny ones profoundly soothed them, while possibly healing uncuddly parts of herself in the process.

Dee learned that newborns going through drug withdrawal often tend to be fussy, have fever, sometimes tremors and vomiting. Dee found she was particularly drawn to these tiny strugglers, imagining Christ-energy gently infusing the tiny body, cleansing cells, being caressed by the loving touch of Mother Mary.

Dee's baby cuddling brought a bonus with Cynthia who was now finishing her master's degree in the specialty of elementary school reading. Cynthia had long had a silent "edge" to her critique of Dee, or so it seemed to Dee.

Dee surmised Cynthia felt becoming an elementary school reading specialist meant she would make life on earth better for those who need extra help learning to read. Zach's work with affordable housing meant he was working to improve life on earth. Cynthia knew Dee was dabbling in fourfold interpretations of Jesus' parables and applied a fourfold perspective to the growth and development of Francis of Assisi, both projects to be shared with Dee's friends, the Brunch Bunch.

To Dee, it seemed Cynthia had a habit of intense scrutiny questioning what Dee was *doing*. What was Dee contributing to make life on earth better when she merely developed topics she shared with a few friends? Dee already had this concern about herself, so to feel Cynthia saw her in this way was a heavy burden to Dee. Becoming a newborn cuddler might give Dee some gravitas with Cynthia.

Dee and Estelle talked about babies and Reggie's memory decline. Estelle observed, "It's about beginning life and ending life. Newborns can be lovingly brought into greater possibility, whereas the old are exiting out of this possibility, here and now, onto some other possibility, it seems to me."

Estelle paused and then shared, "Recently, in the midst of my praying for Reggie, for one thing or another, depending on what is going on with him, I have noticed him become peaceful and co-operative. I'm not sure this is happening more often or whether I am simply more aware of a kind of simple goodness in him when I am calm, patient and peaceful.

"I ask why humanity is so stubborn? I suppose it's the old free-will factor—every person's free-will banging-up against someone else's free-will. But more profoundly, I wonder if our will is always free, or if the will itself is scarred, wounded, in need of healing. Especially if we've been conditioned, taught, learned weird ways, learned strange ways of being. I want answers to these questions," Estelle asserted playfully; less burdened with Reggie's dementia at the moment.

CHAPTER FIFTY-ONE

Sherry

Cynthia's college friend Sherry was a doctoral student in psychology. The two were a contrast in outer appearance. Both attractive, of medium height, Sherry a bit taller and had a look of glamour about her with opulent shiny longish light-brown with golden streaked hair. She wore clothes that magnified her natural appeal; flowing garments and gentle cosmetics highlighting lovely blue eyes accented by only a hint of lip color.

Cynthia dressed more chic-casual-tailored with her darker brown hair in a distinct short style, with greenish-blue eyes, and conventionally moderate make-up. Each seemed secure in her outer personality, confident in her pursuits.

Sherry was vivacious, bubbly, exuberant with a nymph-quality about her. Cynthia had a classically cute face even when intense, serious, sometimes seeming to be an investigative reporter trying to extract facts in an inquiry rather than having a casual conversation.

Cynthia met Sherry in a psychology course a couple of semesters ago. Sherry's real interest in psychology at the moment was the emerging field of psychedelic science. She had had an LSD episode as a high school senior which she still regarded as a life-changing experience in which she "knew" everyone and everything was connected, united in love, after first experiencing paralyzing fear, but then the fear dissipated, while vivid emotions and images remained for some time.

Sherry's story was much like the story of Estelle's seventeen-year-old grandson Dexter who took LSD and confided in his grandmother, leaving her with the quandary whether she should tell his parents. Estelle was worried about Dexter. Sherry's psychedelic experience was one of all-encompassing love. She was a preacher's daughter and heard about God as love all her life, however, her psychedelic venture confirmed God as love.

The preacher's family moved several times in her growing-up years, which had not been easy for Sherry. As a teenager she was resentful of her parents in different ways, and resistant to their best-intentions for her. She felt a lot of guilt about how she treated them which vanished with her psychedelic happening, and thereafter she had a different understanding of her parents, was grateful to them, knew she loved them, but still had moments of psychological resistance to them, and on occasion was impatient and somewhat verbally disrespectful to them.

Now more mature, Sherry respected and loved her parents, realizing her own personality was cut from a different cloth than theirs. The first time she heard the cloth metaphor, it fit precisely what she needed to articulate her relationship with her parents. She simply was of a different mindset, had a different personality approach than her parents and two siblings. This had always been the case, was clearer to her after the LSD experience, and obvious to her now that she was more mature.

Dee and Zach met Sherry in a restaurant for breakfast a weekend visiting Cynthia at the university so Zach could help Cynthia assemble new furniture she'd purchased for her apartment. Dee and Sherry finished their food and lingered in the booth after Zach and Cynthia left for a hardware store. Sherry would later drive Dee back to Cynthia's apartment.

Sherry was talking about her goal of becoming a psychedelic psychotherapist to help those whose maladies seem to be treatment-resistant. She was learning about current research taking place with psychedelics given to people under controlled conditions for whom other medications and techniques had not been helpful to relieve their mental-emotional pain. She knew the power of LSD for opening her own mind, changing her own outlook.

Sherry and Dee talked about changing, stretching the "ego" which means "I" in Greek and Latin. They agreed ego is our habitual reality, the way we are conditioned, our usual mindset, or in the language of computers, our default setting. Dee shared psychotherapist Francine's phrase, "goldfish mentality," likened to the limited environment of a goldfish in a bowl or aquarium. Ego is helpful but limited, they agreed.

Sherry added, "LSD helped me stretch the boundaries of my ego. I guess I could say my ego got rearranged while during the episode my ego was disengaged. I think I was too young to get the full benefit of my experience, but then it may be what my agonizing adolescence needed. It opened me up in some way, which is why I remain interested in how psychedelics might "open" a chronically depressed person who has found no help from other treatments."

Sherry and Dee left the restaurant, drove to Cynthia's fourth floor apartment, settled themselves on the tiny balcony in canvas yard chairs with two small fans blowing on them. Cynthia and Zach had not yet returned from the hardware store.

Dee returned to Sherry's question about Jesus as shaman, which Sherry knew through Cynthia, Dee had read about. Dee prefaced her remarks, "I'm no expert on Jesus or psychedelics. However, the Jewish tradition had prophets, angels, which may have been visual images, just as we experience visual images sometimes mixed with language in sleeptime dreams. The book I've read about Jesus as shaman tells of the Mediterranean shamanic worldview of Jesus' day, which was the view of the men who wrote the Gospels. In the shamanic view the world is made of spirits—spirit energies. In our scientific view, the world is made of particles and energy fields.

"The Jesus-as-shaman book uncovers cultural aspects of Jesus and his followers. The bible book, the Acts of the Apostles, is filled with what we today label altered-states-of-consciousness (ASCs) and what I would consider unusual energy states. We know Jesus fasted, and fasting is a way to enter an ASC. We know he went off by himself to pray. Isolation plus deep prayer plus fasting can create altered states. And again, he lived in a shamanic culture with different explanations and expectations than our scientific culture."

Dee added, "Perhaps if we as a culture can access the right-brain-hemisphere intuitive in us, while continuing to value left-brain-hemisphere rational-scientific abilities, we may be fulfilling the task of our time, which is to become whole-brain functioning, just as I believe Jesus fulfilled his task of healing humanity into universal compassion in its many dimensions—which is still unfolding."

Startled, Sherry looked at Dee quizzically.

CHAPTER FIFTY-TWO

Oriana

Sherry's surprise was that she found in Dee's description what she needed at the moment: the suggestion of whole-brain humanity; the ideal of whole-brain Christianity. Francine had introduced at the Kendrick patio dinners that special summer, "All religion must deal with left and right brain-hemisphere elements, for this is human biology. Christianity is no exception."

Sherry posed a question about Jesus and psychedelics, with his comment, 'Unless you become as little children, you cannot enter the Kingdom of Heaven.' "My LSD trip was filled with awe and wonder. Was Jesus saying adults who lose their childlike capacity for the numinous become stuck in a mundane mindset, their zest for life becomes dull. I have a toddler niece and she is so alive, intrigued by everything, easily wonder-struck it seems to me. I sometimes believe the Kingdom of Heaven is about a psychological state of openness to what IS."

Dee agreed, "Yes, a kind of amazement about being alive. I've thought Jesus with his remark about children may include awe and wonder, as well as trust, survival needs being met, powerlessness, and all kinds of child-qualities, and I would include a young child's time-free existence, for I have found life built on an unrelenting clock schedule is such a grind. Time can be a tyrant."

Dee was realizing more and more that a great blessing was her years of not being on a strict schedule of going to a job every day. She could pay attention to her dreams, study topics of interest, write, pray, work in the yard, run errands, talk with friends, keep a household running smoothly without marching to the passage of time—without feeling relentlessly ruled by time, which can be insufferable. She was not advocating laziness, but a certain kind of liberation from the shackles of time.

Dee's most recent gift of time was Oriana, a retired humanities professor with swirling, curly, black, and white swipes of hair absorbing humidity, poking its way out from under her broadbrimmed straw hat, a new acquaintance who recently moved into the Kendrick neighborhood. Born in Puerto Rico, moving to New York when very young, she was a grand mix of language, culture, ethnic insight. The somewhat plump retired professor was an early morning walker always wanting to lose weight, occasionally passing by as Dee was tending to her flowers or merely enjoying a cup of coffee in the backyard mingling with the floral beauty in the morning before the day's heat arrived.

Over weeks, then months, Dee and Oriana had short over-the-fence conversations. Dee referred to Oriana as the "sidewalk professor." There was the morning when Dee was basking in the blossoms in her yard, trimming flowers ready for the compost as Oriana was walking by and called Dee's attention to an airplane high in the sky while at the same time in the same field of vision there was a very large bird swooping and gliding in the sky.

Oriana was looking up, saying, "On one hand, the steady path of the human-controlled, human designed and created airplane filled with humans and their expectations on their way to specific destinies is a marvelous example of human ingenuity.

"On the other hand, the large bird humans did not create seems free, going its own way, changing its path, unpredictable, graceful, beautiful, gliding, soaring, an inspiration for humans wanting to fly before the invention of the airplane, a symbol of freedom, liberating spirit.

"These two creatures of the sky remind me of the differences between science and religion today. The airplane is science, the bird alludes to free creative source, timelessness, the eternal. Obviously, the bird inspired the airplane, not the other way round. The bird is more primary, created by a creator, just as humans consider themselves created, not invented, including the intelligence that figured out how to make the airplane. Humans are creators and inventors."

Over time, in their short conversations, retired professor Oriana returned repeatedly to re-emphasizing the broad domain of the humanities in higher education, convinced that elevating the importance of liberal arts courses at the undergraduate level could help heal culture's science-religion tension. To her, humanities was a devalued middle-ground waiting to be rediscovered to ease the religion-science divide. Oriana's comments had Dee feeling increasingly enthused about having majored in medieval literature and this formed a bridge between herself and Oriana.

Oriana observed, "In my last years of teaching I began to notice students in general capable of doing compare and contrast, but not analogy or metaphor. To me, the humanities provide a much-needed prism between science and religion."

Dee couldn't believe her ears. Oriana had said the "m-word," metaphor. Perhaps metaphor not only as description, but also as discernment was awakening in culture, for Dee was aware with Cynthia's friend Sherry, though raised in a literalist church atmosphere not given to symbolic interpretation, Sherry had easily grasped the idea of metaphoric discernment, and the overall importance of reading religion and reading one's own being beyond surface, practical, physical knowing.

Dee wondered again about *ego*, "I", limited conscious awareness. Should one want ego to die? To erase ego? Or more realistically, to relax ego, to regard ego at its best as servant rather than master in the personality—ideally, ego includes awareness of phantasies floating about in the personality: emotions, inklings, inclinations, spontaneous thoughts, each and all with a life of their own.

Oriana talked about "allusion confusion" reminding her of American philosopher Ken Wilber's "category error."[17] Wilber talks about "three

---

[17] Ken Wilber, *Eye to Eye: The Quest for the New Paradigm,* (Boston MA: Shambhala, 1990), pp. 7, 10.

eyes," three ways of attaining knowledge: flesh, mind, and contemplation used by St. Bonaventure (1217-1274). Category error is when one eye attempts to usurp the roles of the other two. And it can occur in any direction: the eye of contemplation is as ill-equipped to disclose the facts of the eye of flesh as the eye of flesh is incapable of grasping the truths of the eye of contemplation. Sensation, reason, and contemplation, disclose their own truths in their own realms, and anytime one eye tries to see for another eye, blurred vision results.

Oriana commented, "Bonaventure almost eight hundred years ago used the metaphor of three eyes to demonstrate a hermeneutic paradigm which was multi-faceted, just as fourfold allegorical exegesis was multi-faceted. This might tell us that earthly existence requires a multi-faceted approach to looking at life, disclosing different kinds of truth. One-kind-of-truth fits-all is not adequate for the complexity, or perhaps fragmented nature of human existence. This life seems to demand we recognize different realms or layers of reality."

The two women's conversations were short, a few comments here and there, which Dee preferred, not wanting to be found lacking in her cultural and educational development compared to professor Oriana.

The day came when Sherry arrived in Sandshell for the Fall semester, moved in with the Kendricks, into Charles' unused bedroom, to begin her practicum with Francine as supervisor, while observing other counselors as well. Sherry would be practicing the art of talk-therapy, where she would be scrutinized, mentored, evaluated by those more practiced in this special kind of fruitful human interaction.

Cynthia was responsible for this arrangement that came to pass for Sherry. Cynthia had a high regard for Francine since that summer of dinners on the Kendrick patio when she could only partly grasp what Francine had to offer, now wanting Sherry to be impressed that the Kendrick family was connected to such a fine mind as Francine, Cynthia was somehow aware that Francine was an accredited supervisor and that Sherry's money was running low.

The university approved the practicum with Francine, and Sherry was able to sublet her apartment at the university, save her money to begin a counseling practice after graduation. Cynthia could be a most thoughtful person. She could also hand-out verbal zingers that hurt.

One day in the presence of Sherry and Zach, Cynthia threw at Dee, "Instead of marrying my dad why didn't take the money you inherited, go to graduate school, get your doctorate and then do postdoc work?" Dee was stunned but was quick to answer, "What a question. I never thought of doing such. That never entered my mind. I obviously wanted to be with your father, you and Charles more than doing anything else." Dee was pleased with her answer which dissipated the awkwardness of Cynthia's abrupt interrogation. Zach felt Cynthia was handing Dee a veiled compliment about being smart enough to do what Cynthia proposed.

Another time, Zach joked that a young married couple (not Charles and Kendal) would have a dozen kids because they were Catholic. Cynthia answered, "You and Dee haven't had a dozen and she's Catholic." Zach was left responding, "That's different," without mentioning his vasectomy after Cynthia's birth. Cynthia didn't let go, "Well, maybe you two haven't had sex." Zach wish he'd been more careful with Cynthia who always a knack for hammering a point beyond where one wanted it to go.

Sherry was astute enough, when alone with Cynthia, to be able to address Cynthia's crass comments without offending Cynthia, who defended herself, "When I was really young, Dad and Charles would tease and joke back and forth, and sometimes I didn't know if they were making fun of me. I think it was then that I learned to throw cutting remarks, poison-arrow questions, to protect myself against whatever they were doing that was beyond my comprehension."

Another time, Cynthia told Sherry, "I don't think I'm clever, funny, or witty, but I can be shocking. I know how to shock with a few well-placed words. I've watched comedians do that. It's not going to be easy for me to give-up scorching comments, because I don't have anything to replace them."

Cynthia later shared with Sherry, "I believe I make my shocking retorts from a place of angry aloneness. When dad, me and Charles lived in the apartment where Mrs. Arndt sometimes took care of us, before we moved into our real house with Dee, I slept in a tiny bedroom by myself while dad and Charles had beds in the other bedroom, and I didn't like being alone. Dad would tuck me in bed, kiss me on the forehead, and then I'd be by myself.

"That's why when we got Lucky and Totem, I liked them to sleep in bed with me, or at least in my room with me, and so I made beds for them in my room. Then I wasn't alone. And that felt good. And it also felt like the pets preferred me over Charles, and I liked that feeling, too. It was all circumstances and my childhood understanding of circumstances. I think a lot of life is not about good or bad intentions of people, but that circumstances hold sway and shape us, until we can understand the situation in a larger perspective." Cynthia was capable of learning about herself on her own terms.

CHAPTER FIFTY-THREE

An Allegory at Christmas

At the right time, Kendal and Charles in Clarksdale KS, became ecstatic parents of a healthy baby boy baptized Montel Christian Kendrick, nickname (Monty). Zach and Dee made frequent trips to see the boy-wonder.

The semester went well for Sherry, so well that Francine, who for some time had talked about retiring, offered her counseling practice, office, and extensive library which Sherry had fallen in-love with, especially the large section on the history of early Christianity, all to be purchased over time by Sherry starting as soon as Sherry graduated and moved to Sandshell. Sherry, at first, was unable to appreciate Francine's offer. Did Sherry want to live in Sandshell? She wanted to live in a coastal city, was infatuated with the beach, but Sandshell??

Christmas Day arrived. Cynthia was home from the university, Sherry was among the Kendrick guests along with Dee's mother Paula, Monty and his parents from Clarksdale, and then Monique, Christiane, "J," Justin, and James. Yes, Christiane's ex, James, had moved to town. Francine and Estelle were with their families.

On Christmas, at a bit past one o'clock, thirteen people were seated at the over-sized dinner table which was exquisitely set, Monty in his high-chair, "J" on a bumper seat. Mealtime grace was said by Zach who included each person in his prayer. Food was passed in a reasonably chaotic manner which somehow made for lots of interaction amongst the randomly seated group—an altogether festive gathering. No one forgot this was Monty's first Christmas in Florida.

The weather was beautiful that day in Sandshell, so a walk on the beach was a given. James had his beach wheelchair with its fat tires in his van. He'd enjoy the beach with Justin's help pushing him to a place where he would absorb the broad expanse of nature, and the variety of beachcombers ambling by. There was a beach stroller in the garage for Monty (and future grandchildren), a Christmas gift from Zach and Dee, given them from a couple down the street who no longer needed such. Fat tires navigate sand; ah, the ingenuity of humans.

Cynthia asked whether Christiane would later lead the group in dance. James said he didn't have a dance wheelchair but that he could clap and sway, which eased any tension on that topic. Sherry could have announced that recently Francine offered, upon retirement, her psychological practice to Sherry, which only Cynthia knew. Sherry and Cynthia said nothing about that.

When someone asked where Cynthia was looking to settle upon graduation at the end of the coming semester, she said she didn't yet know but most likely out-of-state. When Sherry was asked her plans upon becoming Dr. Sherry at graduation, she said she didn't yet know her plans.

The real estate market came up and both Justin and Monique could comment on that as an indicator of the local economy. Talk of winter weather in Connecticut compared to Florida engaged Paula, while her expressions of wonder and endearment of being with her first great grandchild on his first Florida Christmas were heartfelt and happily understood by this very congenial group.

And so on. No one was left out of the conversation which veered to the world of computers, and notice was taken that miraculously, no one at the table was checking a smart phone. There was plenty of talk about the electronic age we live in, and James' work aligned with that. Someone asked about Zach's involvement with affordable housing, strides being made, the great need for more affordable housing, which dovetailed again into the local market and the national economy.

Dee's cuddle career with babies was thoroughly tied to Monty, to "J", to care of the young and how well our culture cares for its young, the aged, our priorities as a culture; our schools, the school "J" attends.

Kendal's practice of law, the kinds of legal help her rural clients seek, the unusual home of Kendal, Charles, and Monty; what it's like to juggle Monty, career, home, and Consuelo (their Mexican-American employee) who helped it all happen, mixed and mingled with Charles living a no-beach life, but having the expanse of sky and wide-open spaces, working in a thriving brick-and-mortar furniture store in the age of buying on the internet, the fullness of life in a small town not far from the attractions of Kansas City without the daily complications of traffic.

Zach spoke of groups feeding the poor and homeless this day; some religious groups that do not celebrate Christmas were volunteering to help in this way. And how if the golden rule in each religious tradition could reign the world really would find peace.

No topic prevailed until Monique told of a book, a gift from a client, which she'd just read. Monique explained at length with enthusiasm and exceptional clarity, "The book is allegory, main character female Much-Afraid, member of the Fearing Family, orphan brought up by aunt Mrs. Dismal Forebodings with sons Gloomy, Spiteful, Craven Fear, a great bully. Much-Afraid is crippled with crooked feet, a crooked mouth distorted expressions of her face and speech. Much-Afraid knows compassionate Chief Shepherd, she knows about the Kingdom of Love, she knows the phrase, "Perfect Love casts out fear," and wants to go to High Places beyond the Fearings. The Shepherd helps her get to safe High Places, while she learns love and pain go together.

"There are others: cousins Coward and Pride, helpful neighbor Mrs. Valiant. Twin sisters Sorrow and Suffering are guides on journey. A tiny plant is Acceptance-with-Joy. Then, there is the great sea of Loneliness, Wonder of Nature, also Bitterness, Self-Pity, Resentment. Bearing-the-Cost, forests of Danger and Tribulation, Valleys of Humiliation and Loss.

"Finally, no longer Much-Afraid, her name is now Grace and Glory who can see that even things in the Bible can be misunderstood; that truth comes from personal growth and development, seeing from higher perspectives, from High Places which originate in the depths of one's heart. This how I understand this allegory."[18]

Monique's book review, though uninvited, was well-received with clapping; an amazingly coherent presentation from Monique who could muddle even the simplest conversation.

---

[18] Hannah Hurnard, *Hinds' Feet On High Places,* Published by Fleming H. Revell Company, 1973.

CHAPTER FIFTY-FOUR

Conversation at the Beach

Prior to Christmas day, Cynthia had explained the history of Monique's family to Sherry, who, knowing Justin might be gay wondered why this attractive man, in her eyes, seemed to be giving her special notice across the table from her during the Christmas meal and who then was walking beside her on the beach having settled James in his wheelchair on the sand.

Cynthia was intrigued pushing Monty in his fat-wheeled carriage, wearing sunglasses, which she found as amusing as Mister's doggles many years ago. Perhaps Sherry and Paula were easiest for Justin to catch-up to as they sauntered behind the others who were walking more briskly. A chair had been left behind with James in case Paula tired and chose to return and sit rather than walk. That time did come and so Justin and Sherry walked Paula back to where James was. Paula was seated by James, and then Sherry and Justin continued walking in the opposite direction of the others.

The conversation between Sherry and Justin was easy. Sherry wanted to know everything she could about Sandshell from Justin's perspective because of Francine's offer and Sherry's need to decide. He wanted to know everything about Sherry because he was attracted to her. She decided to skip trying to make sense of this and simply enjoy their delightful conversation.

Finally, how far had they walked? where were the others? were James and Paula OK? Thank goodness for cell phones. They checked-in with the others and walked on together, delightfully alone with each other.

And then, Sherry decided no harm would be done telling Justin of Francine's offer and her own impending monumental decision, whether it be "yes" or "no" to Francine's offer. This information might help Justin include more perspectives about Sandshell. Instantly, she changed her mind. She didn't tell Justin about Francine's offer.

Just then, Justin was saying, "You may have been told I am gay. There was a time I introduced the idea to my mom to get her off my back, and maybe to pay her back, and then she spread the word. Now I wonder why I thought she needed to be paid back, for I see that life had been tougher for her than I could grasp. I didn't need to pay her back for anything, but she could be so bossy, pushy, in my face controlling. She didn't want me to be like my dad."

He reflected a moment before he said, "Actually, I didn't tell my mom I was gay to pay her back. I did it so she would stop pestering me about getting married. Said she wanted grandchildren. Would ask how were things going with whomever I was dating. She wanted me to marry a woman as capable as she is—in case I couldn't earn a living. I wanted to stop her meddling in my personal life. I knew the word "gay" would stop her cold.

"I needed psychotherapy after my dad's suicide. I may have needed therapy even if my dad didn't kill himself, for my mom and dad were mixed-up in their own ways, personally and their having changed cultures. The idea of therapy never registered with me, perhaps because I didn't know any therapist except Francine and I wouldn't go to her because my mom knew her.

"And so, I struggled on my own, through college, after college drowning in commercial real estate at my mother's direction, my father's abandonment with divorce and his final abandonment, suicide.

"Things changed, I started feeling more stable with work, the economy improved, I discovered my Monique-real-estate-gene. I started to re-evaluate myself, who I am down deep. I've come to realize my dad didn't commit suicide to show his lack of caring for us; he just couldn't deal with life; he couldn't handle being alive. He never could handle even the little stuff, so mom overdid everything. It's amazing Christiane and I are as sane as we are. And mom, too. She's really suffered.

"And then James left Christiane after "J" was diagnosed hearing impaired. And then James came back to Sandshell in a wheelchair after the woman he was with died tragically in the accident which paralyzed him. This must be fiction, one might say, but no, this has all happened—it's really real. Christiane is strong like mom but in a quieter way."

Justin looked up at the sky, stopped, turned, gazed upon the vast Gulf water which seemed an ocean. "I needed a therapist. Still do. Will you be my therapist?" Was he jesting? Then he continued, "Monique says, 'Cooperate with grace; expect grace and work with it.' I believe that's how she's made it through. I was raised Catholic and should probably return to Church." Justin became silent.

They stood, inches apart, their shoes in cool sand, sunglasses shading their eyes in this place of vibrant nature tuned to human nature or vice versa: human nature resonating with earthly nature, the radiance of horizon, sea, and sky. She noticed Justin was tracking birds flying high. If Sherry had to make her decision about Francine's offer at this moment, she'd say "yes" to a life in Sandshell. She found the beach—and Justin—magical.

No one spoke until Sherry offered, "If you're serious about a therapist, through my practicum I know some competent local counselors. I'll give you names and telephone numbers. Are you interested in a male or female, or do you have a preference?"

Justin answered, "I may need both, a team, to put Humpty-Dumpty back together again, though we are told all the king's horses and all the king's men couldn't do it."

He continued, "I've read about Humpty-Dumpty on the internet and what that ditty might mean. If Humpty-Dumpty is an egg as often pictured, an egg embodies potential life—all that we are and can become, sitting on a wall, surveying all possibilities, perhaps being indecisive, or even locked in fear, unable to move. Then, falling off the wall—losing balance, losing control, no longer able to cooperate with grace, as Monique would say. And finally, the king's horses and men, representing human effort and will, cannot put this fragmented potential back together—cannot piece together the broken parts.

"However, I sorta believe time and experience have put Humpty-Dumpty back on the wall for me, helping me see possibility in life, and thus I may be able to cooperate with grace, whatever that means, which may include therapy."

In Sherry's eyes, this male with almond-complexion, black hair and eyes, athletic-build was not classically handsome. His nose was perhaps a bit too large. Yet she liked him, was attracted to him, strongly disappointed if he was gay. She could see he was sensitive and caring, helping ex-brother-in-law James with the beach wheelchair, interacting with nephew "J" in a loving way. He could listen, express himself with humor and authenticity.

Sherry appreciated all of this in Justin that Christmas day as they finally walked to rejoin the others at the spot where James and Paula were seated. Sherry wished their conversation was recorded. Did he affirm he was gay, or was he saying time and experience were having him look anew at that aspect of himself? Well, she certainly wouldn't, couldn't ask him.

CHAPTER FIFTY-FIVE

Sherry's Confusion

Back from the beach, at the Kendrick home, Christmas décor shone brighter as dusk arrived. Some had skipped dessert after the main meal and were now indulging. Others were already ready for sandwiches and finger food after the long walk. Plates were filled buffet-style from kitchen counters laden with desserts, noonday foods as well as sandwich possibilities and finger foods, while food, chatter, and drinks found their way to the dining room with everyone seated randomly at the large table, and then slowly the group, leaving paper plates in the kitchen waste bin, ended in the large living room area with the cozy artificial no-heat fireplace. It wasn't cool enough for a heated fireplace.

Sherry, camouflaged her notice of Justin by interacting with anyone near her. This cagey surveillance of him told her she was not singled out for his attention. She'd been wrong to imagine he found her particularly attractive or interesting. Their conversation on the beach seemed never to have happened. She found herself disappointed, but chose to seem energized, thrilled, a feat she accomplished at an early age to mask strong feelings about a boy when she was unsure about his interest in her.

She would need to keep-up her charade with Cynthia later. Afterall, Cynthia told Sherry Justin was gay, so why did she expect him to find her special. Perhaps Sherry was experiencing the limited possibilities of Sandshell and she didn't want a lifetime of that.

Actually, Sherry was beginning to feel miserable, but remained outwardly pleasant, as if having a fine time. Flattered that Francine was impressed with her, she wished Francine's offer had never been made. Sherry was suffering and wishing she could vanish, leave, be someplace else.

Where would she want to be? On a cruise. Not with her parents on their Christmas cruise, a gift from her father's congregation, however, their current voyage ignited the idea of being on a holiday cruise where she would find romance even if it lasted only the length of the cruise. No, she didn't really want that. But she did want romance.

The practicum this semester had imprisoned her. It was good she was presently aware of how stifling life in Sandshell would be for her. Perhaps she could purchase Francine's library on a slow-payment plan, put it in storage wherever she went, or rent big office space or an over-sized apartment for the books wherever she set-up practice. The library need not stay in Sandshell—unless Francine so specified.

Sherry couldn't stop noticing Justin's every action as he interacted with everyone but her. He was attentive to his mother, despite his comments earlier. She was annoyed with the yearning she had for him. Romantic feelings were actually annoying, she concluded. She wished she was back on campus with lots of guys, though nothing permanent had worked out for her there.

Then, she wished she was older, independent, mature beyond the need for romance. But she'd still want male companionship, lifelong commitment—she was too conventional. She wished she could leave the scene, go into Cynthia's bedroom and sleep. The Kendrick home was ever so familiar to her after a semester here. She hoped always to be connected to the Kendrick family. She needed a therapist, she laughed to herself.

The group was gearing up to dance, a holiday tradition she had never before encountered. Furniture was pushed against walls, carpet rolled up.

She liked how easily this happened, which is why tradition works—everyone knows the rules.

She wanted to merely observe others dance, but no, she joined the group led by Christiane; there was line-dancing, individual dance movements, everybody reacted to the lively music. Young "J" always had another dance partner. The adults took good care of him. Charles was able to re-join the group after putting Monty to bed. Sherry watched Justin, saw how naturally he danced in the familiarity of this Christmas tradition.

She poured herself another glass of wine and became more relaxed in the gaiety of the group. She mentally retracted the word "gaiety," as in the word "gay" and laughed inside herself. She didn't care about Francine's offer or the big library or the impending decision she must make. Sherry began enjoying herself; dancing freely.

Towards the end of this natural group levity, Christiane announced a ballroom dance, perhaps wishing the fellow she'd been dating for some time was here, but he was with his children and other family members, a divorced person. It would have been weird for him to be here with James in the wheelchair. But maybe not. Humans can adjust to many situations, Sherry told herself, just as Justin asked her to ballroom dance. She was thrilled with their physical closeness.

Her wine-affected perception was elated, as they danced through the dining room, into the empty kitchen, where he asked if he could call her tomorrow, saying he needed a therapist and her telephone number, dancing out the other side of the kitchen back into the dance area just as the music ended.

Everyone clapped at their comic waltz through the kitchen. Or were they clapping because this was the last dance? Sherry's wine-fuzzy mind couldn't know and didn't care. She was happy, ever so happy as he hugged her at the moment the last note played. They both laughed, but Sherry wished he'd said he wanted to be with *her*—not with a therapist.

Christiane announced a final line-dance. "J" was a very tired boy, she observed. And hadn't they all had a wonderful day together! Sherry now knew the line-dance movements in her head and her body happily embraced the routine.

After that line-dance, the carpet was rolled-out, furniture replaced; with so much help, the room was quickly restored without Sherry's help, for she'd gone to luggage in the bedroom to fetch her practicum business card with her telephone number for Justin and discreetly gave it to him.

There were heartfelt thanks and good-byes. Justin showed Sherry no special affection in his farewell. Yet she teased in her mind, "He is perhaps a closet heterosexual," and smiled inside.

CHAPTER FIFTY-SIX

Dining with Justin

Justin lived and worked in Fort Hayden, a larger city than Sandshell, on the coast just south of Sandshell. Justin telephoned Sherry the next day, late morning, to ask her to dine that evening. He asked whether she had a preferred restaurant, which she didn't have, but said she'd choose a restaurant with a view of the sunset, if there was such.

He said, "The best place for a restaurant sunset is in Fort Hayden, but for this evening we can do Sandshell, since Hayden is not familiar to you." She agreed and assured him, "My trusty GPS will get me there."

And then, she told Cynthia she'd be dining with Justin, exchanging information about local therapists they'd talked about on the beach walk yesterday. This, she hoped would not be true, but did have names and telephone numbers for Justin, in case this was the sole reason of their dining together.

Sherry and Justin met at the beach restaurant at 6:00. He'd reserved a sunset-view table for two. Sherry, today without the influence of yesterday's wine, was still enamored of him. Despite her attraction to him, Sherry was realistic. She and young Monty were the only new faces at Christmas this year, and Justin chose to interact with her over young Monty. She would keep this in mind, she humorously told herself.

At the restaurant, they didn't hug-hello, though he momentarily put his arm around her shoulder as a friend might. Seated, they laughed about the audacity of them looking at menus after yesterday's feast of foods. They ordered mixed-drinks and studied the menu. "We live in the land of plenty," Justin offered, "Fortunate folk are we." After giving their food choices to the waitperson, Sherry said she brought names and numbers of therapists. Justin responded, "Good for you, but I already know you are the therapist of my choice." She laughed, but it was a laugh of perplexity. What did he mean?

He was forthright, "I told you yesterday that to get my mom off my back about marriage and grandchildren, I said to her, 'For all you know, I might be gay,' and then she spread the word that I was, indeed, gay. Now, I relate distantly to mom, who knows she can't talk to me about my dating practices."

Sherry didn't want to sound like a therapist or a reporter and ask how that makes him feel. She wanted to fill the moment with what might be relevant, by saying, "Sexuality and gender stuff is more fluid than what was once believed." He repeated the word "fluid," in a quizzical way, but didn't say more.

He seemed to expect more from her, and she did continue, "Androgyny was known to the ancient Greeks, the male (*andro-*) and the female (*gyne*), form the word androgyny. It's part of the psyche, human psychology.

"You mentioned Humpty-Dumpty yesterday. Androgyny is like the yolk and the white in an egg; the two facets exist in everybody. All males have some female hormones, and vice versa, but not in equal amounts. Imagine, when Humpty-Dumpty fell off the wall, that the egg and yolk got mixed together, which is why the situation couldn't be fixed. Instead, now imagine the membranes of the yolk and egg didn't break in the fall, only the shell cracked. One can gently crack the egg shell and then carefully separate egg white from yolk as a recipe requires.

"Perhaps in people the same is true. In some people the masculine-feminine energies are scrambled together. In others, the two are held-in check, kept separate, intact. Strict gender-roles, division of labor roles, social roles in general play a part in this." Sherry stopped. She felt she'd said enough.

Justin asked, "Well, which is better, to be a scrambled Humpty-Dumpty or an unscrambled Humpty-Dumpty?"

Sherry was not daunted by the simplicity of his question, "When it comes to the human personality, we are complex, more complex than eggs or Humpty Dumpty."

Justin was sure of one thing, "I'm a scrambled personality. I know that. I'd like to be Humpty intact, sitting on a wall, gaining perspective on myself, figuring myself out. Isn't this the goal of therapy?"

"Pretty much," Sherry agreed, while wishing she'd brought Francine's moebius band about feminine Yin and masculine Yang. But no, she corrected herself, she didn't want this to be a therapy session.

To change the topic Sherry could mention Francine's offer; she could get his perspective on Sherry making her home in Sandshell. However, just then, their attention was on a glorious sunset. "Each day, the time of sunset changes, and that intrigues me," Justin observed, as purples and oranges pulsed radiant beauty, leaving a glow of colors after the sun vanished below the horizon. They were quiet, awaiting food. It was as if melancholy was at the table with them, Sherry sensed. Justin's depression? He never used that word about himself.

She resolved she was not going to make-conversation, as Justin began, "Tell me about yourself. I know nothing about you except that you are Dr. Therapist." She corrected, "Not until I graduate at the end of the semester," and then gave him a brief overview of her family, her interests, but didn't mention Francine's offer, which she knew would have opened the door to extended conversation, which would give her another perspective on Sandshell, maybe. She didn't want to conflate the conversation, her situation.

Actually, Justin was an easy conversationalist, and she found him appealing, the shape of his head, his mannerisms, even his hands; she was attracted. She asked him about the commercial real-estate business of which she knew nothing. He gave her a somewhat humorous, flip, overview. Clearly, he wanted more personal talk and asked, "Are your parents psychologically healthy?"

"Reasonably so," she replied. "I'd say my mother is more sound and solid than my dad. You might think being a minister he'd be more together, but I wouldn't say that's the case. She does an enormous amount to help him be effective in what he does."

Justin observed, "Well, Monique has always had to do more than her share. And then, it seems by choice, she overdoes what she does, like yesterday's lesson at the table on allegory. Did she have to go on and on?"

Clearly pained, he added, "I wish my dad could have found his own way without relying so heavily on her. And we know how that ended. Actually, my dad was likeable; easier to be around than her, but she had the grit and guts to keep things together. And why am I still talking about this? Nothing I say is new. It's the same old stuff."

Sherry quoted, "According to the famous psychiatrist, Carl Jung, nothing has a stronger influence psychologically on children than the unlived life of the parent. In other words, children carry the burden of what parents aren't aware of in their own personalities. Stuff is passed-on generationally, sometimes obviously, often subtly."

Justin reflected, "I know almost nothing about my dad's family. Both my parents' families moved from Algeria to France two or three or a dozen generations ago. Who knows what went on in Algeria that made them change countries. And then this country was too hard for him. Round and round I go with these same facts in my head. As to how they impact me, that seems to be *the* question. Or is it all genetics?"

Sherry remembered Francine saying Swiss psychiatrist Jung believed he had had to deal with things or questions left incomplete and unanswered by his parents, grandparents and more distant ancestors, and that psychotherapy pays too little attention to these generational matters. She mentioned this to Justin and added, "Francine advocates paying attention to one's dreams, which invites helpful awareness of what's going on in the personality. I've seen what Francine can glean from dreams."

Justin questioned, "This psychiatrist fellow was saying we inherit personality as well as biology?" Sherry didn't want to be too definite, "We learn, become conditioned, to live in ways that keep us from living fully. Fears, anxieties, worrisome, fretful living such as your mother mentioned yesterday in the allegory she talked about, where the main character, Much-Afraid, belongs to the Fearing family."

Justin quickly responded, “I thought Monique was grandstanding which I found unnecessary.” Sherry said, “Since she’s not my mother, I didn’t react to her behavior, I thought she simply shared with people close to her something new and important in her life.”

“Maybe, but she is my mother and I find her over-the-top performances annoying.” He immediately retracted, “She’s OK. I’d just rather not be around when she grabs center-stage. So maybe she doesn’t have to change, maybe I do. If I didn’t feel so responsible for her. I’ve learned to laugh at her either outwardly or just inside myself. I’d like to feel more neutral towards her behavior, not towards her, but about what she says and does. Does this make sense?”

CHAPTER FIFTY-SEVEN

Learn How to Suffer

"How do you feel about the allegory itself?" Sherry asked. Justin was puzzled, "Well, everyone seemed to enjoy it, talked about it. I don't know. I'm no expert questioner, but I wonder why love and pain must go together?" Sherry said she wondered about that, too, and wished someone at the table, including herself, had asked Monique.

Justin said he felt his mother identified with Mrs. Victory in the allegory. Sherry corrected, "I think it was Mrs. Valiant." Justin agreed, "Yes, it was Mrs. Valiant. At any rate, it would have to be someone courageous, never cowardly, never fearful. But I happen to know Monique has an enormous fear."

Sherry looked at Justin intently, "How do you know this?" "Because it's about me. She's terrified I'll be like my father. That's her biggest fear." Sherry understood. Henri did commit suicide. Justin elaborated, "She's afraid I'll be weak, ineffective, can't earn a living. Sometimes I remind her that I'm her son, too.

"It took a while for me to learn commercial real estate, but I stuck with it. She helped me when the economy bellied-up at one point. But I do have her real-estate gene. I'm more and more confident of that. Confidence is what I lacked. That's what I still lack in relationships. I'm not confident that in the long run all our fuss and fury in this life amounts to anything. Yet, we are here, so make the best of it, but then I always wonder WHY? What's it all about?"

Sherry ventured, "Maybe that's why love and pain go together. If you love life, the price you pay is that it's often a bummer. So, don't love anybody or anything and it won't hurt so much if you lose them, or if they disappoint you. Don't commit, don't give anything your all. Detach. There is some wisdom to that, it seems to me."

They sat quietly until Sherry continued, "I wonder if it is possible to get to a High Place, or High Places of thinking and feeling where everything else is small stuff and you don't sweat the small stuff because you are grounded in what is really real, which is creative love, but it is painful to get to such a place because you have to learn how to suffer through loss, failure, disappointment. You can't go around them. You have to suffer through them to go to a higher place of understanding. Someone once told me with every setback in life you get either bitter or better, depending on what you do with the pain."

Sherry talked about her experience of universal-love using a drug in high school. She said having had the experience, she now feels, "The experience could have ruined me if I went running back for another drug-induced experience, and didn't grow and mature by suffering through the hard spots. Growing up, I was taught not to take the easy way out, but to do the right thing while trusting in something beyond me, greater than my pain, my fears, to take me to a psychologically safe High Place—rising above the situation. I guess that's what the allegory means to me."

Justin had listened carefully, "Monique also mentioned the heart. As you were talking, it occurred to me that the heart is about feelings. A High Place seems more about thoughts, thinking. If we could get our thoughts and feelings straightened out, wouldn't that be good. Where do you go to do that?"

Sherry said, "Prayer where you pour-out your most profound pain, is one place to go. It can lead to Higher Places. I know from experience. And I've seen Francine's ability to help patients puzzle-out their dreams.

Dreams take us to different psychological places, and dealing with dreams can take one to Higher Places of truth which set us free."

Justin responded, "Ah, to be free. I watch birds and want their freedom. They soar and see more. Gravity doesn't hold them down. Freedom, liberation. I love those words as conquerors of depression; being held down." Justin had figured out a lot on his own. Or had he been to other therapists?

Sherry realized she was feeling freer; Francine's offer had been a burden. However, the sunset, wine, conversation with Justin, made her know she could be satisfied living in Sandshell. *It's not where you live, but who lives there*, Sherry believed—mostly, or maybe, at that moment.

CHAPTER FIFTY-EIGHT

Momentarily Content

The evening with Justin ended with a friendly hug at Sherry's car, and Justin's lighthearted comment, "Thanks for a therapeutic time." She felt exhilarated on the way home. Out of her own mouth had come the truth about Francine's ability with dreams. Francine knew how to help people relate to their dreams.

None of Sherry's professors had dream expertise or talent to the degree Francine was endowed with it, nor did the other therapists she worked with during the practicum. Francine offered more than any of the professionals in the field Sherry encountered thus far. It was clear to Sherry she need not stay in Sandshell the rest of her life; she now saw Francine's offer in new light. She now had the answer to Francine's offer.

She saw clearly she was a beginner and that Francine was a pro who offered herself as mentor. How often does it happen that someone like Francine offers not only her practice and library, but her vast experience, unique talent—and the beach! Sherry was elated; she could begin her psychological practice with the road ahead paved. How could this not have been obvious to her before this evening?

What if Sherry's attraction to Justin wasn't about Justin, but he was merely the person to take her to her own truth about Francine's offer. Does Life work in such ways? Do we sometimes unwittingly hold keys to another's pathway? Was this what unknowingly attracted her to him?

She hoped to recall her strongest romantic attractions in the past to see if or what she learned about herself through the attraction; the person. She had had attractions where she didn't like the personality, yet the attraction persisted. But she liked Justin, the little she knew of him. He seemed an honest person, and didn't feel like a needy guy. Perhaps he'd learned how to conceal his neediness, pretending nonchalance about wanting therapy, a therapist. She knew she could not be his therapist.

She thought about her future in Sandshell; all she would learn from Francine. But what if Francine died soon, for she was in her late 70s. But then, the future offers no guarantees, Sherry reminded herself. She'd always assumed she'd marry and have children. She had plenty of time for that.

Sandshell had been generous with Sherry. The Kendricks' free room-and-board was something that had fallen into her lap. Besides free room-and-board, Dee's fertile mind was inspirational, and Zach's altogether lovable, teasing, sometimes over the top personality ever-enjoyable. These people were extraordinary to Sherry.

She learned about sacramental Christianity through Dee and Francine, and Sherry was drawn to the Eucharist, Holy Communion, the ritual of the Last Supper. Yet women couldn't become priests in the Catholic Church. On this count, she might someday need to join the Episcopal Church, she concluded to herself that evening.

That night, the short drive to the Kendrick house was pregnant with possibility; feeling elated, she hoped sometime to watch another sunset with Justin, and was grateful to Cynthia for both Francine and Justin. If all turned out as now expected and soon to be accepted with Francine, Sherry would, not far down the road, be living in her own place in Sandshell. This was her final decision, it seemed. And she felt momentarily content.

CHAPTER FIFTY-NINE

The World Without Metaphor

Shortly after Christmas, Dee's mother Paula returned to Connecticut. Julia from Kansas and Dee were telephoning more than usual, for Julia was suffering the loss of her mentor-friend, psychiatrist Lenore, who died.

Lenore's funeral, which Julia attended, was not long past when Julia received a telephone call from Austin TX from Beth's daughter that Beth's life was ending. Julia was devastated; the death of Lenore and impending demise of Beth crumpled two mainstays in Julia's life. With Beth's death, Matti's generation would be gone.

Julia telephoned Dee suggesting the two of them meet in Austin for the inevitable funeral, which came to pass. When, together in their hotel room, the two reminisced about their last time together visiting Beth. At that time, Julia's concern was Marc shouldering the furniture store by himself, with no inkling that son-in-law Charles would be working at the store. At that time there were no clues on the horizon that Julia and Dee would become mothers-in-law, grandmothers of Monty.

They looked back at Ann Dramm's funeral where they'd met. Only Julia and Dee could appreciate Beth as the last of a foursome: Matti, a smart but semi-tragic person; Ann, who kept Matti's secret, a mystical type. Gabby, the fertile mind that initially uncovered allusion confusion and metaphoric discernment; Beth, consummate community volunteer, who promoted the Twelve Steps that influenced Gabby's discoveries, and Beth saved Matti's computer, as well as arranged Julia meeting her birth father, Cal, and further, was the catalyst behind Ann and Lenore's trip to Lenore's ancestry in Kansas.

Reminiscence can be painful, also beautiful, Julia and Dee re-discovered together in Austin. Julia kept returning to how little we know of the future, while reflecting on the many changes since she and Dee were last together in Austin, where Matti lived out her life remembering the baby girl she'd birthed, now adult Julia.

Julia commented she was now older than Matti when she died. Dee wondered what Matti-traits young Monty might eventually exhibit, and Julia said she'd thought about the same. She'd been too busy with her own children and too disconnected from Matti at the time to be wondering about Matti traits in her own children when they were young. At one point, Matti had come to loom so large in Julia's life that she forgot her biological father Cal's traits. Julia's affection for Cal had grown over the years, and they still kept in contact.

Dee was home in Sandshell after being in Austin with Julia, and feeling hollow inside, for her mother had returned to Connecticut, Sherry and Cynthia were back at campus for their final semester. Cynthia, finishing her thesis and applying for a position in a Kansas City area school district, as she wanted to live near Monty, loving the little guy as she did. Sherry, putting final touches on her dissertation, and then she'd be moving to Sandshell and Francine's counseling practice and library.

While Dee understood Cynthia's affection for Monty, and applauded it, she was sad that maturing Cynthia was moving out of state. The Brunch Bunch was scheduled to meet on Saturday. Estelle was struggling with whether Reggie needed to be placed in a memory care facility. The prospect made her feel both relieved and grieved.

At this same time, sidewalk professor Oriana happened by early one morning with a quote from a contemporary British author writing about metaphor as an invaluable part of life. The quote captured Oriana's ongoing concern about the cultural preference for science over the humanities. The author's words articulated what Oriana and Dee expressed the day they saw the airplane and large bird together in the sky. The quote does not undermine the efforts of science; it merely highlights science's limitations. The British author wrote:

> It would be nice if people were to understand that science is a special exercise in perceiving the world without metaphor, and that, powerful though it is, it doesn't function as a guide to those very large aspects of experience that can't be perceived except through metaphor.[19]

The author's words 'very large aspects of experience can't be perceived except through metaphor' thrilled Dee. A little more talk over the fence between the two women, and Oriana continued on her walk, while Dee went with the quote on the piece of paper Oriana gave her, to sit in the shade on a yard chair this fine sunshine morning.

Dee's thoughts turned to the fourfold formula for dealing with experience which Gabby and Matti adapted from the old exegesis, while remembering that Aunt Tess said Jesus' parables didn't always make much sense to her.

Professor Oriana had recently thanked Dee for magnifying for her the importance of allusion in the personality, saying. "Allusion, allusion, allusion. I've come to wonder, what might we know about ourselves, our most intimate being, should psychological allusion uncovered by metaphoric discernment become widespread and commonplace in culture. We would then be more enlightened about our own being, even me with my weight problem—could be."

---

[19] Francis Spufford, *Unapologetic: Why, Despite Everything, Christianity Can Still Make Surprising Emotional Sense* (London UK: Faber and Faber Limited, 2012), p. 222.

CHAPTER SIXTY

Holy Water

Seated in tree shade that morning, Dee repeatedly re-read British author Spufford's quote which Oriana had given her: 'very large aspects of experience can't be perceived except through metaphor.' Of course, the enormous metaphoric experience for Dee had been deciphering the purple aura cat mental image which she could easily have disregarded, but instead uncovered metaphorically with Ann Dramm.

After the metaphoric uncovering, Dee returned to Florida, for Zach had already encouraged her to come back, and by then she had the independent means psychologically and financially to return. She immersed herself with the Kendrick family and made the decision to marry Zach. She had not thrown away rationality when choosing to marry Zach. Rational processing was part of her decision *after* metaphoric discernment helped her know herself better.

Comfortably seated in the shade of the backyard after tending the flower garden, remembering the book Oriana mentioned about Christianity making 'emotional sense,' Dee was at peace with herself. The air seemed filled with timelessness; eternity. In her own back yard, she was to some degree experiencing the myth of the fulfilled life in the Garden of Eden. She knew also, the Eden story includes destruction of the fulfilled life, whereupon restoration was needed. The Christian myth/story tells how potential was restored in and through The Crucified One.

Dee knew myth not as falsehood, but rather as Truth too big to be expressed, except as a story dripping with layers and possibilities. Christianity is myth, filled with every aspect of living—including emotions. She thought of the deep emotions Estelle was dealing with regarding Reggie's recent death.

Reggie had been in a memory-care facility only twenty-three days when, at around 8:30 p.m., Estelle's telephone rang and a caregiver at the facility gave Estelle the news that Reggie had died in his sleep. Estelle immediately telephoned son Lee.

While waiting for Lee to arrive, in her shocked state Estelle cried to the heavens for a "sign" so she could know that Reggie was OK; since he'd died alone in his room at the facility, she had a desperate need to know Reggie was OK, whatever that meant.

Though in shock, she looked for information about the funeral home the memory-care facility would need to contact. She found the telephone number, which she gave to Lee when he arrived, whereupon he telephoned the facility. While talking to the facility caregiver, Lee distractedly looked at a bookcase, noticing one book noticeably sticking-out, not in line with the others, whereby he aimlessly pushed the protruding book to line-it-up with the others.

However, something behind the out-of-line book kept the book from sliding into place, so finished with the telephone conversation, in his dazed state, Lee took the book from the shelf, put his hand into the hole on the shelf and pulled out a small, slim bottle of clear liquid which had a typed-label that read, "Holy water from the Shrine of St. Joseph." He showed his mother.

Though overcome with the shock of what they were dealing with, she remembered, "Yes, your father and I got that years ago when we were in Arizona." On automatic pilot, Lee asked, "What is it doing in the bookcase?" Estelle didn't know how it got there, but suggested she may have placed it on the shelf temporarily for some reason and then forgot about it while it got shoved back, hidden, perhaps when the shelf was dusted by a housekeeper. Actually, she had no clue.

Despite her crazed bewilderment with Reggie's death, she amazingly recalled, "Saint Joseph is the patron saint of a happy death." A happy death. The words clicked. She knew this was her "sign" that Reggie was OK. Lee whipped out his smart phone and found, yes, Saint Joseph is, amongst other designations, the patron saint of a happy death.

Estelle told Lee about her asking for a "sign" that Reggie was OK, and now, this quickly, yes, Lee found hidden behind a book, the holy water bottle from the shrine of St. Joseph. The synchronicity was overwhelming. The heavens provided what was needed at this crucial moment.

Lee said, "It feels like dad's death has come full circle." They hugged and wept at the prospect of Reggie having had a happy death; at least he now was free from the shackles of this life, the loss of his memory, the confusion of his hallucinations.

Ah, the peace that came to Estelle and Lee at that moment, and then to others they later told of the holy water synchronicity. As if heaven revealed itself perfectly at this critical time for Reggie's family.

In days that followed, Estelle, aware of her emotional state, remembered the solace praying the rosary used to bring. She hadn't prayed the rosary in a long time, though as a child, she kept her rosary under her pillow, praying it as she fell asleep. She began saying the rosary again at bedtime, and sometimes in the morning before getting out of bed.

At this time in her life, she wanted to remember always, two days before Reggie died, walking into his room at the facility where he was sitting the short way across the bed, pillows propped behind his head against the wall, feet on the floor. He had long legs and could do this.

Estelle asked if he was comfortable. He made it known he wanted to sit as he was, so he could spring into action if need be. This seemed to be what he was indicating. She could feel his fear. He felt threatened and had contrived a way to defend himself.

Realizing this, Estelle sat down on the bed with him, crying hard for him, the state he was in, his deterioration, their fifty-five years together, the enormity of change. Actually, she didn't know why she wept, but she couldn't stop, as she gently laid her head on his chest, in his partially-reclined position, he put his arm across her back, and there they were, she didn't know for how long in this unwieldy embrace.

She had rarely wept this hard in her adult years; certainly not in a very long time. After Reggie died, upon reflection, she felt this embrace had been their mutual good-bye, deep affection, bonds beyond words, the good and not so good, everything, everything, everything, a summation of their life together for both of them.

These days when she re-imagined that emotional embrace, she realized no words were said, yet felt everything that needed to be expressed, had been. It was a sublime good-bye and upon recall brought a feeling in her chest, the area of her heart. She had loved Reggie imperfectly, conditionally, and was sorry what they had together wasn't more perfect. Yet, even now, it seemed, healing was taking place.

Praying the rosary made Estelle think about the limitation of words, for with the rosary, one is saying the same words over and over. Was she always thinking about those prayer words with the rosary? No. More importantly, the prayer words seemed to be praying themselves while the rosary-in-hand reinforced the praying process. Usual brain chatter continued—but not only brain chatter, for simultaneously the words of the rosary brought peace, a sense of well-being.

CHAPTER SIXTY-ONE

Covid-19

Only weeks after Reggie's death, the nation and the world, was introduced to the coronavirus, Covid-19. Wearing face-masks, staying-at-home, social-distancing became commonplace. In Sandshell, the Brunch Bunch did not gather.

Brunch Bunch members found ways to contribute during this time of seclusion: Estelle began sewing face masks for neighbors when the retail supply ran out. Monique and daughter Christiane daily fixed a hot meal for Christiane's "ex," James in a wheelchair, and delivered it to him because his routine had been to go to a restaurant, and restaurants were now closed. Anyway, he couldn't be going out in public with his compromising health issues.

Francine continued her lifetime habit of reading challenging material, while also face-timing with clients. Dee, no longer allowed to cuddle newborns, planted a vegetable garden in case fresh vegetables became scarce. She also continued extrapolating Jesus' parables.

Zach worked from home. University campuses closed. Cynthia moved home with Dee and Zach. Sherry moved to Sandshell to begin finalizing takeover of Francine's counseling practice. Sherry and Cynthia graduated "virtually" at the end of the semester.

TV statistics and watching devastating news of the virus became a national habit. The Kendricks in Sandshell and their significant others were on-hold; adapting, wondering, waiting, learning and loving their way through Covid-19, which is told in the novel *An Empty Ache.*

ACKNOWLEDGMENTS

Special thanks to Maureen Lumley, PhD, who connected the author with Jennifer Leigh Selig, PhD., publisher of Empress Publications.

www.ingramcontent.com/pod-product-compliance
Lightning Source LLC
LaVergne TN
LVHW010651110826
845149LV00014B/3032
* 9 7 8 1 9 5 7 1 7 6 1 0 9 *